Geraldine
EVANS

DEAD
Before
Morning

WORLDWIDE.

TORONTO • NEW YORK • LONDON
AMSTERDAM • PARIS • SYDNEY • HAMBURG
STOCKHOLM • ATHENS • TOKYO • MILAN
MADRID • WARSAW • BUDAPEST • AUCKLAND

DEAD BEFORE MORNING

A Worldwide Mystery/November 1995

First published by St. Martin's Press, Incorporated.

ISBN 0-373-26184-5

★

The doctor gave a mirthless laugh. "It's obvious you don't know many medical men, Rafferty. But in this instance, no, I'm not suggesting it was murder. Not necessarily, anyway, though, of course..." He let his voice trail off suggestively. "A medical man wouldn't necessarily need to commit murder to get hold of a convenient body. Perhaps one of his patients had a fall, fractured her skull and died, and rather than embarrass himself, he decided to embarrass me, damage my reputation by dumping the body here, mutilating her to make it look as bad as possible for me."

"But what about the patient's relatives?" Rafferty asked reasonably. "Even a doctor can't just lose a body without being asked."

"You'd be surprised."

★

"For most collections."

—*Library Journal*

"A nice sense of comedy..."

—*Wilson Library Bulletin*

For George, my husband, with love and appreciation for
his endless patience and understanding

For Georgia, my best friend, with love and appreciation for

ONE

'IS IT YOURSELF?'

Detective Inspector Joseph Aloysius Rafferty winced as his mother's voice threatened to pierce his eardrum, and, although briefly tempted to plead not guilty, he had perforce to agree that yes, it *was* himself. Surely, he demanded of his reflection in the hall mirror, a hangover, a murder, *and* his mother all in one morning were more than any man should be expected to cope with? Especially at six thirty in the morning and after less than four hours' sleep. 'I can't stop, Ma. Sergeant Llewellyn will be picking me up any minute.'

'I won't keep you then, son, but I didn't know who else to turn to and what with the wedding and all...'

Rafferty frowned. News of the murder had already taken its toll on his hungover wits, but the word 'wedding' on his ma's tongue was even more worrying and he struggled to get his brain into gear. 'What wedding?'

'I know Jack's only a distant cousin,' she remarked briskly, 'but surely you haven't forgotten that he's over from Dublin to marry my niece Deirdre?'

That wedding. How could he have forgotten that Jailhouse Jack, the world's most incompetent criminal, was preparing to plight his troth and pass his genes on to the next generation? What a wonderful addition to a policeman's family the bridegroom would be, he thought ruefully. Thank God the happy couple would be going back to Ireland straight after the wedding and surely even Jack could stay out of trouble for the few weeks he'd be...

'He's in a spot of bother, Joseph.' After shattering his hopes, his mother didn't pause for either of them to catch their breath, but went on to explain that his troublesome cousin was being held at the Harcombe nick on suspicion of lifting a lorry-load of whisky. 'I know what you're going to say,' she continued before he could get a word in, 'but this time I'm convinced he didn't do it.'

That *would* be a first, Rafferty concluded cynically, thankful that between them the Irish Sea and a three-times removed cousinship usually kept Jack from embarrassing him.

'It would be a shame if he got put away right before the wedding. Can you go and see him and sort it out, son? I wouldn't ask, only I've had Deirdre here half the night crying her eyes out. She's scared she'll have to cancel the wedding.'

'Now that *would* be a shame,' he replied caustically. Wasn't a murder enough, he wondered, without being expected to sort out Jack's little problem? Especially as he knew that as soon as he set foot in the Harcombe nick and revealed his mission of mercy the shit would hit the fan. His family were the limit, especially as some of them were of the opinion that if they must have a copper in the family, he might at least have the decency to be a bent one. He consoled himself with the thought that at least he hadn't made a firm date with the looming fates. Jack could cool his heels for a bit. After all, he now remembered, the wedding *was* still two weeks off. He had plenty of time.

''It's not everyone that avoids matrimony like you, Joseph,' his mother told him tartly.

Rafferty broke in quickly before she got into her stride. The hoped-for remarriage of her braw boy was ever close to his mother's heart. 'Now, Ma,' he warned. 'Don't go getting any ideas. I'm perfectly happy as I am.'

She treated this statement with withering contempt. 'Don't talk so foolish. How can a man on his own be happy? No, what you need is a wife. Your Uncle Pat's girl, Maureen, for instance. She'd be a fine catch for any man. I only want to see you settled.' Cunningly, she injected a quavering note of pathos into her voice. 'I'd like grandchildren before I die.'

'You've got eleven grandchildren already, Ma, and another on the way,' he reminded her. 'How many more do you want?'

'I may have a dozen,' she retorted briskly, imminent death evidently forgotten. 'But they're none of them Raffertys; they're all your sisters' children. I want one or two from my eldest son, my greatest pride. How else can the name get carried on?'

'I'm sure the fifty-odd Raffertys in the phone book will do their best to continue the line,' he observed. 'Why don't you call and spur *them* on a little?' And leave him alone. He glanced out of the window of his Essex flat and shivered. The day was bleak, the mist off the North Sea was thick and he could barely see the shoreline. Unfortunately, he had no trouble making out the lugubrious folds of his sergeant's face as he turned the car on to the forecourt. Llewellyn consulted his watch, then gazed up at Rafferty's window, his expression mournful.

Rafferty scowled. It was going to be one of those days. He felt it in his bones. 'I really must be off,' he told her firmly. 'Llewellyn's here.' He paused, wishing he didn't have to tell her, but he'd never hear the end of it if she had to find out from the papers. Taking a deep breath, he told her quickly, 'There's been a murder and...'

'A murder!'

'Mm.' His attempt at calm nonchalance was singularly unsuccessful and he went on briskly. 'Rather a nasty one. A young girl.' According to the desk sergeant, the girl had been brutally battered, her face left in such a state that it would have looked more at home on a butcher's slab. 'She was found at that private psychiatric hospital at Elmhurst and—'

'A loony bin?' His ma's gasp of horror echoed down the line. 'It'll be one of them dangerous cyclepaths escaped. They're always doing it. The people in charge of these places should be locked up. You stay well away, son,' she advised firmly. 'Let that superintendent sort it out.'

'I *am* a policeman, Ma. And I'll be in charge of this one. They just promoted me, remember? Just because the girl was found in a psychiatric hospital doesn't mean one of the patients did it, you know.'

'Doesn't mean to say they didn't, either,' she retorted. 'Very sly some of them. And they expect you to catch him?' She tutted worriedly. 'You watch your step, my lad.'

He intended to. 'I've got to go.' No doubt the rest of the team would already be there working hard and calling him rude names in his absence. 'About Jack, Ma, stop worrying. I'll see to it.' He didn't have much choice.

To his relief, she kept any further anxieties to herself. 'Thanks, son.' Now pride edged some of the worry out of her voice. 'I'll tell Deirdre that my son the Police Inspector's got it in hand and Jack's as good as free.' Rafferty wished he shared his ma's confidence that springing the prospective bridegroom would be as easy as catching him usually was, but he made no comment. 'Well, I won't make you late for your murder. Look after yourself, Joseph, and don't take no nonsense from any of them high and mighty doctors at that hospital. Arrest the lot of them if you have to.'

'I'll bear it in mind, Ma,' he told her drily. 'Goodbye.'

THE CONSTABLE beckoned the car forward and as the heavy hospital gates thudded together behind them, Llewellyn's dark eyes took on a mystic light and his long face became even more lugubrious as he remarked, 'There'll be trouble over this one. Mark my words.'

Having delivered this cheering prognostication, he said no more and Rafferty, determined that the Welshman's black prophecy wouldn't undermine his confidence, did his best to ignore him. He was helped by his first sight of the house. He came from a long line of builders and house renovators, and its classical Georgian elegance—which the well-tended grounds framed so perfectly—brought Rafferty a few precious moments of delight in a day unlikely to contain many pleasures. The handsome seven-bay house was built of pale Caen stone, a popular import in such a stone-impoverished part of the country. The projecting central section was crowned by a graceful pediment, and the ground floor, raised above the semi-basement, was reached by stone steps. Slender pillars flanked the canopied front door and they were flanked in turn by single windows with two more on either side of the recessed sections of the house. Perfection. Just then, the sun came out from behind the early morning cloud, and he stared as all thirteen of the large sash windows seemed to wink at him, like all-seeing eyes, as though mocking his ability to discover what they had witnessed in the night; a sight undoubtedly shared by the secretive, half-closed dormer eyes of the attic floor. The optical illusion fanned the flames of the superstition that Llewellyn had already successfully kindled, and as they passed the house he switched his gaze determinedly ahead of him as his Welsh prophet of doom drew up behind the earlier arrivals.

'Dr Dally's here,' Llewellyn remarked unnecessarily, with a sidelong glance at Rafferty. 'He must be nearly finished by now.'

'We all know quick and speedy doesn't always win the race, Sergeant,' Rafferty retorted, stung by the dig. 'Not that Sam Dally's *either* when it comes to letting us have some results.' Not for the first, nor the last time that day, he reflected that it was a pity the girl had chosen a mental hospital in which to get herself murdered: on his first serious case since his promotion too. Now he wondered uneasily if an unpropitious fate was about to enjoy some fun and games at his expense. It wouldn't be the first time. As they walked round the shrouding screen, Dr Dally, the police surgeon, raised a shaggy grey eyebrow teasingly.

'Late again, Rafferty?'

Dally's jocular greeting merely earned a scowl, and as Rafferty got his first view of the corpse, he had to swallow hard, again regretting the quantity of celebratory drink he'd polished off the night before. The girl was lying on her back and someone had certainly made mincemeat of her. What might once have been a pretty face was now a soggy mess—her teeth were gone, her eyes were gone, her nose was gone—all smashed to a bloody pulp. It looked as if someone had taken a sledgehammer to her. 'The press will have a field day with this one,' he remarked grimly.

Considering it was April, the previous night had been quite balmy, yet surely he was only imagining the sickly scent of corruption? Behind him, Llewellyn remarked in funereal tones, '"So will we all decay. The past is the only dead thing that smells sweet."'

Rafferty gave him a jaundiced look. 'Thank you, Dylan Thomas.' Trust Llewellyn to enliven the proceedings, he groaned.

'Edward Thomas, actually, sir,' Llewellyn corrected and launched into a mini-lecture, apparently believing that it was his duty to lighten the darkness of his boss's ignorance. 'Killed in action in World War One. Then there's R. S. Thomas, the Welsh vicar. He—'

'All right, all right,' Rafferty broke in, irritated as usual by Llewellyn's display of erudition, sure he did it out of some deep, mischievous desire to get under his skin. 'This is neither the time nor the place to set about completing my education, Sergeant. I'll thank you to remember that.' His puce complexion regained some of its usually fresh colour as he put Llewellyn in his place, but it drained away again as he gazed at the dead girl. Poor bitch, he thought. Whoever, whatever she was, she surely hadn't deserved such an end? Curiously, the naked body was unmarked and as his eyes travelled over the slim cadaver, he wondered at the unfathomable ways of women. Why would a natural blonde dye her hair black? 'The first priority is going to be to find out who she was,' he remarked to Llewellyn. 'Tell "Fingers" Fraser I want her prints run through the computer yesterday.' He hoped to God they were on file.

Otherwise...Rafferty's insides continued to threaten the most unprofessional behaviour and he swallowed hard before he turned to the doctor. 'What can you tell me, Sam?'

'Little enough, Rafferty, little enough. She's certainly dead, though, I can tell you that much.' Dr Samuel Dally had a whimsical sense of humour and liked to tease. The rest of the team carried their gear to the vans, leaving them alone, and now Sam's tubby body rocked back on its heels. Behind his spectacles his eyes lit up with relish as he watched Rafferty's face. 'You look a bit green, my boy.' He dug his hand in his back pocket and pulled out a flask. 'Have a medicinal nip. Doctor's orders,' he added firmly as Rafferty hesitated.

Forgetting his scruples, Rafferty reached gratefully for his medicine and took a swig. 'Should be on prescription.' He grinned as the whisky hit the spot. 'Irish?'

Sam Dally snorted. 'It's only the best that the Highlands can offer. I can see it's wasted on you.' Taking the flask back, he had a quick nip himself. 'Ah. That's better. Nothing like a hair of the dog for setting a man to rights. And I should know.'

Rafferty brightened, glad to know he had company in his suffering. Especially when that company was in the rotund shape of the tonic-toting Dally. 'I gather you had a heavy night?'

Sam nodded. 'Doctors' do at the George,' he explained. 'Annual event. Wouldn't miss it. Our erstwhile chairman's wife, Lady Evelyn Melville-Briggs, organizes it, so it couldn't fail to go like clockwork. Shame she didn't seem to enjoy it. Not surprising she was so quiet, of course. Her old man was in a towering rage when they arrived.' He snorted. 'Some hoo-ha about the door-man. I didn't stop to listen to it.' He put

the flask back in his pocket and became briskly professional. 'Been dead at least seven hours. Rigor mortis
has started to set in around the head and neck. The blow
to the back of the head is probably what killed her.'

Rafferty raised his eyebrows. He could have come to
that conclusion for himself. Even with the body lying on
its back, he could see the skull was caved in, making an
amorphous mess of bone and brain. 'Could a woman
have done it, do you think?'

Sam nodded. 'Wouldn't need as much strength as
you'd think, only stealth to creep up on her and then
determination to keep whacking, like Lizzie Borden.'

Raising his eyes from the gory horror on the ground,
Rafferty caught sight of a well-dressed man pacing with
barely contained impatience at the edge of the trees, and
he nodded in his direction. 'Who's that?'

Sam followed the direction of Rafferty's eyes, and,
in an echo of Llewellyn, he remarked, 'That's Trouble,
Rafferty. Trouble with a capital T.' Rubbing his hands
together with childish glee, he continued. 'That's the
owner. Consultant Psychiatrist Dr Anthony Melville-
Briggs. But you'll find plain "Sir" will do. Husband to
the Lady Evelyn, etc., etc. I wouldn't like to be in your
shoes when he finds out a lowly inspector's in charge of
the case.' He gave Rafferty a sly look. 'Perhaps you
should listen to your mammy and get married again.
Old Tony certainly shows what marriage can do for a
man.'

Rafferty's lips curled. Sam Dally, compassionate
doctor of medicine, could always be relied upon to hit
a man below the belt. One marriage had been enough
for him. In spite of his mother's continued attempts to
persuade, push, and cajole him into matrimony a second time, Rafferty wasn't having any. Still, he mused,

at least it gave her less time for her other little hobby, and unlike that, it didn't carry with it the risk of a jail sentence for the pair of them. 'Got any more unwanted advice?' he now enquired.

Sam shook his head. 'Why cast more pearls before swine, laddie?' he asked sweetly. He glanced again at Melville-Briggs and a beatific smile lit up his face as he set about removing the glow of the restorative whisky. 'I was at medical school with him and he barely had a bean before he married Lady Evelyn. You could see he was determined to go places even in those days.' Sam Dally took off his glasses and gave them a brisk polish before continuing. 'Well in with the Chief Constable, so I understand. Me, I don't mix in such exalted circles.'

The last remnants of Rafferty's good humour vanished as he studied the chief constable's friend. Dr Melville-Briggs had that sleek self-satisfaction that only a man with the good fortune to marry money acquires. He was in his early fifties, Rafferty guessed, but had kept himself in shape. With his pure white hair swept dramatically back from his high forehead, he could have been taken for a Shakespearean actor awaiting the plaudits of the crowd after a lunch-time performance in the park. Rafferty hoped he didn't intend to indulge in any histrionics this morning, but after what Sam had said he wasn't optimistic. Dr Melville-Briggs's cheeks wore an unlovely hectic flush probably caused by a combination of temper and shock and he came to the depressing conclusion that the doctor was taking the crime as some kind of personal affront. But then he was rich and successful and probably imagined that his select establishment would, by its very exclusivity, be shielded from the sordid world outside his gates.

Reflecting that it must have come as an unpleasant surprise to find that his little kingdom wasn't quite as inviolate as he had imagined, Rafferty prepared to give him his second surprise of the day.

TWO

WITH LLEWELLYN dogging his heels, Rafferty made his way over to the exalted one and introduced himself. Bloodshot blue eyes surveyed him without enthusiasm and he got the impression that neither his shiny new rank nor his shiny new car cut much ice with the doctor.

'The constable at the gate said that the CID were on their way.' A faint frown marred the smooth perfection of Melville-Briggs's brow. 'I take it the Chief Inspector will be along shortly?'

Although the doctor's voice was as fruity as a greengrocer's stall and polished to an almost glossy perfection, stress had brought out a hint of his Midlands origin and Rafferty guessed unhappily that the Brummie boy made good would expect the very best and cut up rough when he didn't get it. He broke the news to him gently. 'I'm afraid the Chief Inspector won't be coming, sir. We're a bit short-staffed at the moment.'

'I think you'll find you're mistaken about that, Rafferty.' A professional smile briefly dazzled. 'Obviously the station doesn't know who I am. The Chief Constable's a personal friend of mine and once I've telephoned him, he'll be glad to oblige me.' Presumably satisfied that Rafferty now realized his star quality, Melville-Briggs patted him on the back in a consoling manner as he dismissed Rafferty's skills. 'Don't take it personally, Inspector. But this is a very *select* establishment. A certain diplomacy is called for if my patients aren't to be upset. I'm sure you understand?'

Oh yes, he understood all right, Rafferty reflected grimly. What it didn't need, Melville-Briggs was implying, was some heavy-footed oaf like himself. But it was very tactfully put. He hoped the doctor would be as sensitive to his feelings in a minute or two. 'There's been no mistake, sir. There really *is* no one else available. And the Chief Constable's on holiday. Trekking in the Himalayas, I believe,' he added faintly.

'Trekking in the Himala—?' Melville-Briggs's lips pursed tightly, but they opened sufficiently to murmur, 'I see,' in clipped tones, as he gave Rafferty's off-the-rack suit a swift, assessing appraisal. Perhaps he liked the style, Rafferty mused, but somehow, he didn't think so.

The doctor concealed his disappointment well, Rafferty had to give him that. Melville-Briggs fingered his jaw thoughtfully and smiled again; a smile of singular charm that immediately put Rafferty on his guard. 'Now. How can I put this? It's a trifle—delicate, and I wouldn't want you to think me insensitive, but it *is* important that this distressing matter is cleared up as quickly as possible. The publicity...' He winced as if in genuine pain, before putting his hand inside his beautifully cut pearl-grey suit, and murmuring, 'Perhaps a donation to the Police Benevolent Fund will ease things along a little, hmm?'

Although the doctor's attempted bribery was discreet, Rafferty was under no illusion that bribery was what it amounted to. What did the man expect him to do? he wondered. Fit up a likely criminal with the murder? Or did he imagine the crime could be swept under the carpet like last week's dust and conveniently forgotten? Wishing he could forget the doctor's high-placed friend, he gave a grim little smile. 'The police are always grateful for such generosity, but perhaps it would be best if you sent the cheque directly to the Fund? We don't want anyone getting the wrong idea, do we, sir?'

The doctor withdrew his hand from his pocket. 'Of course not,' he agreed smoothly. He was a cool customer, all right, thought Rafferty. 'Excellent idea. I can't imagine why I didn't think of it.' Balked of an early reduction in the crime statistics, Melville-Briggs's voice lost a little of its silken charm. 'You know, Rafferty, I've been thinking and I'm convinced that there was an ulterior motive for this crime. Someone wants to ruin my reputation and that of my hospital. I haven't any evidence, of course,' he admitted as Rafferty stared at him, 'but a man in my position makes enemies and why else would anyone dump a corpse here? It's obvious when you think about it.'

Rafferty blinked. It wasn't obvious to him. 'Was there any particular reason for you to think that, sir?' he asked guardedly.

'Ask yourself, who has most to lose by this murder? I have, of course,' he answered his own rhetorical question. 'This crime was intended to cause me maximum loss, inconvenience, and embarrassment.'

Rafferty was tempted to remark that the victim had suffered a greater loss. 'I'll do my best to minimize your *inconvenience*, sir,' he promised drily. 'Now. Have you any idea who the dead girl might be?'

The doctor shook his head. 'None.'

'Are any of your staff missing, for instance?'

'No. I've already checked that. And the current patients are all accounted for.' He frowned. 'It's rather a mystery *who* she could be, as visitors can't gain access to the grounds without signing in at the lodge—fire regulations, you know.'

'Mm.' Rafferty had hoped the girl's identity would be easily established, but now that that hope vanished, he became brisk. 'We'll need an official statement from everyone here, and as you're anxious for us to get this crime solved speedily, perhaps I can ask you to start the ball rolling?'

'Certainly. You'll find my statement's very straight-forward. If you'd like to take this down, Sergeant?' Llewellyn whipped out his notebook. 'Between the hours of eight p.m. and two a.m. on 11/12 April, I was at a medical dinner at the George in Hamborne. No doubt the door-man will remember us arriving.' Who did he think he was? wondered Rafferty, bemused. God or visiting royalty? 'I was accompanied by my wife, Lady Evelyn, and I didn't leave the hotel during the entire time. If your sergeant would like to get that typed up, I'll sign it.'

'Certainly, sir,' Rafferty agreed. 'We'll need to see your wife, of course. Just a formality,' he added diplomatically as the doctor frowned. 'Will it be convenient if I call at your home at, say, five p.m. this afternoon?'

'I'm afraid you'll have to make your own arrangements with my wife, Rafferty. I shall be in the flat here this evening.' He fixed Rafferty with a firm eye. 'I *do* hope you'll make every effort to catch the perpetrator. If the case lingers on it could be unpleasant.' He didn't specify for whom—he didn't need to as the question that followed reminded Rafferty on whom any retribution would fall. 'When's the Chief Constable due back, by the way?'

'Not for another fortnight, sir.' Pride made him briefly optimistic. 'But I'm sure we'll have this case wrapped up before he returns from leave.' As soon as the words were out of his mouth he regretted them, but of course the cavalry of common sense arrived too late to do any good and, with a sinking feeling, he hoped he'd be able to live up to his incautious boast.

'I'm glad to hear it, Rafferty.'

There was the faintest suggestion of respect in the doctor's eyes and it gave him confidence. He'd noticed a wooden door set in the wall a few yards from the body. It was locked, but its nearness to the corpse piqued his curiosity. 'Just as a matter of interest, sir, who would have a key to that side door in the perimeter wall?' The quick answer surprised him.

'Apart from myself, no one.' Melville-Briggs looked uneasy at this admission and Rafferty wondered if he realized that, should his alibi not check out, possession of that particular key raised him to the unenviable status of chief suspect; if he did, he soon recovered. 'The staff all use the main gate. I insist upon them clocking in and out every day.'

You would, thought Rafferty, still smarting from the doctor's earlier dismissal of his detecting abilities. He was the type who would be sure to extract his pound of flesh from the wage-slaves.

'All the keys are kept at the lodge,' the doctor went on, 'and they must sign for them, at the end of the shift they hand them back to the lodge-porter. The key to the side gate isn't on the general rings.'

Once again, there was that faint unease. Rafferty made no comment. He would allow Melville-Briggs's well-polished skin to sweat a little. It would do him good. If anyone else did have a key to that door, the gate-porter would be able to tell them.

'As I said, I'll need to speak to the staff and patients as well, sir. Is it possible a room could be put at my disposal?'

'I'll speak to my secretary,' he agreed briefly. 'I'm sure we'll be able to come up with something suitable.' Fixing Rafferty with a determined eye, he added, 'Though I must insist that my patients are disturbed as little as possible. Frankly, I fail to see any reason to question them at all.'

Rafferty thought it likely that Melville-Briggs's concern was less for his highly strung patients and more for the possible loss of revenue from his patients' wealthy and easily alarmed relatives. 'I'm afraid it is necessary, sir.' His voice was firm. 'This was a particularly brutal murder and before I charge anyone I want to be sure we have a water-tight case. The patients may have seen something that would put the identity of the murderer beyond doubt. Perhaps one of them . . .' Even did the deed, he had been going to add before he thought better of it.

Melville-Briggs's small eyes narrowed as though he had followed the train of Rafferty's thoughts. 'Assuming the girl died some time last night, they'd have all been in bed and sedated with nurses in constant attendance.' Melville-Briggs's voice was sharp. 'Anyway, the patients sleep in the bedroom block and their windows overlook the rose-garden, not the gate.'

Rafferty persisted. 'Even so, we still need to take their statements and eliminate them from our enquiries, sir. They may have seen someone suspicious hanging about earlier yesterday.'

Melville-Briggs gave in ungraciously. 'Oh, very well.'

'We'll be very discreet, sir,' Rafferty soothed.

Melville-Briggs didn't look convinced and, after a pained glance at Rafferty's unruly red hair and loud pink tie, he closed his eyes briefly. 'Now, if you'll excuse me, I must get back to my patients.' Rafferty wasn't sure if he'd imagined the, 'while I've still got some left,' tagged on to the end of the doctor's reply. With a curt nod, Melville-Briggs made for the house.

Rafferty sighed. Just his luck to get landed with a murder in a nut-house; such cases always caused unpleasant complications—a nice simple mass murder would be less troublesome. Melville-Briggs was going to be a problem, he could sense it. Just because, so far, he'd been reasonably accommodating, didn't mean it would last. 'Dally was right,' he remarked gloomily to Llewellyn, as he watched the doctor's retreating back. He even *walked* rich. 'Gentleman Jim's going to be trouble. Did you notice the charm beginning to wear thin?'

'He just needs a little careful handling, sir,' remarked Llewellyn smoothly. 'As the Bible says, "A soft answer turneth away wrath,"' adding, as Rafferty stared at him, momentarily speechless, 'Proverbs 15 verse—'

'Yes, all right!' Rafferty interrupted, not altogether surprised to discover that Llewellyn had a Machiavellian side to his nature. 'I had enough of Bible thumpers at school without you starting. Anyway,' he added flatly, 'I'm not here to massage Melville-Briggs's inflated ego.' But he *was* a friend of the CC, he reminded himself unhappily. Perhaps Llewellyn had a point, though he didn't intend to give his sergeant the satisfaction of knowing he was right. He was unbearable enough as it was. 'So, you catch more flies with honey than you do with vinegar,' he remarked sardonically. 'I'll bear it in mind.' But he knew he'd have to do more than that. It went against the grain, but he knew if he didn't want him to start a loud and angry buzzing, Melville-Briggs was one ugly bluebottle he would be wise to coat in as much honey as he could muster.

Dr Dally and the scene of crime team had finished their work and the body was ready to be taken to the mortuary. Rafferty stood and watched as the shrouded corpse was placed in the back of the ambulance. So lost was he in silent, brooding contemplation, that he jumped a foot in the air as from behind him there came a cackle of maniacal laughter. He turned and found himself eyeball to eyeball with a man in pyjamas, presumably one of Dr Melville-Briggs's precious patients. The man's pupils were wildly dilated and his curly dark hair and long beard gave him a Biblical appearance, which his first words did nothing to contradict.

'So the whore has gone, then?'

Rafferty nodded, all senses suddenly alert. 'Did you know her?' The idiocy of his question was apparent as soon as the words were spoken. Melville-Briggs had probably been correct when he'd said the patients would have been quiet and sedated at the time of the murder. And if that was so, how could this one even guess at her identity, especially as her features had been rendered unrecognizable, even by her own mother?

The man didn't seem to think his question in any way odd. 'Of course I knew her. Doesn't every man recognize that foul, naked wanton, the Whore of Babylon?' As the ambulance came round the far side of the house and continued up the drive, he raised a wiry pyjama-clad arm and pointed. 'Jezebel has gone now. The devil will find a place for her in hell. So shall end all fornicators.' Lowering his condemning arm, he began to pound his bunched-up fist into the palm of his other hand.

Rafferty noticed that the man's skin was stained with a red substance that looked very like blood and with a little chill he wondered whether Melville-Briggs might have been wrong? Was it possible this poor, sick creature had somehow evaded the nursing staff and gained entrance to the grounds? His confidence plummeted. Having an outsider commit the murder would be awful enough, from the doctor's point of view, but to have one of his patients proved the guilty one would be very bad for business. Very bad indeed. He would probably prefer the case not to be solved at all. If one of the patients was the murderer, it was evident he would have a fight on his hands. And he suspected that Melville-Briggs was the kind of man who would fight dirty.

THREE

LLEWELLYN BROKE INTO his reverie. 'I had a word with Constable Hanks. Seems the body was found this morning by one of the gate-porters.' He consulted his notes. 'Name of Gilbert. Apparently, he was just coming on duty by the side gate.'

'He had a key to that gate, did he?'

Llewellyn nodded.

'You're sure, man?'

Llewellyn looked down his long nose at Rafferty's sharp tone. 'Quite sure, sir. Gilbert's at the gate-lodge now should you wish to question him about it yourself.'

Stifling a sigh, Rafferty remembered that his superior Welsh sergeant had been educated at public school and had then gone on to university to read English and Philosophy. His notebook certainly testified that he held degrees in the correct use of the English language, which perhaps explained why he looked so peeved that the secondary-modern educated Rafferty should question its accuracy. He'd even toyed with psychology, by all accounts.

Quite why Llewellyn had decided to join the police was a mystery to Rafferty. He hadn't even come in on the special entry scheme for graduates that offered accelerated promotion, which got his grudging respect. But, like so many university types whom he encountered on the force, Rafferty considered the Welshman had little 'nose' for things, and he thought smugly of his own extremely sensitive nasal member. 'So,' he remarked finally. 'The chief suspect now has company. Pity.' Dr. Melville-Briggs was either a liar or a fool who didn't know what went on in his own hospital. Or did he expect his orders to be obeyed without question? Surely, he asked himself, a psychiatrist, of all people, knew that rules were made to be broken? If Gilbert, the gate-porter, had a key to the side gate it was possible that others had too. Was it likely a lowly gate-porter would be permitted a privilege allowed to no one but the boss? Rafferty made off briskly towards the gate-lodge. Hampered by his still bruised dignity, Llewellyn followed more slowly.

Gilbert, the gate-porter, was a sharp-featured little man, who gave the appearance of having a grudge against the world. He sat, nursing a pint mug of tea, looking very sorry for himself. The mug was inscribed with the legend 'work is a four-letter word', and Rafferty got the impression that it stated a large part of Gilbert's limited philosophy of life.

'Yes,' he admitted, with a show of reluctance when Rafferty began to question him, 'I found the body. Gruesome it was.' His eyes swivelled sideways at Rafferty and he whined self-pityingly, 'By rights somebody should take me 'ome. Ain't right to expect a man to carry on working after seeing such a sight.' He took a sip of his tea. 'Ain't right,' he repeated glumly, as though he felt he was being unfairly deprived of a legitimate day off.

'I'm sure Dr Melville-Briggs will let you go just as soon as you've answered a few questions.' Rafferty's lack of belief in Dr Melville-Briggs's compassion for his fellow man was evidently shared by Gilbert, whose face became even more glum.

'Him?' He snorted. 'Not likely. There's more chance of me getting the sack than sympathy from him.'

Despite the aura of gloom that surrounded the man, Rafferty got the distinct impression that Gilbert was enjoying himself in a rather perverse way. He was star for the day. Tonight he would probably hold court in the local pub and expect to be bought free drinks all night as he told and re-told his grisly tale. Rafferty thought Gilbert and Llewellyn should get on well together; they both seemed to get pleasure from looking on the black side.

'Have you any idea who the victim might be, Mr Gilbert?' Rafferty questioned. Gilbert shook his head. Although Melville-Briggs had told him no one from the hospital was missing, Rafferty wanted to double check. 'Are there any girls with long dark hair amongst the staff or patients?'

'There's one or two, but they're away at the seaside, lucky so-and-sos. Wish I was.'

'I believe you have a key to the side gate. Is that right?'

Gilbert nodded once, guardedly, then added, with the air of one who—if he had to take the road to hell—wanted to make sure that it was on the coach during the staff outing, 'Mind, I'm not the only one. I like to oblige people when I can. Do 'em good turns like.'

Gilbert was a most unlikely do-gooder, thought Rafferty, eyeing him without enthusiasm. Fiddling the tea-money and stocking his freezer from the hospital kitchens would be more his line. Scared that possession of the key would incriminate him, was Gilbert confessing to the lesser sin of providing half the staff of the hospital with illicit keys? Rafferty groaned softly, but he needed to be clear on the point. If so, it immediately threw the list of suspects wide open. 'I understood from Dr Melville-Briggs that no one else besides him had a key to that gate and that all the staff had to use the main entrance.'

Gilbert snorted again. It seemed to be his favourite mode of expression. 'Supposed to. Only this morning I was a bit late, like, and thought I'd sneak in. Jack the night porter would 'ave covered for me and clocked me in as usual.' He sighed heavily. 'Now I suppose when 'is lordship finds out, I'll be for the 'igh jump.' His voice rose indignantly. 'What did she want to go and get herself murdered 'ere for? On the very morning I was late, too. It ain't fair.'

The wretched victim seemed to have discommoded everybody. Rafferty probed a little deeper. 'Jack, the other porter, did he see anything?'

Gilbert grinned with sour amusement. 'Old Jack? No. Didn't know nothin' about it till I told 'im. Likes to get 'is 'ead down of a night, does Jack. No chance of that on the day shift, worse luck.'

He could do with a bit of shut-eye himself, Rafferty thought, rubbing his gritty eyes and forcing himself to concentrate. 'How many of the staff have keys to that side gate?'

Gilbert's grin faded. 'Most of 'em,' he replied gloomily. 'I suppose you'll want a list?'

Rafferty agreed that it would be helpful and with several mutterings and mumblings, Gilbert provided it. As he wrote, he continued his explanation. 'I go through the pantomime of locking the rest of the keys up in this cupboard 'ere.' He indicated the metal key cabinet that hung on the wall. 'But it's only to keep old smarmy-pants happy, cos they all keep the keys to the side gate. They usually 'ang around the staffroom for coffee before they start and I bring the keys over in bulk then, before ol' Tony puts in an appearance. I do the same in reverse before they leave, so they can use the side gate. I'd let 'em keep the keys if it was up to me, less trouble all round, but you can never tell when 'is lordship might decide to check up. He can be right sneaky like that.'

Rafferty wondered whether Melville-Briggs would be pleased to discover the reluctant admiration behind the complaint of his gate-porter. 'But I thought they had to sign in and out as well as hand over the keys?'

Gilbert's eyes slid away and Rafferty concluded that Gilbert supplied a certain skill as a forger along with his other services. Quite an enterprising fellow. 'Never mind. Go on,' he prompted.

Gilbert seemed relieved that Rafferty was so obliging as to gloss over his little difficulty and now he became confiding. 'As I said, most of us come and go as we please through the side gate. It's more convenient like for the bus.'

'Does ol—' Rafferty caught himself in time. 'Does Dr Melville-Briggs keep keys himself or does he hand them in to you?'

'Not 'im.' Gilbert looked aggrieved. 'He's always 'ad a key to that side gate as long as I've been 'ere and that's gettin' on for seven years now. Makes more use of it than the rest of us put together 'an all.' He sniggered as though he had said something amusing and then he looked speculatively at Rafferty. 'Do you reckon 'is lordship done it?'

The idea seemed to appeal to him. How may titles did the blasted man have? Rafferty wondered. 'Does 'is lordship . . . ?'

'He's not a lordship!' Gilbert sneered at the very idea.
'I just call 'im that because he acts as if 'e *was* one. It's
'er that's the ladyship. 'Er dad were an earl or a lord or
somethin'. He's only a sir because 'er money greased a
few palms. It's 'er title, 'er money, even 'er bloomin'
name.'

'What do you mean?'

Gilbert grinned slyly. 'She insisted 'e take her name,
Melville, when they got married. She's got a brother,
but even then, 'e showed no signs of producing an 'eir.
'E's a bit...' He flapped a limp wrist graphically.
'Herself and her brother were the last of the line and the
name would have died out, see?' He sniggered again.
'Though if you saw her precious son, you'd think she
might have saved herself the trouble. I can't see her
gettin' an 'eir out of 'im!'

'Oh? Is he...?' His flapping wrist was every bit as
graphic as Gilbert's had been.

'Supposed not to be—he's gettin' married after all.
But whenever 'e's been 'ere on the cadge from 'is old
man 'e looked as limp as a week-old lettuce leaf to me.
I 'eard as 'ow 'e's got himself a fancy car-renovation
business in London, paid for by his ma, complete with
muscular mechanic. I reckon 'e's only marrying that
horse-faced Lady Huntingdon's daughter to keep in
with his mum.' Gilbert sniggered. 'Probably rather
shack up with that mechanic, 'Arry. Mind, if you saw
the bride, you might agree wiv 'im. She was 'ere at
Christmas with some bigshots ol' Tony was showing
round and you'd think she'd been sucking on a lemon
from the sour puss of 'er.' Gilbert was well into his
stride now and had perked up considerably. 'Lady E.
gave him all this, you know.' He waved his arms to take
in the beautiful house and grounds and all that went

with it. 'My ol' woman 'elps out at the 'all when they
'ave big dos and not much gets past 'er. You'd be surprised at what people let slip after all them fancy wines.
Rivetin', some of it,' he added with a certain bright-eyed
satisfaction.

Rafferty made no comment, but he wondered if Gilbert fancied his chances at extracting a little blackmail
money from the well-to-do diners? He wouldn't put it
past him.

' 'Er brother had let the whole estate go to wrack and
ruin.' Gilbert continued his confidences. 'She 'ad it all
tarted up. No expense spared, so I 'eard. She organized
the whole show. Even acted as 'is secretary while he got
'imself established. Very capable woman is Lady Evelyn, no airs to 'er—not like *'im*. She encouraged 'im to
be one of them 'ead shrinkers. Mind you, she's right,
there's money in it. All them neurotic women he
treats—very profitable, I reckon, though few of them
seem to ever get cured. Why wave goodbye to the goose
that lays the golden egg? Think he's a god, they do.
Mind, I don't reckon her ladyship would agree wiv 'em.'

'Oh?' Rafferty's ears pricked up. 'Why's that?'

'My ol' woman reckons they don't get on. He's got a
flat on the top floor 'ere and often stays there at night.
That's why he finds the side gate so convenient.' He
winked and tapped his nose. 'Very cosy that flat is too,
for 'im and his assorted lady friends. Regular proces-
sion of them there is.'

Lucky old Tony, thought Rafferty. Not only a rich
wife to buy him success, it seemed she put up with his
bits on the side as well. 'She must be a very understanding woman,' he remarked.

'I don't know about that. She's one of the old
school—the put up and shut up sort. Believes in duty,

the stiff upper lip and all that. Mind, I don't 'old that against 'er. It's the way she were brought up and at least you know where you are wiv 'er. Not like 'im.' Belatedly, he seemed to realize he had been a trifle indiscreet and now he looked anxiously at Rafferty. ''Ere, you won't tell 'im I've told you all this, will you?'

'Think of me as a priest, Gilbert,' Rafferty reassured him. 'I hear everything but repeat nothing.'

Rafferty's reassurance didn't seem to comfort him at all. If anything, he looked gloomier than before, as though he found the possibility of a cop keeping a confidence pretty unlikely.

Rafferty borrowed Gilbert's telephone to get the house-to-house organized. The search for the murder weapon and the victim's clothes was also got under way and now Rafferty left the team to it while he and Llewellyn made for the house. He prayed that the victim had a record, because if she hadn't it was likely to be a long case, and after his boast to Melville-Briggs, he didn't fancy having to break the news to him if he should turn out to be wrong. He didn't think he'd get any more sympathy than Gilbert was likely to receive. Still, at least he should have found them a room by now. Presumably the man was capable of working out that parading his patients past the gutter press for their interviews at the police station was unlikely to improve his profits or his reputation.

MELVILLE-BRIGGS WAS half-way down the stairs when they entered the house. There was none of the usual institutionalized scrimping here, Rafferty noticed. The carpet was thick and luxurious; the stairs magnificent; the open strings of the tread-ends were decorated with scrolls and the treads carried turned banisters with graceful refined curves. Of solid oak, like the panelled walls, they hugged the side of the house as they rose to meet the first floor.

Tearing his mind and eyes from the beauty of the house, Rafferty reluctantly relieved him of the role of chief suspect. 'I've just been talking to Gilbert, the gate-porter, sir, and it seems that most of the staff here have keys to that side gate. Naturally, that widens the entire scope of the case.'

Melville-Briggs's eyes narrowed and the look in them boded ill for the unfortunate Gilbert. He subjected Rafferty to a thoughtful scrutiny before commenting, 'Well, if this case is to be solved, you'll want to get on, I'm sure.' He led the way briskly up the stairs.

Rafferty asked conversationally, 'Have you managed to find us a room, sir?'

Melville-Briggs nodded. 'I've spoken to my secretary and we've sorted out something suitable.'

Suitable for what? Rafferty mused. His lowly rank? Was it to be the attic or the basement, he wondered, as he followed Melville-Briggs's broad and expensively tailored beam up the stairs. He hoped it wasn't the attic. The thought of all those stairs was enough to bring on his smoker's cough. Ex-smoker's cough, he corrected himself. There was to be no backsliding this time. He was determined on it. 'I'll need a full list of the staff, sir.' One of the first things to do would be to get their movements checked out.

Melville-Briggs didn't pause in his regal ascent, but waved his arm irritably. 'I think you might save such requests for my secretary, Mrs Galvin, she's perfectly capable of dealing with such matters.' Apparently the great man didn't soil his hands with clerical work. They reached the landing that ran around three sides of the

hall and Melville-Briggs paused and glanced speculatively at the two policemen. 'You know, Rafferty,' he
began. 'I've been thinking.'

Rafferty waited to hear the results of these delibera-
tions. He hoped he wasn't to be treated to another little
lecture on the importance of the hospital and its residents. But as Melville-Briggs went on, he discovered
he'd wronged the man.

'You remember I mentioned I thought someone had
a powerful motive for leaving the body of that poor girl
on *my* premises?' Rafferty nodded. 'I've given it some
more thought and realize that it's my duty to give you
the name of the man I suspect.'

This unexpectedly helpful attitude made Rafferty
wary. Was the doctor trying to settle some old score by
his allegations? he wondered. He didn't doubt he was
capable of it. Most people had ulterior motives for what
they did and they all came out of the woodwork in a
murder investigation. You're just an old cynic, Rafferty, he told himself. Perhaps the doctor was simply
improving with acquaintance. The thought was encouraged by the fact that for the first time, Melville-
Briggs had mentioned the unfortunate victim with every
appearance of compassion. Up till now, it had been
only himself and extensions of the same—his hospital,
his patients, his patients' relatives—that had merited his
consideration. 'Yes, sir?' he said encouragingly. 'Go
on.'

'This is strictly confidential, of course, but I suspect
a man called Nathanial Whittaker. He's the owner of
the Holbrook Clinic a few miles away.'

'Have you any reason to think he might wish you
harm, sir?'

'He threatened me only last night. In front of witnesses, too. Rather a coincidence, don't you think?'
Rafferty remained silently non-committal and Melville-Briggs went on in the manner of a man with a
deeply felt grievance which he felt wasn't being given
sufficient consideration. 'Shows what was on his mind,
to my way of thinking. I think his lack of success has
unbalanced him. It does that to some men and, of
course, his entire life's been a disappointment. No
wonder his wife left him. You might find it interesting
to look him up in the Hospital Yearbook and send for
some of his literature. You'll be able to see just how
unimpressive his place is. Bitterness and failure can do
sad things to a man's morals, Rafferty. In your line, you
should know that. You must encounter such people all
the time.'

'But surely he wouldn't go as far as murder just to
damage you, sir,' Rafferty remarked quietly. Still, he
mused, it might sound a crazy motive for murder, but
it was incredible what people *could* get up to and for the
strangest of reasons. And Melville-Briggs would make
enemies with the greatest of ease. Hadn't he taken an
instant dislike to the man himself?

The doctor gave a mirthless laugh. 'It's obvious you
don't know many medical men, Rafferty. But in this
instance, no, I'm not suggesting it was murder. Not
necessarily, anyway, though, of course...' He let his
voice trail off suggestively. 'A medical man wouldn't
necessarily need to commit murder to get hold of a
convenient body. Perhaps one of his patients had a fall,
fractured her skull, and died, and rather than embarrass himself, he decided to embarrass me, damage my

reputation by dumping the body here, mutilating her to make it look as bad as possible for me.'

'But what about the patient's relatives?' Rafferty asked reasonably. 'Even a doctor can't just lose a body without questions being asked.'

'You'd be surprised. Doctors still need bodies for experiments and Whittaker does a lot of research.' He gave a derisive laugh. 'None of it very successful, I might add. Some men would do anything for fame and Whittaker's one of them.' He paused to let that sink in and then continued. 'I grant you, any patient such a doctor might lose would never be an *important* patient. Good Lord, no,' he added, as though the bemused Rafferty had just accused him of something quite shocking. 'Not that Whittaker attracts that type of patient. Dropouts and dregs are more *his* line, you'll find, the sort who wouldn't be missed, and Whittaker takes a lot of National Health patients. Well,' he smiled sardonically, 'he has to, few *private* patients would be foolish enough to go to that mismanaged clinic of his. His patients tend to come and go as they please. Why should anyone think it odd if the occasional one vanishes? Such people discharge themselves all the time without bothering to go through the official formalities. Sometimes they die—from an accident or an overdose or an accumulation of the abuse to which they've subjected their bodies. Sometimes they just give up and turn their faces to the wall.'

A murder victim that hadn't even been murdered. It was a somewhat bizarre suggestion, Rafferty reflected, as his eyes met the enigmatic gaze of his sergeant. Bizarre, but not impossible. 'Would he have access to a key, though, Doctor?'

Sir Anthony sniffed. 'As it appears that Gilbert handed them out like Smarties, it's not beyond the realms of possibility, Rafferty. Or,' he added tartly, 'beyond the powers of the police to find out.'

FOUR

MELVILLE-BRIGGS opened a door on the first floor that overlooked the drive. 'These are the investigating policemen, Mrs Galvin.' He didn't bother to introduce them. 'I believe I mentioned that they required a room?'

She glanced at Rafferty. 'I imagine you require details of our staff, their duties, hours of work, and so on?'

Rafferty nodded encouragingly. Her voice was pleasant; low and musical. She was perhaps in her early thirties. An attractive, delicate-featured woman, there wasn't a strand of dark hair out of place in the ruthlessly neat French pleat and Rafferty wondered what hidden depths such an outwardly controlled appearance might be concealing. There appeared to be an air of constraint between her and the doctor. Intrigued, Rafferty glanced speculatively at them both, but Melville-Briggs, having made his wishes known, wasted no more of his valuable time, and went out, shutting the panelled door firmly behind him, as much as to say 'don't bother *me* with minor details.'

Mrs Galvin opened the top drawer of the filing cabinet and extracted two thin files and handed them to Rafferty. 'The green file lists all the staff who are on duty this week and the buff file covers the full complement of staff, from the medical staff through to the cleaners. Though, of course, most of the nursing staff are away on escort duties at the moment. We usually take our patients away for their short spring holiday about this time, so there's only a skeleton staff and a few patients here.'

Rafferty brightened. That was the first glimmer of good news he'd heard all morning. 'And they're all accounted for?' Mrs Galvin nodded. 'You'll understand that we need to establish the victim's identity as speedily as possible. Have you any idea who she might be? What she might have been doing in the grounds?'

'I'm afraid not. I finish work at five thirty, so have no idea who might frequent the premises after that time.'

There had been a certain distaste in her voice. Rafferty wondered who *would* know? Perhaps his earlier guess about one of the night staff smuggling in a girlfriend would prove accurate? He hoped so, as it should make establishing the victim's identity easier. Now he gave Mrs Galvin one of his more winning smiles. 'Can you tell me what sort of patients you treat here?'

'We accept a variety of cases, but we specialize in drug-dependency, and most of our patients come into that category.'

'How long do most of them stay?'

'We tend to take in the really hopeless cases, I'm afraid, those that have been assessed and treated unsuccessfully elsewhere. You could say we provide a permanent and secure home for the sadder elements of society.' Few empty beds then, mused Rafferty, very profitable. 'They lack for nothing,' Mrs Galvin went on, as though anxious to remove the cynicism Rafferty suspected might be apparent in his blue eyes. 'Perhaps you don't realize that in the grounds we have an extensive range of facilities to keep them happy and occupied? For instance, we have an indoor heated swimming-pool, a jacuzzi, a gymnasium for our younger clients, and of course we encourage them to

develop an interest in gardening—it's a very soothing
occupation for disturbed minds, we've discovered.'

As well as making a small saving on gardeners' wages,
Rafferty reflected. Rather convenient.

'Do you handle really violent cases at all?' asked
Llewellyn, getting to the heart of the matter.

'Occasionally,' she admitted cautiously. 'But the patients are carefully supervised at all times. There is no
possib—'

'I'm sure they are,' Rafferty interrupted soothingly.
Remembering the patient he had encountered in the
grounds, he asked, 'Could you let me have a list of the
in-patients?'

Her manner became brisk. 'Not without Dr Melville-Briggs's authority, I'm afraid. Most of our patients come from very distinguished families and we
have to be discreet.'

Rafferty didn't press the point. They could always
apply for a court order to release the files if he thought
it necessary.

After giving him a searching glance from steady grey
eyes, she added, 'You'll find the staff lists clearly
marked to show those on sick leave or holiday leave,
those on escort duty and so on. All the symbols are explained at the base.'

'You keep a tidy filing cabinet, Mrs Galvin,' Rafferty complimented. 'Really first class.' He thought
ruefully of his own untidy and neglected paper work.
When this case was over, he resolved, he really must
tackle it.

Her grey eyes held a hint of amusement as she remarked, 'It's my job, Inspector, I hope I'm reasonably
efficient at it.'

She handed over another document with the comment, 'This is a plan of the hospital and its grounds. You might find it helpful.'

Rafferty nodded. 'Would you have a Hospital Yearbook? Dr Melville-Briggs thought we might find it useful.'

'Really? I can't imagine why, but yes, of course, I have a copy.' She reached over to the book rack on her desk and passed it to him. 'It's this year's.'

'I'm obliged to you. I'll let you have it back as quickly as possible.'

She nodded and walked briskly to the door. 'If you'll follow me, I'll show you the room you can use.'

She led them along the corridor and back down the stairs. She opened a door at the far end of the hall and they descended another short flight of steps, though these had no fancy scroll work and were plain and serviceable. After negotiating several dusty corridors and interconnecting empty rooms, Mrs Galvin at last led them to their temporary office.

The room allotted to them was in a rather mouldy smelling semi-basement at the back of the house. Rafferty turned on the light. The naked bulb illuminated a cheerless little box, empty but for half a dozen rickety-looking chairs and a battered table upon which countless schoolboy hands had carved their initials. He guessed that Melville-Briggs had chosen this particular room for them as punishment for not falling in with his wishes over the attempted bribe. Two telephones rested on the table and he picked one up to check that it was working.

'That one has an outside line,' Mrs Galvin told him. 'The grey one is for internal calls. I'll supply you with a list of the various extensions.'

He nodded his thanks before glancing up. There was a small window high up in the wall, but all it illuminated were the cobwebs festooned around it. Rafferty gave a wry smile as Llewellyn murmured predictably, 'Be it ever so humble...'

Mrs Galvin looked embarrassed. 'Perhaps I could try to arrange something a little more... a little larger.'

Rafferty surmised that her boss was unlikely to take kindly to the idea, especially if, as he suspected, his slanderous accusation against a fellow medical man proved so much hogwash. 'Don't trouble yourself, Mrs Galvin.' He tried his smile again and this time there was a definite softening in the dark grey eyes. 'This will do us very well, won't it, Sergeant?'

Llewellyn looked around the room with a marked lack of enthusiasm. 'It'll serve our purpose, sir.'

His dour tones gave the impression that, once installed in the room, they intended to wield truncheons with vigour, and Rafferty winced, half-expecting the Welshman to enquire if it was sound-proofed. But perhaps he was being unduly sensitive, as Mrs Galvin didn't seem to read any more into the remark.

'If you need anything else, please ask me. I'd rather you didn't trouble Dr Melville-Briggs.'

Her sentiments echoed Rafferty's. Until they had identified the victim, the less he saw of that gentleman the better. Gallantly, he escorted her to the door. 'Thanks for your help, and I promise I'll try not to trouble the doctor more than strictly necessary. I'm sure he's a very busy man.'

A slight flush tinged her delicately boned cheeks. 'Oh yes. I think you could say he keeps himself fully occupied.' Rafferty detected a certain bitter irony in her tone, but at his sharp glance her voice immediately softened.

'He has much with which to concern himself. The patients can be very demanding and he has to think constantly of their welfare.'

He'd have to if he wanted them to keep laying, was Rafferty's cynical thought. 'Dedicated type then, is he?' he enquired.

'Dedicated?' Her voice was lightly ironic. 'Oh, yes, I think you could say that. Hence the flat. Lady Evelyn doesn't encourage him to bring his work home.'

Especially not the blondes, brunettes, and redheads whom Gilbert had more than hinted at, Rafferty thought. Perhaps the faceless lady would turn out to be one of them.

THEY'D WORKED their way through the files that Mrs Galvin had given them and soon had several impressive-looking lists of their own. After careful checking, it was firmly established that no one from the hospital was missing and all the staff and patients currently on holiday on the Dorset coast had been accounted for, which meant that the victim had certainly come from outside. It was curious, because he had earlier dispatched Constable Hanks to question Jack, the night gate-porter, before letting him home, and the man had been adamant that not only had no unknown visitors been signed in the previous evening, but that everyone he had signed in had been signed out again. As Gilbert had told them, Jack hadn't seen or heard anything; as far as he was concerned, it had been a quiet night. It pointed to the dead girl being very much an *unofficial* visitor, as he had suspected.

Rafferty looked at the clock. 'Right. It's time to go a calling.' Bundling his files together, he handed them to Llewellyn with a sigh of relief. They had an appointment for five o'clock. 'Perhaps Lady Evelyn will be kind enough to drop the great Narcissus in it?' he remarked hopefully. 'Wouldn't that be nice?' As expected, Llewellyn contradicted him.

'Unlikely, sir. Besides, there must be plenty of other witnesses to confirm what Dr Melville-Briggs said.'

'Well, I can hope,' Rafferty retorted, adding caustically, 'Get a move on. We don't want to be late twice in one day.'

ELMHURST HALL WAS the only property down a quiet country lane and was well concealed from prying eyes. Rafferty had made Llewellyn stop off at the public library to borrow a book on local history on their way to see Lady Evelyn, and the hall featured prominently. He was looking forward to seeing it.

The high wrought-iron gates were open and Llewellyn turned the car into the drive. The building was mainly early Tudor, but Rafferty's part-trained builder's eye recognized that the great hall was medieval. The old stained glass glowed with an unearthly light, well set off by the simple black and white timber-framed walls and he stared blissfully, absorbing it all.

The manservant who opened the door must have been warned to expect them, for after checking their names he led them through an inner high-arched door, which, to Rafferty's delight, led to the original hall. It was magnificent and as he looked round him a lump formed in his throat.

The roof timbers soared fully fifty feet above the floor and looked as though they had been crafted by a giant's hand. Enormous king posts rested on collar-beams, which, in turn, rested on moulded braces, all coated with the rich patina of centuries. His gaze took

in old battle banners, swords, and shields hanging from
the wall, enormous serving dishes, and a vast oak table, which must easily hold thirty people. Barely aware
that he had stopped to stare, it was only when Llewellyn cleared his throat that he remembered why he was
here.

The butler opened another door and introduced
them. Lady Evelyn rose from her chair and came to
greet them. 'Inspector. Won't you and your sergeant
come and sit by the fire? These large rooms grow a little chilly at this time of day.'

Rafferty was glad to sit at the vast hearth and warm
himself. Llewellyn settled himself and his notebook at
a short, discreet distance.

Lady Evelyn sat opposite Rafferty on the other side
of the hearth. 'You'll both take coffee with me? It's all
ready.'

Rafferty nodded his thanks, and while she served him
he studied her. He guessed her to be around the late
forties. She was tall, and although the fine skin and
grey-flecked auburn hair were her only real claims to
beauty, she had an indefinable quality that no cosmetic
could provide, and he wondered what she had seen in
old Tony. Her grey worsted skirt and high-necked white
blouse were plain, the blouse adorned only with a discreet gold brooch on which there was some Latin in-
scription, the meaning of which Llewellyn would, no
doubt, take great delight in explaining to him later.

Taking his cup, he settled back comfortably as she
served Llewellyn. It was a restful room, and if the chair
upon which he sat lacked cushioned modernity its
straight back and high curved arms offered repose.
Even Llewellyn seemed to have relaxed, Rafferty no-

ticed with amusement, and looked as contented as the unfortunate composition of his features would allow.

Rafferty glanced curiously around the room, at the well-worn but presumably expensive rugs, at the many paintings of fierce-looking earlier Melvilles, each neatly labelled, the photographs that adorned the desk top and mantelpiece. He was reluctant to introduce the unpleasant topic of murder into such peace, but, he reminded himself, as he was here as a policeman and not an invited guest, he'd better get on with it.

Putting his cup down, he began. 'As I believe my sergeant explained on the phone, we're taking statements from everyone in any way connected with your husband's hospital, Lady Evelyn. In most cases, it's just going to be a formality, of course, but we need to eliminate as many people as possible from our enquiries.'

She nodded. 'Naturally, I'll help in any way I can.' Her eyes shadowed. 'A most distressing business. I understand her face...' Lady Evelyn paled and stumbled to a halt. It was a few moments before she was able to go on. 'Forgive me. It's all been rather a shock.' She gave a moue of distaste. 'My husband rang me earlier and revealed some of the more... unpleasant details. Her poor family—have you been able to identify her yet?'

Rafferty shook his head. 'Of course, it's early days. You've no idea who she might be, I suppose?' he asked hopefully.

Lady Evelyn shook her head. 'I rarely visit my husband's sanatorium these days, Inspector. Even the staff are mostly strangers to me now.' She gave a faint smile. 'A consequence of a busy life, I'm afraid. At one time, I used to know them all.'

'I see. I understand you and your husband were at the George in Hamborne last night?'

'That's right. A medical dinner. It's held every year.'

'It went on till two a.m., I understand?'

'Yes.' With a tinge of irony, she added, 'I found it a rather long night, but as the proceeds were in aid of the local nursery and I'm on the committee, I felt obliged to attend.' She smiled self-mockingly. 'A case of *noblesse oblige*, as they say.'

Rafferty nodded understandingly. How often had he felt obliged to do what he would rather not? His wife, Angie, had made any number of scenes whilst he had been studying for his sergeant's exams. Too often, for the sake of peace, he had abandoned his studies to escort her to some function or other and they hadn't even offered the consolation of supporting a worthy cause. That was why he had failed his exams the first time. She had hated the police force and its anti-social hours of duty. 'Duty, duty, it's always duty,' she had often screamed at him. 'What about me—my needs? Don't they count?'

A log crashed noisily in the grate and brought him back with a start. He found he had relaxed once more and forced himself to sit more erect in the chair. 'Were you both present at the George for the entire night? Your husband...'

'Anthony?' She stared at him. 'Surely you don't suspect my husband?'

'No, no,' he reassured her. 'As I said, it's probably only a formality, so if you can assure me that you were both there all evening we won't trouble you any further.'

'But I can't.' Lady Evelyn fingered her gold pin and gave him a bleak little smile. 'This is rather unfortunate. We weren't together the entire evening, you see, Inspector. Once the meal was over I saw little of him, so I'm afraid I can't give him an—alibi, I suppose the term is. As you can imagine, on these occasions the men talk shop and wives tend to be left to their own devices.'

She spoke lightly as though it were a matter of little moment, but Rafferty had been in enough similar situations in his own marriage and knew what it was like to be ignored, left on the side-lines while one's partner joined more congenial companions.

Almost as though in defence against his silent and unasked for sympathy, Lady Evelyn brightened. 'I'm sure it will be a simple matter to prove that he was there the entire night. There were enough people present and as Anthony seemed to know most of them, someone's sure to be able to confirm what he says.'

'How did you get to the George that night, ma'am?' asked Llewellyn. 'I understand you have a chauffeur?'

'Yes. But as it happens, it was his long weekend off and I'd stupidly forgotten to ask him to change it—so annoying. And by the time I did remember, he'd already left. Normally, of course, for such a function, we would use the Bentley and Anthony was rather put out when we were reduced to my car.'

'But surely you could still have used the Bentley?'

'I'm afraid not, Sergeant. The Bentley is a manual and I only drive automatics. When we discovered that Anderson our chauffeur had left for the weekend we both knew that I would have to drive.' She smiled faintly. 'There are usually excellent wines at dinner and on such occasions my husband likes to let his hair down with his colleagues.'

'A rather unfortunate start to the evening, ma'am,' Rafferty commented sympathetically.

'Yes.' She sighed. 'Of course, in the way of such things, it got worse. The lights on my car had been accidentally left on and the battery was flat. Anthony rather blamed me, but both he and my son, when he's home, tend to use my car as a spare. Anyway, after some completely pointless recriminations, we used jump leads from the cook's car. By the time we finally got going, it was rather late.'

'It might have been a better idea to borrow the cook's car in the first place,' Llewellyn commented dryly.

'I did suggest it, of course—it's an automatic like mine, but it's a little old and shabby and my husband feels he has a position to maintain. He didn't want to arrive in such an... unsuitable vehicle.' She went on. 'But as it happened, it wouldn't have mattered. By the time we got to the George, the carpark was full and the attendant wouldn't let us in. We had to drive round and round the streets till we could find a parking place. Anthony wasn't very pleased. He gave the door-man rather a hard time, though, of course, it wasn't his fault, poor man.'

Rafferty could imagine how Anthony Melville-Briggs would take such an affront to his dignity. No wonder he had been so sure the door-man would remember them. The good doctor in a rage would certainly be a pretty spectacular sight. Swallowing the appreciative chuckle, he glanced over at Llewellyn. The Welshman's dark head was bent over his notebook as though its contents engrossed him and he wondered if it was possible that his sergeant shared his amusement.

Although the day outside had turned bleak, and the old house groaned from the buffeting of the wind blowing straight off the North Sea, the winter parlour was warm, the panelled walls reflected the glowing red

and gold flames from the heaped logs burning steadily
in the hearth and Rafferty felt lethargy steal over him.
Curious to discover more than his quick perusal of the
guide-book had revealed, he asked, 'Has Elmhurst Hall
always belonged to your family, ma'am?'

'No, only since the late fifteenth century,' replied
Lady Evelyn. 'My great-great-great, etc., grandfather,
a landless knight, backed Henry Tudor at the Battle of
Bosworth, and as you probably know, the Tudor won
the day.'

'And your family were rewarded with the Hall?'

'In a roundabout way. Henry Tudor was reluctant to
give rewards out of his own pocket, being a mean man
by nature, but Edward Melville was given something
even better—a rich heiress in marriage: Lady Cecily
Aimering. It was through her that we acquired the Hall,
amongst other things. At that time, of course—' She
broke off and he looked enquiringly at her.

'I'm sorry.' She gave an apologetic smile. 'I didn't
mean to give you a history lesson.' Rafferty glanced
slyly at Llewellyn to see if this sensitivity had penetrated. Llewellyn met his eyes with the inscrutable expression of a Merlin as Lady Evelyn continued. 'My
husband tells me I bore people to death talking about
the house.'

'You're not boring me,' Rafferty assured her. He
managed to get a little dig in for Llewellyn's benefit.
'Give me someone who knows their stuff and can tell it
without talking down to people and I'm happy. Besides, I'm a bit of a history buff myself. Houses are a
hobby of mine,' he explained, 'and it tends to go with
the territory.' But there was work to be done, he reminded himself, signalling to Llewellyn as he got to his
feet. 'We'd best be off. Thank you for your hospitality,

ma'am. If you could possibly pop into the station some time and sign the statement?'

'Of course. Tomorrow morning? About ten?'

He nodded. 'That'll be fine.' Rather sheepishly, he pulled the little library book about the Hall from his pocket as they headed for the door. 'I understand you occasionally open your home to the public, ma'am? I wouldn't mine seeing it myself when this case is over.'

'Why don't you give me a ring when you're able to make it and we'll arrange a time?'

Rafferty was happy to agree and finally they left, but he couldn't help wondering if Lady Evelyn would still be willing to show him round her home if the case ended with her husband being arrested for murder. He rather doubted it. In spite of his air of confidence, Melville-Briggs's alibi wasn't nearly as sound as he'd led them to believe. If his own *wife* couldn't vouch for him for the whole evening, was it likely that anyone else could?

FIVE

LLEWELLYN LOOKED UP from his study of the Hospital Yearbook, which Mrs Galvin had so obligingly lent them, as Rafferty entered their temporary office the next morning and flung himself into a chair. 'Still no sign of the murder weapon?' he questioned Llewellyn.

Llewellyn shook his head. 'They should finish searching the hospital and its grounds today. Has Dr Dally been able to give you any idea what the weapon might be?'

'Hasn't a clue.' Rafferty pulled a face. 'Won't admit it, of course. I don't suppose any blood-soaked clothes have shown up, either?'

Llewellyn shook his head again. 'Neither have the victim's fingerprints been traced yet. They're still working on it. Fraser said he'll ring back if they come up with anything.'

Rafferty nodded. 'Perhaps I should ask my old ma to light a few candles for us? We'll need all the help we can get to solve this crime if we can't even discover who the victim was. You'd think *someone* would have missed her by now.'

Llewellyn tapped lean fingers on the book lying open on the desk in front of him. 'The Holbrook Clinic that Dr Melville-Briggs mentioned, sir, it's only about three miles away.'

Rafferty grunted. 'I know. I asked Gilbert. But never mind that for now. Whittaker isn't going anywhere. If he intended to, he'd have gone by now and he hasn't. I checked.' He got up restlessly. 'Get on to the station. I want more men up here. I don't care how many officers you have to drag off leave. I want those clothes and the weapon found.'

After Llewellyn had organized the extra manpower, he studied Rafferty with probing dark eyes. 'Do you really think there's anything in this professional jealousy theory of Dr Melville-Briggs's, sir?'

Llewellyn's voice sounded doubtful and, sensing an unspoken criticism, Rafferty frowned. Aware that he was being over-sensitive, but unable to stop himself, he took a high moral tone. 'An experienced policeman keeps an open mind, Sergeant,' he replied loftily. 'There certainly seems to be a lot of bad feeling between the two men. According to Gilbert, they nearly came to blows a month ago, apart from their disagreement on the night of the dinner. Seems Whittaker accused Melville-Briggs of spreading malicious rumours about him. Gilbert swears Whittaker hadn't obtained a key to the side gate from him, but he did drop a heavy hint that Miss Gwendoline Parry, the Administrator here, is rather sweet on Whittaker and she has a key. She's on leave till Tuesday. She'll keep. We've plenty to occupy us till then.'

The phone rang just then and Rafferty snatched it up, hoping there might be some good news at last. A delighted grin split his face as he scribbled a few quick notes on the scrap pad in front of him. 'Yes, yes, I've got that. Thanks. Thanks very much.' He replaced the receiver slowly, as though savouring the moment, and gave Llewellyn an elliptical glance.

'Good news, Taff.' The use of the nickname was quite deliberate. As he had guessed, the Welshman didn't take kindly to it—well, *he* didn't take kindly to being thought of as an ignorant Mick. Maybe Llewellyn would take the hint and stop acting so damn superior. Tilting his chair back at a dangerous angle, he challenged, 'I bet you a pound to a pinch of shit that this'll bring a smile to that mournful Welsh mug of yours.'

Llewellyn merely murmured, 'Oh?' before issuing a cautious warning, 'I wouldn't tip your seat back like that, sir. These old hospital chairs aren't up to such rough treatment.'

Rafferty waved the caution aside. 'That was Fingers Fraser on the phone. He's matched the prints, so ma won't have to light those candles after all. The victim's identity will point us to the man who killed her. It's bound to.'

Llewellyn's expression didn't alter, but his laconic reply succeeded in wiping the smile off Rafferty's face. 'I wouldn't be so sure. Identifying a victim does not a murder solve.'

Rafferty scowled and brought all four legs of his chair back to earth with a crash. The crack of splintered wood proved Llewellyn's forebodings correct and he landed in an undignified heap on the floor as what was left of the chair collapsed under him. A faint smile took fleeting possession of Llewellyn's features and he murmured softly, 'Pride goeth before destruction, and an haughty spirit before a f—'

'Oh shut up!' Rafferty retorted childishly. Bloody sanctimonious know-all, he silently cursed his sergeant. He got up gingerly. The legs of the chair had parted company with the seat—permanently by the look of it. He pushed the evidence of his vandalism into the adjoining lumberroom and shut the door on it. Not that Dr Melville-Briggs was likely to show his face down *here*, but you never knew. It would be just like him to send in a bill for the damage. Thrusting his hands in his pockets, he demanded belligerently, 'Don't you *ever* look on the bright side?'

Llewellyn gave a tiny shrug. 'I don't believe in courting disappointment. There is one thing I don't understand though.'

'Only one? You surprise me. And what might that be?'

'Why you assume the murderer was male.'

Rafferty hadn't assumed any such thing, the use of the male pronoun had just seemed the most obvious in the circumstances, but now he felt stung to defend his choice.

'Elementary, my dear Llewellyn,' he replied, determined to regain the advantage which he had so abysmally lost. 'The victim, Linda Wilks, was on file for prostitution.'

Just then, he heard a faint shuffling noise outside the door. Putting his fingers to his lips, he crept to the door and quickly hauled it open. Gilbert was standing there with a tea-tray. Startled, he nearly dropped the lot.

'What do you want to go and do that for?' he complained. 'Gave me the fright of me life.'

Rafferty's eyes narrowed. 'Have you been listening?' He wouldn't put it past him. Perhaps that was why Dr Melville-Briggs hadn't sacked him yet. Men like Gilbert had their uses.

Gilbert got on his high horse. 'I've got better things to do with me time. Mrs Galvin thought you'd want tea, and asked me if I'd be good enough to oblige.' He sniffed. 'But I shan't bother again.'

Rafferty took the tea-tray. 'Thank you, Gilbert.' He stood pointedly in the doorway, waiting for the porter

to go. 'Was there anything else?' he asked. Grumbling
to himself, Gilbert took the hint.

'We ought to get a key to that outside door, sir,'
Llewellyn suggested quietly. 'We don't want him
snooping around.'

'I'm aware of that, Sergeant,' Rafferty replied tartly.
'Unlike you, I'm also aware that Gilbert's likely to have
duplicates of all the keys in the place. It's a bolt we
need.' There was one on the inside door, he noticed.
He'd better bring a drill and screwdriver in with him
tomorrow and move the bolt to the outside door if they
didn't want the entire staff to be privy to their discov-
eries. Slamming the door, he set the tray down on the
table. 'You can be mother. Now,' hooking his foot beneath the front rung of another chair, he dragged it towards him and sat down. 'Where was I?' he asked.

'You were explaining why you think the murderer is
a man, sir,' replied Llewellyn expressionlessly as he
handed him his tea.

'So I was.' Rafferty laced his fingers behind his head
and assumed his most nonchalant pose, wishing he
hadn't started this conversation as Llewellyn could be
relied upon to pinpoint any flaws in his hastily con-
structed theory. 'How likely is it that a London prossie
would come all the way out to deepest Elmhurst to see
a woman?'

Llewellyn replied coolly, 'More likely, I would have
thought, than coming all the way out here for just one
customer.'

'Unless he could pay well enough to make it worth
her while,' Rafferty countered swiftly. Which ability, in
his book, put Melville-Briggs back as odds-on favourite.

He was savouring this thought along with the hot, sweet tea, when Llewellyn, true to form, spoiled the flavour of both. 'High class then, was she, sir?'

'Not exactly, no,' replied Rafferty flatly, regretting his desire to put his sergeant in the wrong. He might have known that Llewellyn would immediately put his finger on the weak points in his argument. It was probably his university education, thought Rafferty resentfully, as he was forced to concede that his hasty theory might have a few holes in it. Linda Wilks had been far from high class if the police at Streatham were to be believed.

Although he accepted that it was a bit early to jump to conclusions, Llewellyn's criticisms made him reluctant to wave goodbye to his conjectures entirely. Particularly if there was a chance of involving his favourite medical man in a juicy murder trial. The starring role in such a case would take the satin finish from Melville-Briggs's smoothly emulsioned mug with all the efficiency of a blowtorch. It would even be worth suffering Llewellyn's scepticism to see that. Aware that his own personal feelings ought not to come into it, yet determined not to let his sergeant get the better of him entirely, Rafferty added, 'Let's just say she was an obliging sort of girl—went in for the kind of parlour games that stimulate jaded sexual appetites—whips, chains, that sort of thing. Saucy outfits too, apparently. When Streatham nick picked her up last time, she claimed she was an actress.' He snorted. 'A likely story. The only acting she did was when she played Madame Whiplash for a paying customer. Fancy a guess as to who the customer might be?' Llewellyn didn't take him up on his offer. 'Who do we know who's got a nice cosy flat, right on site? Whose sexual appetites—according to friend Gilbert—have had a surfeit of sweeties? Who's high powered enough to enjoy the titillation of a little role reversal? The great, the greedy, the goose-egg gatherer himself, that saviour of womankind, Dr Anthony Melville-Briggs, that's who. No wonder he tried to dump our suspicions elsewhere. It's well known that the rich are a weird lot where sex is concerned. Their goings-on swamp the pages of the Sunday tabloids every week. Even you must have read about Madam Cyn from Streatham, the luncheon-vouchers bordello queen.'

Llewellyn looked down his long nose at the suggestion. 'I make a point of avoiding such sordid sensationalism.'

You would, thought Rafferty, as he murmured, 'That's rather a pity. I've always thought a policeman should keep up with the scandal sheets. All in the line of duty, of course,' he added drily. 'Call it a getting to know our future customers exercise, if you like. Anyway, Madam Cyn's main business came from the intellectual type's fancy for "correction".' Rafferty eyed Llewellyn mischievously as he got the dig in. 'Same sort of line as Linda Wilks.' He grinned. 'Perhaps the good doctor likes to be tied up by a bit of rough trade occasionally and smacked on his plump pink behind?'

'Aren't you being a trifle melodramatic, sir?' Llewellyn questioned deflatingly. 'We've only just discovered the victim's identity. It might be advisable to find out first if there *was* any connection between them before jumping to hasty conclusions based on suppositions and hearsay. Besides, we've still got the rest of the skeleton staff to interview yet. We can't begin to settle on a suspect until we've got an overall picture.'

Rafferty sighed. Trust Llewellyn to want to go by the book. Rafferty had always found it made a case much more interesting if he ignored the book. There was nothing wrong with a bit of good dirty speculation, he told himself. As far as he was concerned, he'd be delighted if old smarmy-pants proved to be a mass of nasty perversions and a murderer to boot, friend of the Chief Constable or not. If he *was* their man, Rafferty wouldn't allow such a consideration to prevent him making the arrest. Besides, the CC would be pretty quick to distance himself from the doctor if he *was* the culprit and Rafferty's job should be safe enough. He couldn't resist teasing Llewellyn a little more. 'Perhaps she decided to up her rates and he wasn't keen. I like it,' he added decisively as the grin stretched even further.

Of course, Llewellyn wiped the grin off his face with his usual efficiency. 'I doubt the Chief Constable would—not without some proof and so far there isn't any.'

'Not yet,' Rafferty agreed stubbornly. 'But as you so rightly pointed out, we haven't finished interviewing yet. Lady Evelyn didn't give her husband the foolproof alibi he probably hoped for. Perhaps the others at that convention won't either.'

Like the voice of conscience, Llewellyn immediately piped up. 'Sam Dally was there. And he didn't remark on any obvious absences on the part of Dr Melville-Briggs. He *was* the chairman, don't forget. He'd be sure to be missed.'

Rafferty scowled. He'd forgotten that Sam Dally had mentioned that his prime suspect was chairman of the committee and probably responsible for making sure that everyone, especially himself, had a whale of a time. No wonder Melville-Briggs had been so unlovable yesterday morning. He'd probably been nursing a hang-over as formidable as Rafferty's own. He could almost like the man for that, almost, but not quite. 'It's not far to drive from the George,' he pointed out. 'He could still have nipped out during the evening, driven back here, killed the girl, and nipped back. I imagine there was a large crowd. Nothing could be easier than to dis-appear for half an hour or so, especially once the din-ner was over and he started to mingle.'

But apparently, Llewellyn had pumped Sam Dally a little more and now he wasted no more time in giving Rafferty the rest of the good news. Apparently, the role of chairman called for a lot of speechifying and prize-giving; Dr Melville-Briggs had been centre-stage dur-ing the greater part of the evening, no doubt holding forth on his favourite topic—himself, thought Rafferty sourly. And as Llewellyn had said, even Sam hadn't been able to recall any great gaps in his presence. With regret, Rafferty put his suspicions of Melville-Briggs temporarily aside. He couldn't even console himself with his madman theory. It seemed the pyjama-clad denouncer of women had several strange habits, one of which consisted of covering his hands with blood, any blood, he wasn't particular. Yesterday morning, before the nurse could stop him, he had dashed out of the day room and entered the kitchen where he had smeared his hands with blood from a large joint of beef which was just about to go in the oven.

'Did you check with Charge Nurse Allward about the possibility of the rest of the patients being able to get out?'

Llewellyn nodded. 'Nothing there. He told me that either himself or the little Filipino girl, Staff Nurse Estoce, sat at the end of the bedroom block, right by the locked door all night. No matter how devious they might be, none of the patients could get out without being seen. The windows can't be opened by the patients. I haven't yet spoken to the Staff Nurse, but I imagine she'll confirm what Allward said.'

Disappointed, Rafferty nodded and bent back to his lists. There was no way they were going to avoid checking out everyone's movements. 'Right,' he said. 'Let's get on. We'll have Friday night's duty doctor in, Llewellyn. Dr Simon Smythe. Round him up, there's a good man.'

Left alone, Rafferty leaned back in his chair and gazed at the small square of blue sky visible through the window. *Someone* had opened the side gate and let the girl in, presumably, someone who was expecting her, and in spite of Llewellyn putting the dampers on his theory he still thought it most likely to have been a man that the girl had come to see. All right, he admitted, Sam had said that a woman *could* have killed the girl, but it didn't seem a woman's crime somehow. It would, he was now convinced, turn out to be a relatively simple case. Some on-duty member of staff had organized Linda's visit as a bit of light relief that had gone badly wrong, and, frightened by what he'd done, he'd panicked and smashed her face, perhaps hoping to divert suspicion to one of the more violent patients. Though, he mused, if so, surely he'd have had the wit to arrange an escape?

Just then Llewellyn opened the door and ushered Simon Smythe into the room. A long and bony man, Dr Smythe looked to be in his late twenties. His old-fashioned horn-rimmed glasses seemed too heavy and rather overwhelmed his face. Already, he'd lost most of his blond hair and what remained was stretched lankly across as much of his nobbly scalp as it could cover.

Rafferty summoned a smile. 'Thank you for coming so promptly, Doctor. Won't you sit down?' Smythe did so, and Rafferty sat companionably beside him on the desk, while Llewellyn and his notebook took the other chair. 'Now, then, Doctor, as you probably know, we're interviewing all the staff and patients about the murder.' Smythe nodded. 'I understand you were duty doctor on Friday night?'

'Yes, yes, that's right.' Smythe's watery eyes looked quickly at Rafferty and away again. 'I—I generally am at holiday times like this.' A tinge of resentment crept into his voice. 'Dr Melville-Briggs likes to get away, but even when he's in the flat here, he becomes very annoyed if I disturb him.'

Understandably, if he was 'entertaining', thought Rafferty. 'I see. So, you were the only doctor on the premises?'

Smythe nodded quickly, as though he would prefer to deny it. His hands began to tremble slightly and he tucked them in the pockets of his white coat out of sight and cleared his throat. It sounded very loud in the small and otherwise silent room and the noise seemed to agitate him.

'It must be a great responsibility.'

Apparently, he had touched a raw nerve. 'It is. A great responsibility, Inspector.' Rafferty nodded sympathetically as Smythe began to pour out his grievances. 'Of course, in an emergency I can always contact Dr Melville-Briggs, but,' his mouth turned down like a sulking child's, 'he doesn't always agree what constitutes an emergency. He can become quite abusive if one disturbs him unnecessarily.'

I'll bet, thought Rafferty. 'Bosses aren't always very understanding, sir,' he commiserated. A picture of Superintendent Bradley in full hectoring mode came into his mind and he added quietly, 'It's much the same everywhere—the way of the world.'

Smythe nodded sagely, as though Rafferty had revealed a great truth, and for a few moments they both pondered the extent of his profundity.

Judging the moment propitious to press on, Rafferty asked quietly, 'Can you remember anything unusual about that night, sir? Anything at all?'

Smythe hesitated and then shook his head. 'No. It was a quiet night. That's why—' he broke off and looked guiltily at Rafferty.

'You were saying, sir?'

'Nothing. Really.' He clamped his lips tightly together as though scared he might say more than he intended. 'It, it's just that I still can't quite believe it. That poor girl must have been murdered while I was watching the late film.'

Strange, thought Rafferty, as far as he knew, the approximate time of death hadn't been revealed. However for the moment he didn't pursue the point. Looking thoughtfully at Smythe, he replied, 'She died quickly. It's not as though you could have done anything to help her.'

Smythe brightened at this. 'You're right, of course. I couldn't have helped her, even if...' His voice fumbled into silence once more.

'Just a few more questions. When you're on call, I imagine you're expected to stay on the premises?'

Smythe nodded slowly and his eyes slid away again. He behaved as guiltily as a shop-girl caught with her hand in the till, but confident that he would winkle his

secret out of him sooner rather than later, Rafferty
contented himself with continuing the interview. 'And
when you're on call, where would you usually be?'

'I'd be either in my office or the staff lounge. They're
both in this building on the first floor,' he added helpfully, as Rafferty consulted the plan of the hospital
which was open on the desk. 'I carry my bleep so I can
always be contacted straight away, no matter where I
am. It reaches several miles.'

'I see. And how long would you be on call?'

'From nine at night to seven in the morning. I was in
my office when Gilbert found the body and came to get
me.'

'So, you'd be available the entire night and either in
your office or the lounge—is that correct?'

Smythe blinked owlishly, then nodded.

Rafferty wondered if he had filled in part of the long
night with bashing in Linda Wilks' head? He seemed the
type who would need to turn to a prostitute for sexual
gratification. Of course, he reflected, Smythe's odd behaviour mightn't have anything to do with the murder.
A lot of nervy types worked themselves into a state
when they were interviewed by the police. After a few
more questions, he terminated the interview. Smythe's
eagerness to be gone was apparent, as was his dismay
when Rafferty let him get as far as the door before calling him back. 'Just as a matter of interest. Does the
name Linda Wilks mean anything to you?' If he had
hoped to startle Smythe by revealing that they knew the
dead girl's name, it was a wasted effort. Perhaps Gilbert had already spread the word?

Smythe's red-rimmed eyes looked blankly back at
him through the thick lenses. He shook his bony head

vigorously, as though relieved that he had been asked a question that held no fears for him. 'Should it?'

Rafferty smiled at him. 'Probably not.' If he had known the victim he mightn't have known her by that name. Vice girls commonly used several aliases in an attempt to keep one step ahead of the law. This time, Smythe made it safely through the door.

SIX

'HE COULD HAVE done it,' said Llewellyn. 'He was here alone. He said himself it was a quiet night. He could have slipped out, or even brought her into his office, with nobody being any the wiser. Even if he didn't do it, he might have seen who did.' He leaned over the plan of the hospital and pointed. 'I've been checking the layout of the house and from both his office and the staff lounge you can see over the side gate. Of course, even with the outside lights, it would be pretty dark, but he could still have seen something or someone.'

'We'll have another word with him, but not just yet,' Rafferty decided. 'If he knows something, it shouldn't be too difficult to get him to talk. We'll have Staff Nurse Estoce in next, and then Charge Nurse Allward. They were both on duty on Friday night. You'll probably find them waiting in the staff lounge if you give it a ring.'

With her flawless skin and graceful movements, Staff Nurse Estoce was quite exquisite, thought Rafferty, but as with so many oriental girls, she was shy and self-effacing. Still, she managed to answer their questions clearly enough, at least until they asked about her duty colleague on the night of the murder; then her eyes became clouded and Rafferty had to remind himself to concentrate on her answers rather than her face.

'You say that Charge Nurse Allward was late back from his early break, Staff. Did he give a reason for that?'

She nodded. 'One of the patients had a bad dream. Charge Nurse Allward settled him and stayed with him till he slept.'

'He didn't ask for your help?' She shook her head. 'So you didn't see the patient at all during this time?'

'No. I checked on him later, of course.'

'And you say Mr Allward returned at eleven forty-five p.m.?'

'Yes. I noted the time particularly before I went for my own break as I do not like to be late back.'

'Didn't you hear the patient cry out yourself?' Again, she shook her head. 'Why was that?'

She gave a tiny shrug. 'I imagine it was only a little cry and Mr Allward comforted him before he became too upset.'

'You didn't notice anything unusual that night? You didn't hear a scream for instance?'

'No. But in a hospital screams are not so unusual.'

'Have you any idea what the victim might have been doing in the grounds?'

Interestingly, a delicate rose colour tinted her olive skin and her reply was defensive. 'N-no. I couldn't say.'

Couldn't—or wouldn't? Rafferty wondered. 'You don't seem very certain, Staff,' he remarked gently. 'The victim's name was Linda Wilks. She was about your age. Perhaps you'd like to think about that and get back to me?' She nodded once and her eyes looked anxiously at the door, before returning to his face.

Why was it everyone was so anxious to get away from him today, Rafferty mused. First Simon Smythe and now Staff Nurse Estoce. If this kept up he'd have to seriously consider changing his deodorant, which would be a pity, as he still had twenty bottles of the stuff that his ma had got wholesale. At least, she'd *said* they were

wholesale, he remembered uneasily. Staff Nurse Estoce
was still staring at him with her great dark eyes, making him feel like a thug, and he let her go. It was obvious *something* was worrying her. What on earth could
she be hiding? Was she protecting someone?

'Find out if she's got a boyfriend amongst the staff,'
he instructed Llewellyn. 'Let's have Allward now.'

There was nothing meek or self-effacing about
Charge Nurse Allward, Rafferty noted. He couldn't
have presented a greater contrast to Simon Smythe.
Allward was in his early thirties and only about five or
six years older than the other man, but they might have
been light-years apart. He was tall and elegant from his
glossy, expensively styled brown hair to his burnished
black shoes. He seemed completely at his ease and he
sat on the hard hospital chair with a faintly sardonic air,
as though he found it amusing to be interviewed by the
police.

'The sergeant said you wished to see me, Inspector?'

'That's right, sir. Just a few questions.' After going
through the previous spiel that he'd used with Smythe,
he asked Allward for his movements on the night of the
murder.

'As you probably know, I was on duty in the male
bedroom block with Staff Nurse Estoce from eight
forty-five p.m. till seven a.m.'

Rafferty nodded. 'I understand you were late returning from your eleven fifteen p.m. break? Fifteen minutes late. Why was that?'

Allward's sardonic expression became more
thoughtful at this and he sat up a little straighter, as
though realizing he should treat the interview more
warily. Perhaps he hadn't expected his loyal little Staff
Nurse to mention his lateness, Rafferty mused.

'I was delayed by one of the patients,' he explained calmly.

'Which one?'

'Old Mr Tompkinson. His room's at the end of the corridor, near the little cubby-hole where we make the hot drinks.'

'I see. What was the matter with him?'

'Just a bad dream.'

'You didn't need to give him any medication?' He knew that would have to be entered up on the patient's records.

'No. I just got him a drink and settled him down again.' He smiled easily. 'He's a nice old boy. Pathetically grateful for anything you do for him. He and I came here on the same day so I've always regarded him as one of my special charges.'

'You didn't see anything unusual that night?'

'Depends what you mean by unusual. This *is* a psychiatric hospital, Inspector,' Allward teased gently.

'Anything out of the ordinary, then?'

Allward shook his head. 'No. But then I didn't look out of the windows, if I had I might have seen something, I suppose. I'm afraid I can't help you, Inspector.'

He even managed to look and sound as though he was genuinely sorry not to be of more assistance, which made Rafferty feel unreasonably irritated. But Allward was far too smooth for Rafferty's taste and he was too human to keep his feelings completely hidden. He wondered how it was that Llewellyn's professional composure never seemed to be ruffled by personal antagonisms? The thought added to his irritation.

'The victim's name was Linda Wilks. Did you know her?'

For a moment, he thought he saw a brief flicker of—
something—in Allward's eyes, but it had vanished before he could decide whether it had been recognition,
fear, or surprise at their speed of identification that had
caused it.

'I'm afraid I can't help you, Inspector. But, of
course, if she was a visitor to one of the female patients, I'd be unlikely to meet her. Perhaps one of the
porters would know her?' he suggested helpfully. 'They
get to see all the visitors.'

'Surely, Gilbert's told you they didn't know her? That
they had no idea what she was doing here?' replied
Rafferty sharply. 'Neither has anyone else—or so they
say. She's a regular mystery woman. Very strange. She
wasn't a member of staff or a patient. She wasn't a visitor—at least, not an *official* visitor—which, given what
we've found out about her, lead me to suppose she had
a less than above board reason for coming here. She was
a prostitute, Mr Allward,' said Rafferty bluntly. 'Who
do you think might have booked her services that
night?'

Allward met his eyes squarely. 'I can't imagine.'

'Try,' suggested Rafferty. 'There were six members of
staff on duty that night. One of them yourself, three of
the others were women, which would seem to rule them
out, and the others were Dr Smythe and Fred Brown,
the night porter. A limited field for your imagination to
work in, I think.'

'Are you inviting me to smear a colleague, Inspector? Hardly ethical. Besides, any of the other members
of staff could have returned easily enough. The hospital would be a convenient place to take such a woman,
I would have thought, away from prying families, es-

pecially as most of the patients are away at the moment and there are plenty of empty bedrooms.'

'They've already been exonerated, sir,' Rafferty told him with satisfaction. But it was clear that Allward wasn't about to confess. After he had gone, Rafferty pulled his coat off the back of the chair and shrugged into it. 'We'll do the rest of the interviews later. Guess who's got the happy task of breaking the news to the dead girl's parents?' He headed for the door but stopped when he heard the swiftly indrawn breath behind him.

'Can't the Met do that?' Llewellyn asked sharply. 'Surely we're not expected to go all the way to London to break the news. I hate—' He broke off and closed his mouth tightly, as though aware that he'd already said too much.

Surprised at this unexpected outburst, Rafferty eyed Llewellyn with a certain degree of sympathy. Breaking news of sudden death was one of the more unpleasant aspects of police work. Nobody liked it and he was startled to discover that the controlled Welshman should show his distaste so openly.

Llewellyn's pale face flushed and he made an awkward attempt at an explanation. 'It's just that, as a child, I had often to accompany my father when he broke the news of sudden death. He was a minister,' he went on in a strange stiff voice. 'He told me it was part of my training for when I went into the ministry.' The flush had faded now, leaving his pale face starkly etched with lines of pain. His lips twitched in a ghostly semblance of a smile. 'I've hated having to break such news ever since.'

Embarrassed, Rafferty remarked gruffly, 'Bit of a problem that in our line. How have you managed?'

'Wasn't too bad in the little country town where I was stationed before. Most of the sudden deaths were of farmers driving home drunk at the end of market-day and the uniformed branch dealt with them.' He squared his shoulders. 'I suppose I've become a bit rusty, especially since my father died.'

'Look,' said Rafferty diffidently. 'If you'd rather, just this once, I can take a WPC along.' He shuffled his feet awkwardly and avoided Llewellyn's eye. 'Ease you into it gradually, like, especially as this job's likely to be particularly gutty.'

'Thank you for the offer, sir, but no.' Llewellyn's stern self-control was back in place—just. 'Avoidance is no answer. I'd rather get it over with.'

Rafferty nodded. 'As you like.' He returned to Llewellyn's previous remark, glad to get away from such an uncomfortable topic. 'I didn't know you had a religious vocation, Taff.'

'I didn't.'

'Oh.' He said no more. If Llewellyn wanted to confide in him, he would do so. Relieved to have discovered a more human side to his sergeant, Rafferty felt the stirring of a little fellow-feeling and, as they went out to the car, he explained, 'The victim rented one of those anonymous and tacky bed-sits in Streatham for her trade. But her family live near here, according to the Met. Only about half a mile from the hospital.'

Llewellyn had brought the car round to the front earlier and now it stood gleaming in the April sunshine. The Welshman took little pleasure in anything else, but the car was the joy of his life. He probably offered such ritual cleanliness up as a sacrifice to his dour Welsh god, thought Rafferty, and his earlier sympathy dissolved a little. 'I'll drive. Got the car keys?'

Reluctantly, Llewellyn handed them over. Rafferty knew he didn't like anyone driving "his" car—particularly him, whom Llewellyn considered both fast and reckless. His expression resigned, Llewellyn got in, wincing as Rafferty revved up.

Reaching to take his cigarettes from his pocket, Rafferty remembered he'd given them up and instead he pulled out a bag of boiled sweets from his pocket, unwrapped one, and popped it in his mouth. Glancing at Llewellyn, Rafferty noticed that the Welshman's eyes were still shadowed, even though he kept his gaze stiffly eyes-front. Anxious about the coming interview, Rafferty surmised, sucking hard on his sweet. That made two of them.

THE PRIVET HEDGE surrounding the Wilkses' small front garden was fussily neat and clipped as efficiently as a sergeant-major's moustache, but to Rafferty it had more of the appearance of a green plastic wall than a living thing. As he advanced up the path, he took in the sparkling white nets draped across the louvre windows of the terraced house, each of their full folds a neat one inch from its neighbour, and sighed. The short back and sides on the hedge had hinted at it, but the curtains confirmed that he and Rafferty were likely to be regarded by the murdered girl's parents as little better than murderers themselves. Murderers of reputation and respectability and pride. He glanced at Llewellyn as he raised the door-knocker and realized the Welshman had reached the same conclusion. His face was stiff, as though it had been dipped in a bucket of Robin's starch.

The door was opened a bare three inches and a woman's face appeared. Rafferty felt a momentary shame at the relief that flooded him when he saw her eyes were

red-rimmed with weeping; they must already know, he
decided, mystified yet grateful that someone else had
broken the bad news to them.

'Who are you? What do you want?'

'Police, Mrs Wilks,' Rafferty explained in a low
voice, holding up his identity card for her to see. He
cleared his throat of a sudden frog. 'It's about your
daughter, Linda.'

Her head shot up. 'Linda? What's happened? Has
she been arres—' Her voice broke off abruptly. Biting
her lip, she reluctantly opened the door wider. 'You'd
best come in.'

Exchanging puzzled glances, they followed her past
the well-buffed horse-brasses and flower-patterned
carpet of the hall. Rafferty wondered apprehensively if
it was possible they'd had other bad news, something
totally unconnected with the case?

Although it was still bright outside, the curtains were
pulled across the windows and the living-room was
shrouded in gloom. But the curtains were unlined and
allowed sufficient filtered light through for Rafferty to
confirm his earlier conclusions about the Wilkses' respectability from a swift survey of the room. Everything was spotless and fussily neat. No books or
newspapers created the usual friendly muddle that filled
most people's homes. Each item had its place and remained in it. There were still more flowers here; on the
fitted carpet, full-blown pink roses on the faded chintz-
covered suite, delicate, tightly enclosed buds on the
wallpaper.

Rafferty felt Llewellyn give a start, when behind
them, and so far unnoticed in the gloom, a man's figure rose to his feet. Linda's father, Rafferty guessed,
and introduced himself and Llewellyn. Like his wife,

Mr Wilks didn't seem surprised to see them. What *was* going on here? he wondered.

Sidney Wilks was not an impressive man. Short and wiry, under sparse pepper-and-salt hair his face was brick-red and a curious selection of expressions passed, one after the other, over his features—shame, resentment, anger—and a quickly hidden fear which Rafferty found even more baffling.

Invited to sit down, they eased themselves gingerly on to the edge of the chintz settee, Rafferty now almost as anxious as his sergeant for the job to be over and done with.

'Well?' Sidney Wilks barked at them suddenly. 'Why don't you get it over with? What's stopping you? Though I don't know why it takes *two* of you.'

Beside him, Rafferty felt Llewellyn jump and he quickly found his voice in case his sergeant's stern self-control gave way and he said something they'd both regret. 'I'm sorry, it's just that I thought you knew, Mr Wilks,' he began. 'You seemed . . .'

'Knew? Of course we knew,' Daphne Wilks broke in before he could go on. 'Why else would we be so upset?' She glared at him, then, slowly, her gaze swung to Llewellyn and her face changed as though she saw something in the Welshman's stiff, white demeanour that suddenly made everything clear to her. All at once her face became ashen and she sat abruptly on the armchair behind her and gazed accusingly at Rafferty. '*You're* the one in charge of the murder. It was in the local paper.' Her voice was now no louder than a whisper. 'Oh, my God, no! It's her isn't it? The girl found murdered at that hospital—it's our Linda. *That's* why you're here. And I thought . . .' She gave a faint, hysterical laugh. 'Stupid of me. Why else would you come

to see us? She is—was—of age after all. What concern
is it of the parents if a girl decides to pros—'

'Mother!' Sidney Wilks's voice was sharp. 'They're
not interested in that. That's our business.' He scowled
warningly at her before he turned to Rafferty with an
apologetic smile. 'I'm sorry. She's not herself. It's her
age, you know?'

Rafferty stared at him, conscious that he'd made a
terrible blunder. Did Sidney Wilks really imagine they
were unaware of their daughter's extra-curricular activities? The way he had shut his wife up suggested that
was exactly what he did think.

Mr Wilks gave his hand-knitted cardigan a tug
downwards as though to say, 'Glad I've got that out of
the way', before he met Rafferty's eyes once more. 'Was
she right? About Linda being the murdered girl?'

Rafferty nodded and mumbled, 'We know what your
daughter did, Mr Wilks, there's no point in trying to
hide it. I'm sorry.' But Wilks gave every appearance of
not hearing him and he lapsed into silence.

'Perhaps these gentlemen would like some tea?' Wilks
suggested to his wife, in a voice of a man determined to
observe the civilities. His daughter might have been
murdered, its tone implied, but that was no reason to
forget one's manners. Mrs Wilks cast a reproachful
glance at her husband before going out and shutting the
door behind her.

Rafferty found himself watching Wilks with a kind of
horrid fascination. Unlike his wife, he didn't seem
shocked by his revelation of their daughter's murder. Of
course, shock came in many forms, but Sidney Wilks
was a shade too accepting, too unemotional, and Rafferty wondered if he'd already known that his daughter
was dead. But how could he? Unless...? But he was

jumping to conclusions again, he chided himself. It might just be that he was one of those men who considered it unmanly to show strong feelings. He was of the generation to think that way. And it seemed likely that Linda would have been the sort of girl to think nothing of disappearing for a few days without a word to her parents. Even so, his manner made Rafferty feel increasingly uncomfortable and he had opened his mouth to speak when Wilks's lack of emotion was dispelled in an outburst that was as sudden as it was furious.

'Wanted to be an *actress*!' His voice scorned such an ambition. Now he seemed to need to talk, to explain feelings he had been keeping pent-up. 'I told her not to be so stupid, as if such jobs were for people like us. Security, I said, that's what you need, my girl. Told her if she persisted no good would come of it and I was right, wasn't I? No good *has* come of it.' He sounded satisfied that his prediction had been proved correct. Perhaps he realized how this must appear, for his voice became quieter, more intense. 'I fixed her up with a good job at the Electricity Board when she left school,' he told them, as though he still didn't understand why his daughter should reject what had been good enough for him for forty years. 'Typing. They were even willing to train her on the word processors, send her on a little course. But no—that wasn't good enough for Madam Linda. She had *ambitions*, she told us. Ambitions!'

Mrs Wilks came back with the tea. Rafferty wasn't surprised that the bone china tea service had been brought out. More roses decorated the matching teapot and crockery. He was beginning to find the flowery theme of the room oppressive and he longed to loosen his tie and fling open the windows.

Mrs Wilks poured the tea and passed it round. It seemed to restore her, for now she began to explain. 'We had a row, the night—the night before she was found in that hospital. When I heard about it, I wondered if it could be our Linda. She hadn't come home, but then that wasn't unusual.'

'Used this place like a hotel,' Sidney Wilks interrupted. 'Thought her mother was a launderette and restaurant combined. I told her...'

'Please, Sidney.' Obviously distressed, his wife cut off his flow, before going on quietly: 'Besides, I didn't want to think about it. I persuaded myself it couldn't be her. I didn't want to face...' Her voice trailed away and Rafferty came to the conclusion that Daphne Wilks would always shy away from unpleasant reality. In this instance, he couldn't really blame her. The death of a child, whatever their age, was more than most parents could come to terms with. 'She died very quickly, Mrs Wilks,' he told her, in a futile attempt at comfort. 'She couldn't have known anything about it. The—rest—happened after death.'

Mrs Wilks nodded mechanically, as though she hadn't really taken in what he had told her, and she went on as if he'd never spoken. 'After the row, Linda ran out and Sidney went after her.'

'I couldn't catch her,' Sidney Wilks broke in again. 'She'd disappeared by the time I got to the end of the road.'

'I don't know why you never came straight back,' complained his wife. 'When you knew how upset I was.'

'I was upset too,' he defended himself aggressively. 'I wanted to be alone for a while, to think what was best to do. She told us she was moving out permanently,' he explained for Rafferty's benefit. 'She wasn't here much at the best of times. Staying with friends, she used to tell us she was. Anyway, she said she'd fixed up to move into a flat in London with some girlfriends. God knows who they were, she never mentioned any names. Had it all planned and not a word to us.'

'Was that what caused the row?' Llewellyn asked quietly, apparently having got himself back in control.

'No,' replied Mrs Wilks. 'It was the—other business. You see I found her dia—'

'Mother!' Sidney Wilks warned sharply. 'They don't need to know about—that.' He turned back to the policemen, as though his word settled the matter, but Daphne Wilks had decided to face facts and she overruled her husband.

'It's no use, Sidney,' she told him. 'We can't hide it. Linda must have had a criminal record, don't you see? How do you think they were able to identify her, when according to the papers...?' She took a shuddering breath. 'Anyway, it might help them find out who did this dreadful thing. I owe her that much. We both do.' She turned back to the policemen, ignoring her husband's ugly flush. 'I found her diary, you see. Usually she locked it away, but that evening she must have forgotten. I was so stupid,' Daphne Wilks went on. 'At first, I thought she'd written a series of little plays. They were all set out like that, you see. But they were all on the same theme. That was what made me suspicious. She always took a particular case with her when she went up to London. Her "auditioning" gear, she told me it was. I forced it open. She kept it hidden at the back of her wardrobe. No wonder. Inside there were the most...'

She stopped for a moment to wipe her reddened nose with a damp handkerchief and then went shakily on. 'All I could think was why? What could have made her do this to us?' She gave a half-shamed glance at her husband, before continuing. 'Sidney had been in the garage, working on the car, and when I heard her come home, I fetched him so we could confront her together. I was in such a state, I didn't even make sure he washed his hands first. He left a dirty smear on the wallpaper.' Her mouth formed into lines of reproach, as if she believed that by concentrating on mundane resentments, she could push the horror to the back of her mind. 'I haven't been able to get it ou—'

'Can I see this diary?' Rafferty interrupted before they started on mutual recriminations.

'We burnt it,' said Sidney Wilks quickly. But not quite quickly enough, as his wife reached beneath the seat cushion of her armchair and brought out a large and expensive looking calfskin-bound book and handed it over.

'You promised you'd burn it!' her husband accused.

'I know.' Her head dropped. 'I couldn't.' Slowly, she raised her head and looked at Rafferty. 'We've just got the gas fire, you see,' she explained with an air of apology. 'I'd have had to burn it out in the garden and I kept thinking what the neighbours would say if any of the pages were to blow away.'

Rafferty guessed that what the neighbours would say had largely governed their lives. Sadly, he reflected that the neighbours would now have enough scandal to keep their tongues wagging for many a long day.

Mrs Wilks was right, he saw, as he flicked through the diary. Linda *had* set it out like a play or a film script, or as near to them as either of them would recognize. The diary contained Linda Wilks's dreams, the film-script-like layout had helped to clothe the sordid reality of what she was doing in the soft-focus lighting of a film seduction scene. Had she managed to convince herself as well that she was merely acting out a role? he wondered. Had she persuaded herself that should the acting become too brutally real the director would shout 'cut'? He turned back to the first pages. Slowly, he began to read.

ACT 1 SCENE 1

The scene opens in a book-lined study. We see an elderly man dressed in a school uniform sitting in front of a desk.

CUT TO: *A young woman wearing a cape and mortarboard enters. In one hand she is carrying a cane which she hits into the other palm. She walks slowly forward till she is standing in front of the elderly schoolboy.*

GIRL: You've been a naughty boy, haven't you, Simpson?

MAN: *Cringes.* Yes, Miss.

GIRL: Do you know what happens to naughty boys? *She swishes the cane.*

MAN: Oh, yes, Miss. I know. *The man's face goes pink. Now he seems suddenly excited.*

GIRL: Lower your trousers then, Simpson, and bend over the desk. *He does as she says.* It's six of the best for you. *Her cape swings open. Underneath she is naked. She gazes at the quivering buttocks of the man and raising her arm . . .*

Rafferty shut the diary with a snap and glanced quickly up as though he had been caught doing something dirty. From his brief flick through, the entire diary seemed filled with similar scenes. That one had been quite tame. 'I'll have to take this,' he told them apologetically.

Sidney Wilks hissed accusingly at his wife. 'You should have destroyed it, as I said. Now the whole world will know exactly what sort of little trollop your daughter was.'

Rafferty wasn't altogether surprised at the speed with which Wilks distanced his own relationship with the girl. The theory was that tragedy brought people together. It didn't—more often it tore them apart in a manner as savage as the original crime. He'd seen it many times and it never failed to depress him. Grimly, he looked at Wilks as he began to taunt his wife.

'At least when that's read out in court, the papers won't need to make up anything worse,' he told her. 'Not that they could,' he added with a vicious spite as his wife gasped. 'This'll give the neighbours something to talk about all right.'

Mrs Wilks gave Rafferty a beseeching look. 'Is he right? Will everyone hear all the details of what Lin . . . what she did? I thought you'd be able to keep it quiet.'

Rafferty looked from one to the other and swallowed hard. How could he tell her the truth? It would be kinder to let it dawn gradually on her. 'It depends,' he temporized. 'The way she earned her living may not have had anything to do with the murder, of course, in which case . . .'

'You don't really believe that though, do you, Inspector?' Sidney Wilks demanded scornfully. 'It'll come

out, especially as she was going to meet another of her
men that night.'

Rafferty felt Llewellyn tense beside him. 'How do
you know that?' he asked, making his second contri-
bution to the interview.

'She had a phone call, didn't she? About half ten that
night, a few minutes after she came home. Taunted me
with it when I demanded to know who it was. "One of
my men friends," she said. "A medical man."' He
glanced at his wife's crouching figure. 'Of course, you
know we'll never be able to hold our heads up again,'
he spat at her. 'We'll have to move.' This was said with
such spiteful satisfaction that Rafferty felt his whole
body cringe.

Mrs Wilks's face seemed to crumple as she realized
that her husband was right. Fresh tears filled her eyes
and she looked round her neat and oppressively tidy
living-room with a tragic expression. She shook her
head slowly, as though that, to her, was more unbearable than her daughter's death.

'Could we perhaps have a photograph of your
daughter, Mr Wilks?' Rafferty asked, wanting to get
done and out of the house as quickly as possible. 'It
might help us to catch her killer.'

'Have one?' The voice was tart. 'You can have them
all. What do we want with them now?'

One by one, he pulled every photograph of Linda
from the fireplace wall and dropped them with a clat-
ter on the low table in front of the settee on which the
two men sat. His wife made no protest, but just sat
rocking herself backwards and forwards staring sight-
lessly at nothing, as though she had retreated to a secret refuge where sordid reality couldn't touch her.

'Ahem, Mr Wilks?' Rafferty began tentatively. 'Can you give us any reason why your daughter should dye her hair dark?'

Sidney Wilks blinked rapidly as he gazed down at the snapshots; family snaps taken in happier times of Linda as a baby propped up with cushions, as a toddler, as a gap-toothed and wriggling tomboy sitting on her father's lap, school photos as a teenager where she looked with sultrily half-closed eyes into the camera—perhaps even then convinced she would be a great actress.

'It was for those acting roles she kept going for,' he told them in a curiously flat voice. 'She thought she'd stand more chance if her hair was the same colour as the character she was trying for.' He reached out a shaking hand and picking up one of the most recent photographs, rubbed his thumb over the glass. 'That was my little girl,' he told them bleakly. 'My pretty, innocent little girl.' He took out a large white handkerchief and after blowing his nose, put it carefully back in his pocket. For a moment, he looked bewildered, as though he hadn't quite grasped what a cataclysm had wrecked his orderly little world. Then, without any warning, his face contorted and he smashed the glass of the frame against the corner of the mantelpiece and yanking out the photo, he threw it at Rafferty. 'Take it. Take them all. We don't want them back. Wearing those short skirts of hers, flaunting herself, the bitch asked for it. She deserved all she got. Deserved all she got,' he repeated, as though trying to convince himself of it.

Silently, they stood up and Rafferty picked up the photograph. Mrs Wilks was still in a world of her own and took no further interest in the proceedings. 'I'd like to look at Linda's bedroom, Mr Wilks, if that's all right?' Sidney Wilks just nodded. He'd washed his hands of his daughter, his expression said. They could do what they liked. 'Erm. Perhaps, while I'm doing that, you could let my sergeant here have a description of what Linda was wearing that night?' he suggested.

Llewellyn shot him a reproachful look and sat down again. Slowly, he pulled his notebook back out and began to write as Sidney Wilks's voice, drained now of emotion, described what his daughter had been wearing.

Rafferty went upstairs, and after finding which of the three was Linda's bedroom he quickly searched it. He found the case that Mrs Wilks had referred to, but it was empty, all the usual erotic items of a prostitute's art removed. Sidney Wilks had obviously been here before him. He must be cursing himself that he hadn't been quite thorough enough.

He returned to the living room to collect a relieved Llewellyn, and, after drawing Sidney Wilks back from whichever hell he had retreated to, they said their goodbyes and speedily left.

SEVEN

LLEWELLYN SIGHED heavily as the door closed behind them, his eyes curtained by the fall of thick black lashes. He gave himself a little shake and the controlled expression was back in place, the deep emotions that had flickered across his features stowed safely away once more. 'An unhappy man,' he commented. 'He loved her very much, in his own way, you could see that.'

Rafferty was about to disagree, then he realized his sergeant was right. Love came in all shapes and sizes, he of all people should know that. Dispiritedly, he began to flick through the diary once more.

Back to normal, Llewellyn began a mournful quote, '"Love is a sickness full of woes . . .",' but broke off at Rafferty's involuntary groan. 'Samuel Daniel, 1562-1619,' he muttered under his breath. Rafferty ignored him.

'Curious that he didn't come straight back when he didn't find his daughter,' Llewellyn remarked after a brief silence. 'It would be more usual for parents to share the shock of such a discovery together.'

'You saw them. There was precious little attempt at comforting one another. They live only half a mile from the hospital,' he went on thoughtfully. 'Discovering that his daughter's on the game would be enough to make any man mad with rage.' At least he assumed so. Not having ever experienced the dubious joys of fatherhood, he had only his imagination on which to draw. It was certainly a strong motive for murder. 'He could

have followed her—he'd been tinkering with the car
when his wife found the diary and called him in. Perhaps, when Linda ran out, he picked up a spanner
without thinking and followed her.'

'He couldn't have done it, of course.' Back in his
stride with a vengeance, Llewellyn threw cold water over
the idea with the ease of long practice. 'Linda was
found *inside* the hospital grounds. Where would he get
a key to that gate?'

'Perhaps he didn't need one.' Rafferty raised his head
from his perusal of the diary, pleased he'd succeeded in
coming up with a theory that Llewellyn wouldn't find
so easy to fault. 'Maybe the person she was meeting let
her in and left the door unlocked by mistake?' He
tapped the slim book with a forefinger. 'Or perhaps, if
she had a regular customer at the hospital, he might
have given her a key. Her father *did* say she was going
to see a medical man that night, and there's no reason
why she shouldn't occasionally earn some money lo-
cally.'

Llewellyn nodded thoughtfully. 'And her father followed her into the grounds? You could have something
there, sir. Wilks is the type to have a complete brain-
storm. All that determined respectability is unnatural.'
He gave Rafferty an inscrutable glance. 'As Freud
said...'

'Never mind what Freud said,' Rafferty broke in before Llewellyn had a chance to start on all that psycho-
logical mumbojumbo. 'We'd do better finding out what
her prospective flatmates have to say. Now that we've
got her name and photograph I'll get on to the papers.
I shouldn't think we'll have long to wait before her girlfriends contact us.' He sent up a silent prayer for for-
giveness after his comforting lies to Mrs Wilks. 'I agree

the father's a possible suspect, but at this stage we can't afford to concentrate our investigations too much on one person.'

Llewellyn looked down his nose at this as Rafferty conveniently forgot his previous enthusiastic concentration on Melville-Briggs. Once again, Rafferty ignored him.

'Her girlfriends might know if Linda *did* have a regular customer at the Elmhurst Sanatorium, particularly if they were on the game themselves.' He opened the driver's side door of the car and was about to get in, when he saw Llewellyn's unhappy expression and relented. 'All right, you drive,' he said, handing the keys over. Rafferty opened the door and climbed in, chivying Llewellyn as he fumbled with the ignition key. 'Hurry up, man,' he grumbled. 'Let's get back to the station. We've got a lot to do.' He tapped the photograph. 'I want you to get copies made of this and give them to the house-to-house team. They'll have to start over again now. And I'll want posters of her put up at bus and train stations. I want everyone within a twenty-mile radius to know her face. Get the photo on the wire to the Met. She presumably met most of her johns there and it's possible there's someone in town who knew her in both identities.' Certainly better than her parents seemed to, he added silently to himself.

Llewellyn was still taken with Rafferty's previous idea. 'If her father did do it...' He glanced back at the house as he started up the car. Someone had been watching them. As he turned his head, he just caught a quick movement as the nets were twitched back into place. 'Why would he strip her?'

'He said she dressed like a tart. Perhaps he thought, naked, she looked more respectable, more innocent than she ever could in her working gear. If it was him, I wonder what he did with them? He wouldn't have been able to burn them easily with no open fires in the house. Perhaps he buried them or threw them in the sea? It's only about a fifteen-minute walk from their house. I want you to notify the search teams to be on the lookout for anything washed up by the tide.'

Llewellyn slipped in a little philosophical comment. 'He'll blame his wife for the girl going to the bad, of course. That type always do.'

'Well, he's got to blame someone,' said Rafferty flatly. 'It's human nature. Especially if he *did* do for the girl. And who else is there to blame?' Perhaps, he mused, if Linda's mother had been a different sort of woman, her father would have been a different sort of man and Linda would still be alive. But of course, he reminded himself, you could say that about anyone.

RAFFERTY HAD been right; they'd passed the photograph to the media in time to catch the Monday papers and Linda's girlfriends had seen the item and the request for information. He and Llewellyn were on their way to see them now.

'Let me do the talking,' he warned Llewellyn. If, like Linda, they *were* part-time hookers, he didn't want Llewellyn putting their backs up before they told them what they knew.

Despite making good time, it was nearly noon when they reached Streatham and then Rafferty spent twenty minutes circling round before he could park. Finally, ignoring Llewellyn's stern exhortations about policemen not being above the law, he left the car on a double yellow line, cursing himself for a fool when he saw the flat. It formed part of a large house and the front garden had a tarmac surface which provided ample space for parking. He should have guessed. Many of the large, formerly family homes around this area had been converted into flats.

Ignoring the sombre-suited Llewellyn's wince of pain, Rafferty straightened his dazzling orange and magenta tie and studied the array of cards and bells by the front door. He pulled a face when he realized they wanted the top floor. 'I hope they've got a lift,' he muttered as he rang the bell. The grill spluttered into life, he shouted his business and the door was released. He cursed as he saw the 'lift out of order' sign. Wasn't it just his luck? he sighed. Blowing like a pair of bellows by the time he reached the top floor, he had to hang on to the banisters for a minute, grinning foolishly at the two young women at the door. Clinging there, he had time to reflect that he had probably stopped smoking none too soon. It didn't surprise him to notice that Llewellyn's breathing seemed perfectly normal. His body was as disciplined as everything else in his life and he worked out twice a week in the police gym; something which earned a few ribald comments from the canteen cowboys at the station.

The girls looked nervously first at each other and then at him. 'Inspector Rafferty?'

Still gasping, he could only nod. Who the hell did they think he was? he wondered. Would any self-respecting rapist knacker himself by climbing all those stairs? As the girls still regarded him with suspicion, he pulled his identity card from his wallet. Reassured, they now became concerned at his speechless condition and one of the girls asked, 'Are you all right?'

'Really, I'm fine,' he insisted, when he was finally able to get a word out.

'The stairs are tough on older people,' she sympathized artlessly, while behind him, he heard a muffled snort from Llewellyn, who was still—just—the right side of thirty.

Her comment did nothing to boost Rafferty's ego. Dammit all, he was only thirty-seven, not seventy-seven. He supposed along with giving up smoking, he ought to start taking more exercise, watch his diet, cut down on alcohol; in short, make himself as big a misery as Llewellyn.

Apparently, the three girls all made a somewhat precarious living on the fringes of show business and although Linda had not only been a friend, but had also been about to move in, they could tell them little about her. It seemed that none of them enquired too closely into the affairs of the others. 'Please try to remember,' he pressed. 'It's very important. Did Linda say anything, anything at all, about any regular men she might see at Elmhurst or where they might meet?'

They looked at one another and shook their heads. The blonde girl, Patsy, said, 'We knew she must have some men friends down there, of course, because sometimes, when she came up to town, she had quite a bit of money with her, money she wouldn't have been able to earn otherwise, but who they might have been, I've no idea. Perhaps Tina would know more, she's known Linda a lot longer than either of us two.' Rafferty looked about him hopefully. 'She's not here. She had a very early flight to the States last Saturday morning. Tina's a dancer,' Patsy explained apologetically, 'and her agent managed to get her a tour booking as a replacement at the last minute.'

'Would you have a number where I could contact her?'

'You could try her agent.' Patsy picked up the phone book and read out his name and number as Rafferty jotted the information down.

'You don't happen to know the names of any of her men friends in London?'

'She rarely mentioned anyone. Men were just— men—to Linda, unless she met someone who could help her career.'

'It was that important to her?'

Patsy smiled at him. 'Oh, yes. In fact, you might say she spent her whole life playing a part.' She handed him a photograph from the sideboard. 'That's Linda, in the middle.'

The Wilkses' family photographs hadn't really captured the dead girl. This photo gave far more of an idea of the real Linda. As Patsy had said, she was pretty enough, in a pale, unhealthy sort of way. Her hair hung over her face and though she pouted in the usual provocative manner at the camera, there was a hint of desperation in her eyes.

'When was this photo taken?' asked Llewellyn, obviously determined to get in on the act, despite Rafferty's strictures.

'Last year. She had a part as an extra in a film and we went to see her on set. She was so excited about breaking into films, was sure her big chance would come from it. But it was never released. They ran out of money.'

'Did Linda ever mention the Elmhurst Sanatorium?' Rafferty queried. He didn't have much hope anything would come of it, but he had to ask. They shook their heads. 'What about Dr Anthony Melville-Briggs or Dr Simon Smythe?' No, they'd never heard of them either. He ran a few more names past them, but they too were unknown to them. Still, that proved nothing.

Linda had not been forthcoming about her men friends. He tapped the photographs with a forefinger. 'Is it all right if I take this?' Patsy nodded. 'I'll let you have it back as soon as possible.' He fished in his pocket for his number and handed it over. 'If you think of anything, please phone me.'

Patsy showed him out. 'Poor Linda. All she wanted was the big break. She never talked about anything else.' She shook her head. 'It's funny, but the last part she played was that of an angel. Another flop.' Her eyes flickered upwards. 'Strange to think that if she's managed to get up there she'll be auditioning for the same part right now. You will get the man who did this to her, won't you, Inspector?'

Rafferty did his best to reassure her on that point, wishing he felt half as confident as he sounded. He was thoughtful as he and Llewellyn walked back to the car. They had learned little and the thought depressed him, but he cheered up a bit when he discovered they hadn't been given a parking ticket. He even let Llewellyn drive and as they left the quiet residential street behind he sat staring restlessly out of the side window. The traffic lights changed to green and they rounded the corner. His ears pricked up as he heard the familiar sound of a concrete mixer. Hadn't his Uncle Pat said he was working on a building site around this way? he mused. Rafferty looked at his watch and grinned. Five to one. Couldn't have timed it better if he'd tried, he congratulated himself. 'Pull up here,' he instructed.

'But it's a double yellow line, sir,' Llewellyn protested. 'I can't just...'

Rafferty sighed, unwilling to go through that all over again. 'Never mind that,' he ordered. 'I'm only asking you to pull up for a minute, not take up squatter's rights.' Muttering under his breath, Llewellyn did as he was told.

In spite of feeling he was beginning to know and understand his sergeant better, Rafferty still found his unrelenting company something of a strain and he needed a break, however short. The craving for a bit of light relief made him feel guilty and the sharp edge had gone from his voice as he added, 'Get some lunch and come back for me in an hour. You'll find there's a decent pub near the common. They serve hot food *and* they've got a car park.'

He got out of the car and slammed the door with the enthusiastic vigour of a convict out on parole. Crossing the pavement he quickly skirted the barriers guarding the building site and a pleased smile settled on his face as he took in the beginnings of a block of rather superior apartments rising from the dust and rubble of some previous building. He stood and watched for a little while, taking pleasure in the almost symphonic movements of the foreman and his men as they laid their bricks. As though obeying the commands of some invisible conductor, they all laid down their trowels at virtually the same moment and with a purposeful air, they followed one another down the ladder secured to the scaffolding. Lunch-time.

Rafferty strolled over. Already he could feel his spirits lifting. Building sites always had that effect on him. He had done some of his best thinking whilst surrounded by the roar of machinery and the good-natured cussing of a building crew.

'Hello, Uncle Pat.' It was a courtesy title as Pat was really a first cousin; his oldest and favourite cousin, in spite of the fact that he was always ready to take a rise out of him. At least he didn't hold his job against him.

The black-haired giant glanced round and his broken-toothed mouth curved into a delighted grin. 'Joseph Aloysius! It's yourself, is it?' His eyes twinkled as he clapped him on the back with a heavy hand. 'What's this I hear about you and our Maureen? Your Ma's told me you're sweet on her.'

Rafferty sighed. Maureen was Pat's eldest daughter and his second cousin. She was very bright and usually managed to reduce Rafferty to tongue-tied inanities in ten seconds flat, an obstacle to love that his ma seemed happy to ignore in her desperation to see him married again. The trouble was that his ma couldn't see beyond the fact that, in a country of increasing non-believers, Maureen was a 'good Catholic girl' and likely to encourage the religiously lax Rafferty back to the paths of righteousness. As if that wasn't recommendation enough for his mother, she came from a good breeding family—his own. Hadn't his ma drawn his attention to Maureen's child-bearing hips more than once? Unfortunately, for his ma they seemed to confirm that the match was made in heaven.

'When's the wedding?' Pat enquired, still grinning. 'Sure an' it'll be useful having a policeman as a son-in-law.' Rafferty winced. 'Don't look so worried, lad. It's only pullin' your leg, I am. My girl knows her worth, her ma's made certain of it. Surely, you know she goes for the intellectual type?' Rafferty hadn't, but it wasn't surprising, as he did his best to stay out of her way. 'She's on the hunt for a professor, at least,' Pat went on. 'I'll give you ten to one she wouldn't think of throwing herself away on a skinny carrot-top copper, whatever your ma hopes. It's my bet you'll stay on the shelf a while yet, Joseph.'

Amazingly, Pat had married an educated woman with ambitions, and, after twenty-five years together, they were still happy. It must be the attraction of opposites, mused Rafferty, uneasily reminded of Maureen.

Pat put his great arm round his shoulders and gave him the same disarming grin that had persuaded the middle-class highbrow Claire Tyler-Jenkins up the aisle and into his arms. 'Chin up, son. A little disappointment in love is good for a man. Sure and you'll get over it.'

Since being bowled over by his uncle's determined romancing, his wife had transferred her ambitions to her children and Rafferty was sure that none of those ambitions included marrying one of her daughters to *him*. Even though his Uncle Pat was a pretty good advert for marriage, Rafferty hoped he was right as Kitty Rafferty had a way of eroding a person's resistance that was positively tidal.

'Enough of this mournfulness.' Pat punched him playfully on the shoulder and he winced. 'Come away in the hut and have a bite to eat with the lads.'

As he sat in the hut, wedged between his Uncle Pat and his son Sean, Rafferty for the moment forgot his troubles. The atmosphere in the hut was cheerful, the tin mug in his hand held tea, strong, sweet and piping hot, and his ma, Llewellyn, the Elmhurst Sanatorium and Dr Melville-Briggs seemed a million miles away. For the moment, he was content.

ALTHOUGH THE A12 was fairly quiet, it was late afternoon by the time they got back to the station. 'Get hold of Dally,' Rafferty instructed the Welshman. 'Remind him that I'm still waiting for the results of the post-mortem. Anyone would think he had a conveyor-belt of corpses awaiting his attentions.'

Of course, there was no answer. Sighing, Rafferty checked down his lists. 'We'd better get on. We've only one or two more members of staff to go and three more patients. Right, let's have...' He paused, unable to read his own handwriting. 'Enrolled Nurse White.'

'Enrolled Nurse Wright is, I think you'll find, the young lady's name, sir,' Llewellyn supplied confidently, secure in the ivory tower of his own perfect script.

'Whatever,' Rafferty mumbled. 'Let's have her in.'

Nearly three quarters of an hour later, Rafferty knew he was in no danger of ever forgetting the wretched woman's name. He felt like cursing it and her from Llewellyn's ivory tower.

Nurse Wright mightn't have been academically bright enough to have studied for the higher RMN qualification, Rafferty reflected, but she was smart enough to know on which side her bread was buttered. It had taken him all that time to drag her story out of her and, even then, it came reluctantly. Was she hoping for promotion to Melville-Briggs's bed? he wondered.

It seemed a young woman had handed her a note for Melville-Briggs just as she had arrived at the side gate for duty on the night of the murder. Of course, she hadn't thought to give it to them when Linda Wilks's body had been found the next morning. She'd actually *thrown* it away. Or so she said, claiming the girl had said she would wait till 11.30 p.m. for Melville-Briggs to contact her. But as the nurse said, she only realized Sir Anthony wasn't in his flat that night when she had got no answer to her knock, and she had thrown it away.

Of course, the note had vanished. Rafferty wondered if she'd handed it to Melville-Briggs at the first opportunity and hadn't thrown it in the waste-basket at all. He cursed as he thought of the hours wasted raking through dustbins. He'd had to take men off the other search teams to look for it. Remembering Nurse Wright's tight white uniform and the fashionably tousled blonde curls under the saucily positioned cap, he hoped Melville-Briggs would be grateful for her attempted discretion.

They'd almost certainly lost the element of surprise in questioning Melville-Briggs about the matter. He'd be expecting them to demand an explanation. Well, Rafferty determined, he wasn't going to—at least not yet. Never do what people expect you to do, was his motto. It left them unbalanced which was just what he wanted. He'd see him when he gauged vertigo was ready to tip the doctor over into some useful disclosures and not before.

IT WAS TUESDAY A.M. and the fresh brightness of the day made Rafferty reluctant to head straight for their grim temporary office. Instead, he lingered in the hospital grounds for a few precious moments of peace. But at a sound behind him, he realized that even that brief respite was to be denied him.

'Psst.'

He stopped and turned, but there was no one in sight. Shaking his head, he told himself he was imagining things.

'Psst.'

There it was again. It seemed to be coming from the trees bordering the perimeter wall. 'Who's there?' he called loudly.

'Shh. Be quiet, can't you?' He was asked in a furious whisper. The voice sounded vaguely familiar and rather irritable. 'Come over here, for God's sake, before somebody sees you.'

Rafferty put his hands in his pockets and, after glancing casually around to see if he was being observed, sauntered as nonchalantly as curiosity permitted, towards the trees and the urgent, whispered summons. He wasn't altogether surprised to find that it was Gilbert, the gate-porter who had found the body, who was indulging in such James Bondian tactics. 'Not got the sack, yet, then?' he enquired drily, which conversational gambit only earned him a scowl. 'What do you want, Gilbert?'

'Got something that might interest you, 'Spector,' said Gilbert, with a quick, guilty glance over his shoulder. 'I meant to tell you before, like, only it slipped me mind.'

What dreadful secret could be pummelling Gilbert's flexible conscience? Rafferty wondered. He had told the little man to consider him as a priest, perhaps he was now to be treated to a confession? He hoped Gilbert didn't realize that full confessional secrecy was not something that he personally had any truck with. 'I'm listening, Gilbert,' he responded, assuming as pious a stance as he could muster. 'Go on.'

'I wanted to tell you about who I saw in the local the night the girl was killed. As I say, I meant to tell you bef—'

'And who might that be?' interrupted Rafferty.

'Simple Simon.'

'Dr Simon Smythe do you mean?'

'That's right. Simple Simon. Only he didn't meet a pieman.' He sniggered at his own wit. Rafferty smiled obligingly and waited for him to elaborate. 'He met a girl. And 'im meant to be on duty, too.' He sniffed, adopting the self-righteous tones of a man who knew his duty and did it, come what may.

'You're sure it was the night of the murder?'

'Course I'm sure. He was in the small private bar, knocking back whisky like it was going out of fashion. 'E didn't see me as the angle was awkward, but I saw 'im all right. I only caught a glimpse of the girl, though.'

'This girl—are you saying it was Linda Wilks?'

'I'm not saying nothin'. I'm just tellin' you what I saw, ain't I?'

'But Linda Wilks was a local girl and Elmhurst's a small place. Are you saying you didn't know her?'

'I wish you'd stop tryin' to put words into me mouth,' Gilbert complained. 'I didn't say I didn't know Linda. I did.' Hastily, in case Rafferty should think *he* had murdered her, he added, 'Just to nod to like, when she was 'ere, which wasn't often. All I'm sayin' is that the girl I saw could 'ave been Linda. But as I only caught a glimpse of the back of 'er 'ead, before the landlord came and served me and blocked me view, I can't swear to it. I can't be sure *who* she was. But Linda must 'ave been in Elmhurst that night, mustn't she?' he remarked slyly. 'She managed to get 'erself murdered, after all. Bit of a coincidence that, to my way of thinkin'. Mind, I'm not sayin' that Simple Simon done it. That's fer 'im to know and you to find out, ain't it?' he remarked complacently.

Rafferty sighed. Who'd have suspected that Gilbert had scruples? For some reason, he wanted to drop Simon Smythe in it, but his strange code wouldn't let him make a proper job of it, wouldn't let him say anything definitely helpful to the police.

'Mind,' Gilbert went on, in a sly, confiding manner. 'If it *was* Linda Wilks, we all know what 'e was doin' wiv 'er, don't we? Simple Simon rarely 'ad a girlfriend. Not a *proper* one, like.' He sniggered. 'You might call Linda Wilks more an *im*proper one, mightn't yer?'

Ignoring the salacious look in Gilbert's eye, Rafferty asked, 'Did they come in together?'

Gilbert shrugged. 'Don't know. I only noticed them at the last knockin's.'

'Can you describe this girl?'

Gilbert screwed his face up, as though to emphasize the difficulty of casting his mind back in time the vast distance of four days. 'Let me see. She had long dark hair,' he finally revealed. 'Admittedly, Linda Wilks was blonde the last time I saw 'er, but I generally never saw 'er with the same colour 'air twice in a row, so that don't mean nothin'. Bit on the skinny side. Meself, I prefer a woman with a bit more meat on her bones.'

'Never mind about that. Get on with it.'

Gilbert tutted. 'I'm tellin' you, ain't I? She was about nineteen, twenty, I'd say. Quite tall, about five foot seven.'

He seemed to be having few problems with his memory now, Rafferty noted drily. He began to suspect the real reason why he was the recipient of Gilbert's news. Had he tried to get Simon Smythe to cough up in return for keeping quiet? If so he had evidently been rebuffed and he wondered at Smythe's hitherto unsuspected bravery. Perhaps the poor sap just hadn't had the wherewithal to buy the porter's silence?

Gilbert continued in a confiding tone. 'I'm not normally a man to snitch, like, but if 'e done it, then it's my duty to 'elp the police. 'Ere,' he looked sideways at Rafferty. 'Isn't there usually some sort of reward offered for 'elping the police? Not that I'm doing it for the money,' he added hastily, as he saw Rafferty's frown. 'But if it's my entitlement, I might as well 'ave it.'

Rafferty sighed. Gilbert struck him as the sort of man who would milk a system for every penny of his entitlements, whether he deserved them or not. Not without a certain amount of satisfaction, he said, 'I'm sorry, Gilbert, but you must have been watching too many cops and robbers programmes on the telly. You're thinking of insurance companies, they're the ones with money to burn, not the poor copper.'

Gilbert looked as if he regretted his confidences, now the chance of profit was gone, and Rafferty decided it was time to get tough with him. 'I must say, I'm surprised it's taken you so long to "remember" what you saw.' Recalling Nurse Wright, he reflected that absent-mindedness must be catching. 'What's the matter, Gilbert? Did Smythe tell you to go to hell?'

Gilbert stiffened, the image of injured innocence. Unfortunately for him, it was at odds with the shifty look in his eyes. 'I don't know what you're talkin' about,' he retorted belligerently. 'I'm only tryin' to do me duty. But if all you're goin' to do is make nasty 'sinuations, I won't bother.' He clamped his mouth tight shut and made to go. But Rafferty grabbed his arm and held it tightly.

'Not so fast, Gilbert. If there's any more I want to hear it.' He smiled grimly into the man's sharp, weasel features. 'After all, you want to do your duty, don't you?'

Evidently Gilbert thought better of playing hard to get. Sticking out his bottom lip, he remarked plaintively, 'I was just about to tell you, wasn't I? You don't give a man a chance.'

'So, I'm giving you the chance now. Take it.'

'All right, all right, keep yer 'air on,' he complained. 'Though I don't know what else you expect me to say. You coppers are always putting words into a man's mouth. I don't want you to think . . .'

'Did they leave together?'

'No,' he admitted, rather reluctantly. 'They seemed to have a bit of a barney. She upped and left and he hung about for a minute, then he followed her out. He could 'ave caught up with 'er easily enough, what wiv those great long gangling legs of 'is.' He eyed Rafferty speculatively. 'Gonna arrest him are yer?'

Rafferty tapped the side of his nose with his finger. 'That's for me to know and you to discover, Gilbert.'

The porter scowled and Rafferty eyed him thoughtfully. It seemed that Gilbert had noticed rather more than a second's glimpse would reveal. It didn't surprise him. Smythe was supposed to be on duty at the hospital and Rafferty could imagine that the porter's shifty eyes would be out on stalks when he saw Smythe in the pub, his grubby little mind working overtime. He must have anticipated a nice little profit for keeping his mouth shut and it was only spite that had made him tell Rafferty what he'd seen when he'd failed to collect what he would have considered his dues. He eyed the man with distaste. 'Would you recognize her again?'

'Doubt it. I told yer, I only saw . . .'

'The back of her head. I know. I just wondered if any more of your memory had inexplicably returned.'

'I'd tell yer if it did, 'Spector,' Gilbert protested, with a show of hurt pride. 'You needn't sound as if I forgot deliberately. I reckon it must 'ave been the shock that made me forget. Yes,' he added firmly, glad to have found a believable excuse for his memory lapse. 'That'll be it. Shock can do funny things to a man's memory, you know. You learn things like that workin' in a 'ospital.'

'Really? Well, we must just be glad that the shock's started to wear off, then, mustn't we?'

Gilbert scowled and his face fell into disconsolate folds. Rafferty ignored him and concentrated on the implications of what the porter had just told him.

If Linda Wilks *had* been with *Smythe* just before she was murdered, it looked as if Melville-Briggs would be off the hook, which was rather a pity. He'd been looking forward to tackling him about the disappearing note. He still might do it, though, he promised himself, as a small reward for putting up with the doctor's increasing harassment. He seemed to expect Rafferty to debrief him on their results at the end of every day and he was getting fed up with it. If it wasn't for the fact that he was a buddy of the Chief Constable...

Rafferty found a pleasant smile for his informant. 'Thank you, Gilbert. You've been most helpful. I expect the Chief Constable will send you a letter of thanks. You could frame it.'

Gilbert snorted. 'Likely story. Seems to me all the likes of me get from the police is nasty 'sinuations.'

'I wonder why?' Rafferty walked away, leaving a disgruntled Gilbert muttering obscenities behind him.

THE PUB WAS BUSY with its lunch-time crowd when Rafferty and Llewellyn walked in. Rafferty caught the landlord's eye and beckoned him over.

'Police. Sorry to trouble you again. We have information that Linda Wilks might have been in here last Friday night. The night she was murdered.'

The landlord frowned. 'Who told you that?'

Rafferty's confidence began to evaporate a little. 'Never mind. Just think about it. She was a local girl. You must have known her by sight. Surely you remember seeing her that Friday?'

'I can't say as I do,' he replied. 'It was a very busy night. Darts final and the bar was packed with supporters from the Horse and Groom in the village. Run off my feet I was.'

'She was in the private bar, not the public.'

'No, she wasn't,' the landlord contradicted. 'She might have been in the public bar, but, as I said, there was such a crush, it would have been easy to miss her.'

'Perhaps some of your regulars could help?' Llewellyn suggested.

Unfortunately, it appeared that the regulars had celebrated themselves senseless after their team had won the darts final, and neither their evidence nor their memories could be relied upon.

'Sorry, Inspector.' The landlord was apologetic. 'It was a bit of a wild night, I'm afraid. We were all a bit sozzled. It's a good ten years since we won the trophy.' He glanced up at the silver cup proudly displayed above the bar.

Rafferty sighed. 'This other girl—the one who *was* in the pub, the one in the private bar. Perhaps you can describe her?'

He nodded. 'Reminded me of the sister-in-law a bit. She was a real classy-looking piece, *and* she had long dark hair, whereas Linda tended to fade into the wallpaper a bit. Now, let me see.' He glanced again at the darts trophy as though seeking inspiration. 'She was about twenty or thereabouts, I reckon. Stylishly dressed. Nicely spoken, too. She stood out, see? Not our usual sort of customer at all.'

Although, as the girl *hadn't* been Linda Wilks, he didn't think it would be relevant to the case, Rafferty's curiosity was piqued. 'Anything else you remember about her?'

'I could tell from her accent she wasn't from around these parts,' the landlord went on conversationally. 'I remember thinking it a bit odd that she should come into my pub, as it's so out of the way.' The landlord fingered his chin. 'I seem to remember seeing her in here a week or two ago, as well, now I think about it. I began to hope we were going to be taken over by some yuppie types. I'd have been able to put my prices up.'

Rafferty wasn't interested in the landlord's lost hopes. 'Those are the only times you'd seen the girl?'

'Reckon so.'

'The second time she came in, I understand she wasn't alone?' Llewellyn put in.

The man's eyes were bright with gossip. 'That's right. She was at first, but later, near closing time, she was drinking with a chap called Smythe from the hospital. Know him?'

Rafferty nodded. 'They didn't leave together?'

The landlord shrugged. 'Don't know. When I came round for the glasses, they'd both gone.' He grinned. 'I was pretty gone myself by that time.'

Rafferty nodded his thanks and they left. So much for Gilbert's confidences, he thought. The porter had been careful not to positively identify the girl as Linda, he remembered, and Rafferty suspected that he had known damn well that Smythe had been with another girl altogether that night. After all, it would seem, from what he'd said, that his single glance had been one long riveted stare. Although Gilbert had merely told him about the incident and encouraged him to put two and two together and make five, he intended to have a few words with Gilbert when next he saw him. It wouldn't do any harm to talk to Smythe. He'd already lied to them about being at the hospital the entire night. It was possible he'd told other lies as well. Linda Wilks could easily have been in the pub that night. Why shouldn't Smythe know her, even if not by her real name? He could have used her services. He could even have been the medical type who had rung her up that evening. Perhaps he had booked her services for when he returned to the hospital from the pub and had tipped her the wink as he'd left.

Rafferty brightened. 'Come on,' he said to Llewellyn. 'Let's go back to the station and call Dally. He might have some results at last.' There was no point in going off half-cocked, he told himself. He wanted more substantial proof against Smythe than the fact that he had been in the pub, drinking, when he should have been on duty, and had lied about his whereabouts at the time of the murder.

Back at the station, Rafferty put his feet up on his office desk and took the telephone from Llewellyn. 'What happened to you, Sam?' he asked. 'I expected the results of the PM before now.'

'We don't always get what we expect in this life, Rafferty,' Sam Dally replied laconically. 'Surely your mammy told you that?'

'My mammy told me a lot of things, Sam—not all of them very wise. But then, a woman who regards all doctors as gods can't be entirely relied upon.' Sam snorted disgustedly at the other end, but Rafferty carried on. 'Have you got any answers for me? Something that'll hold up in court, preferably.'

'Beggars can't be choosers,' he was told. 'You'll have to make do with what I *have* got and that's precious little—a few answers but more questions. What would you like first?'

Rafferty sighed. 'Just give it to me as it comes.'

'Right. She died between ten forty-five and midnight. From the blow to the back of the head, as I told you.'

According to Gilbert, Smythe had left the pub about 11.30 p.m. Ample time for him to meet Linda Wilks and take her back to the hospital. Ample time for murder. The timing was surely too coincidental for any other answer? Rafferty felt the excitement begin to build again. 'And had she had sex before she died?' Whatever other questions might remain unanswered from Sam's findings, Rafferty was confident that this wouldn't be one of them and Sam's firm 'no' muted some of his excitement. He had been relying on obtaining genetic evidence to confront Smythe with the murder. Uneasily, he wondered if it was possible he had been wrong about him? But he brightened again as he remembered that the coincidences connecting him to the girl's murder were pretty strong. The man had probably just lost his head. With a character like Smythe, the slightest suspicion of a sneer on the girl's part could be enough to push him over the brink. No doubt when he saw what his drunken frustration had done to her, his sexual desire had cooled quicker than the corpse.

'No sign of a struggle either,' Sam went on, happy to provide the rest of the questions he had promised earlier. 'Her body was untouched, there was no skin trapped under her nails. Someone just bopped her on the head, laddie, and then turned her over and set about removing her face. Odd sort of weapon, too. Not the usual blunt instrument. Could be some sort of garden tool. There were small traces of rust in the wounds. Obviously matey-boy didn't go to the expense of buying a new tool to bash her head in with.'

'Must have Scottish blood in him,' Rafferty murmured. But he wasn't really in the mood for their usual banter and Dally was, anyway, impervious to insults.

'I've ordered further analysis. You'll get the results all in good time.'

In *his* good time he meant, Rafferty reflected glumly. Talk about Dally by name and dally by blooming nature. Sam's evidence reminded Rafferty of something. Hadn't Mrs Galvin mentioned that the patients were encouraged to help with the gardening? Perhaps they might have been allowed to carelessly leave their tools lying around? 'You mentioned that this weapon could be a garden tool. Can't you be more specific?'

'Could be a fork or a rake, something like that. But don't quote me on it, Rafferty. I'm not sure *what* it is.'

Rafferty frowned into the receiver. At least Dally had finally admitted it. So far, he was getting more questions than answers, as Sam had promised, and he didn't like it.

'Looks like you've got yourself an oddball, Rafferty. Someone who murders just for the fun of it.'

'You needn't sound so pleased about it.'

'Keeps me in employment,' observed the caring doctor, complacently. 'What do *you* reckon the motive could be?'

'The usual,' he replied, still thinking of Simon Smythe. 'He must have hit her harder than he thought and panicked. Still, it's strange that the girl didn't either put up some sort of a struggle or accommodate her attacker's sexual requirements. I mean, a need for violent sex is hardly likely to come as a surprise to a prostitute. Yet, according to you, she did neither. I don't know what to make of it, but I intend to find out.'

'And the best of British to you. Oh, and another thing,' Sam tutted to himself. 'You nearly made me forget, the way you go wittering on. She was pregnant. About two months gone.'

EIGHT

IT SEEMED Smythe had had second thoughts about his lies, for when they got back to the hospital they found a note pushed under the outside door to their office. But arresting Smythe, even if he was the murderer, wasn't a prospect likely to fill Rafferty with triumph. If he had been a hunting man, Smythe was the kind of catch he'd have left for the dogs. Still, he reflected, as he picked up the internal phone and dialled Smythe's number, it would be a relief to get his first murder case wrapped up. But there was no reply. 'Probably sitting up there in his office wetting himself,' Rafferty snorted. 'Let's go and see.'

Smythe's first-floor office was small and rather cramped. The walls housed a pathetic show of achievements: his medical qualifications, and pictures of him at various stages of his school career, prep-school, university, and in a white coat outside some unknown teaching hospital. Each time, he was flanked by a man and woman—his parents presumably.

'You wanted to see us, Dr Smythe?'

After passing his tongue over dry lips, Smythe nodded miserably. 'I suppose Gilbert's spoken to you?'

'You suppose right. You shouldn't have told us lies, Doctor. Did you really think we wouldn't find out the truth?'

'I *meant* to tell you, I'd gone into your office fully intending to, but I lost my nerve.' He licked his lips. 'I thought you might be glad to pin it on me, especially as Dr Melville-Briggs had offered you a bribe.'

'I didn't take the bribe,' Rafferty was quick to point out, annoyed that his morals should be questioned by Simon Smythe.

Smythe looked relieved at this. 'But I didn't know that,' he explained. 'I was called away just then. I'd been watching from my office window and all I saw was his hand go in the pocket where he keeps his wallet and the confident expression he usually wears when he gets his own way. I was a gift, I thought. I was sure you wouldn't believe me if I told the truth. Once I'd told you the first lie, I had to go on. I didn't know what else to do. I found the body, you see, and I suppose I just panicked.' His face looked bloodless and his mouth opened and closed spasmodically, but no words came out. Indeed, he seemed to have trouble breathing and appeared on the verge of collapse.

As Rafferty waited for Smythe to go on, he became aware of the steady tick of the clock on the wall. It was a sturdy-looking thing, perhaps a survivor from the days when the house had been used as a private school. It had a paternalistic air; its large, round face reminiscent of a jolly schoolmaster. Smythe didn't seem to find the deep paternal voice of the clock any comfort. He sat staring down at the hands clenched in his lap, as though a thorough study of them would provide him with the answers he needed to convince them of his innocence. With difficulty, Rafferty kept his features as rigid as Llewellyn's. Sitting either end of the desk as they were, he imagined they must look like a pair of particularly malevolent bookends.

The clock on the wall ticked away another thirty seconds, then, suddenly, Smythe slumped pitiably in his chair as though the weight of their suspicions was too much for him. 'I suppose you think I killed her?' Desperately, he searched their faces for signs of denial. Seeing none, he slumped even lower and his hands gripped the arms of his chair as though they were the only things that stood between him and disaster. 'I knew it. I knew everyone would think I did it. That's why I kept quiet. I've been such a fool. I *didn't* do it, you know.' He began to wring his bony hands. 'You must believe that I didn't do it. You must,' he repeated in a voice hoarse with fear and desperation.

He looked more like a frightened rabbit than a suspected brutal murderer and Rafferty almost reached out a comforting hand, but then a picture of Linda Wilks's destroyed face flashed into his mind. For all that she had been a part-time hooker, she was the innocent victim in this, she the one deserving of sympathy. He would do well to remember it. 'You were the duty doctor that night. You told us yourself you were expected to stay on the premises. Why didn't you?' He leaned forward until his face was on a level with Smythe's. 'What happened when you brought her back here? Did she laugh at you? Is that why... ?'

Smythe shook his head violently. 'No, no, you've got it all wrong. I didn't bring anyone back here. Not the dead girl nor anyone else.'

'You abandoned your responsibilities to go to the pub. Why? Did you have an appointment with Linda Wilks for later?'

Smythe shook his head again. 'I only went out for a drink. I didn't expect to meet anyone.'

'Don't take me for a fool, Dr Smythe. I know enough medical men to know that they are always careful to keep a ready supply of drink to hand. Where did you keep your Dutch courage? In your desk or the filing cabinet?'

'In the desk.' He raised his shoulders and then let them fall again. 'I'd run out. That's why I went to the pub. You don't understand,' he told Rafferty. 'You don't know what it's like.' He looked down at his clenched fists, loosening and tightening them spasmodically, as though unaware of their movement. 'I hate it here.'

'Then why don't you leave?' But even as he asked the question, Rafferty realized that for a man like Smythe, it wasn't that easy. He was hardly the type to impress a selection panel.

'Don't you think I've tried?' The nervous aggression returned briefly, but as though he realized it would gain him no sympathy, he sank back in his chair and his voice quietened. 'It's not that easy. I wanted to be a vet, you know?' He grimaced. 'I've never been very good with people, but my parents had set their hearts on my becoming a doctor. I didn't have the guts to disappoint them. They'd sacrificed so much to give me a decent education. I went into psychiatry because I felt the patients would be less threatening, I hoped I might be able to help them. I was wrong, of course. They've no confidence in me.' He shrugged despairingly. 'I've no confidence in myself, so why should they have any? Not that Melville-Briggs's open contempt does me any favours, either.'

'If he thinks so little of you, why does he keep you on?' asked Llewellyn, coolly logical as usual.

Smythe laughed bitterly. 'Because he gets me cheap, Sergeant. He doesn't let me near his private patients, of course, but I'm good enough for the NHS patients the Health Authority can't accommodate.' His eyes watered self-pityingly. 'Sometimes I think I'm destined to remain here for ever as his whipping-boy. That's why, sometimes, I need to escape, so I go up to the pub. It's not far. It's warm, friendly, and unlikely to appeal to Melville-Briggs. And, for a time, I'm able to forget what a mess I've made of my life. I don't do it often,' he defended himself. 'Only—only, when . . .'

Only when you've booked a tart and her services, Rafferty added silently to himself, and needed something more than thin blood in your veins. Smythe's attempt at self-justification collapsed and he became abusive.

'Just because I was unlucky enough to find the body, doesn't make me a murderer. There's one or two others who could have done it. Dr Whittaker at the Holbrook Clinic, for instance. From what I heard, Melville-Briggs made Whittaker as mad as blazes last Friday night. And he left the dinner early, looking murderous by all accounts. Whittaker would have done anything to get back at him. Then there's Allward the Charge Nurse. He gets up to a few tricks at night, I can tell you. Have you checked *their* alibis?'

'But they weren't in the pub with a dark-haired girl that night,' Rafferty reminded him, deliberately ignoring the fact that Smythe had been with another girl, a stranger. 'You were.'

'But I bet none of them in the pub claimed that the girl I'd been with was the one who'd been murdered,' Smythe retorted.

'No,' Rafferty conceded. 'But neither did they confirm that Linda *hadn't* been in the bar that night.' He fully intended to have the other drinkers in the bar questioned, but from what the landlord had said, their testimonies wouldn't be any more reliable, and, for the

moment, he discounted the witnesses' ability to tie
Smythe in with the victim. Linda Wilks might or might
not have been in the pub that night, but she was certainly dead, and the likely time of death tied in with the
time Smythe had left the pub, which was just a few
hundred yards down the road from the hospital.

'The girl was murdered in the hospital grounds, not
the pub,' Smythe defended himself. 'Anyone could have
killed her.'

'Hardly. Not everyone has a key to that side gate,'
Rafferty reminded him quickly, though Gilbert had
done his best in that direction.

'Charge Nurse Allward has. He could have brought
the girl into the grounds. He's done it before.'

'Why didn't you report him, then?' Rafferty demanded bluntly. Had Staff Nurse Estoce suspected
something similar? he wondered.

Smythe shrugged. 'Why should I? I don't feel I owe
Melville-Briggs any loyalty. But neither do I feel my
contract includes being a patsy for his convenience,
which is why I'm telling you these things now. It would
suit him just fine if I was charged with murder. I'm only
on a short-term contract. He'd make out that I was
some sort of locum doctor and not actually one of his
staff. He'd manage to wriggle out of any possible con-
tamination somehow.' His mouth turned down petu-
lantly. 'He's good at that.'

'If what you say is true, how often did Allward invite girls into the hospital at night?'

'Often enough. Who's to say that he didn't do it last
Friday night? There's plenty of empty rooms at the
moment with so many of the patients away. It would be
an ideal time for him to get up to mischief, especially
with Melville-Briggs absent for the night. What could

be easier than for him to set up a little rendezvous and sneak away for half an hour during a meal break?'

'Like you, you mean?' Smythe scowled unhappily at the reminder. 'Do you know *for a fact* that Allward invited a girl here that night?' Rafferty persisted.

'No.' Smythe's reply was sullen. 'Why don't you ask him yourself?'

Rafferty's smile was grim. 'I intend to, Doctor. After I've finished questioning you, that is.' How on earth had Smythe's parents managed to convince themselves that he was doctor material? Rafferty wondered. It was plain to him that the man wasn't suited to the job. The tragedy was, he would probably have made a good vet. Rafferty looked again at the photographs on the wall. His parents didn't look wealthy, but the pride of achievement shone from their faces; an achievement paid for by the hapless Smythe in years of degradation and humiliation, trapped in the wrong career. Realizing he was again on the verge of feeling a misplaced sympathy, Rafferty sighed and invited Smythe to continue. 'You said you had gone up to the pub for a drink?'

Smythe nodded. 'I only meant to go out for half an hour or so, but I . . . I got chatting to a girl. She was so pretty. It's ridiculous, I know, that I should think...girls have never bothered much with me, but I began to hope...' He broke off and swallowed hard in evident distress. 'She was waiting for someone,' he resumed. 'It wasn't me.' He wiped his face with the sleeve of his white coat and then looked down at his hands again. 'That's why I...'

'Why you met up with Linda and killed her?' Hadn't hurt pride and frustration long been sufficient motives for some men to kill, he mused sadly.

'No! I told you...'

'You'd had a lot to drink—we know that, so you needn't trouble to deny it,' he added, as Smythe continued to shake his head. 'You persuaded her back here. Then, when she refused sex, you hit her.' He still couldn't understand why even a part-time prostitute would refuse sex, but presumably they, too, had their preferences. He didn't quite understand why he should bludgeon her face to a bloody pulp, yet leave her body untouched. If Linda Wilks had been killed in a frenzy of frustrated anger, there would have been blows to her body as well, but there hadn't been. He had been struck at the time by the fact that the body had been unmarked. Struck by it and then promptly forgotten about it, until Dally had remarked on it. Now, the strangeness of it struck him afresh. It hinted that the girl had been killed by someone in control, coolly, deliberately. Not Smythe's type at all.

Altogether, it posed too many unanswered questions for Rafferty's peace of mind.

'Why won't you listen?' Smythe spread out his hands as though beseeching for alms. 'I had an argument, I admit it, but *not* with the dead girl. It was another girl entirely, surely you learned that much at the pub? I wanted her to come back for a drink. It was quite safe, I knew Melville-Briggs would be out at a dinner all night. He does the same thing several times a year.'

'So while the cat was away you decided to play.'

'Why not?' he demanded truculently. 'I told you, I wouldn't be the only one. Melville-Briggs might think he owns me, body and soul, but he doesn't. I'm my own man.'

This defiant declaration was pathetic after what had gone before, but at least it seemed to give him some satisfaction, for now he calmed down a little. 'Anyway, she wouldn't come. She kept insisting that her friend would arrive soon, but when he didn't, she left. I left soon after. On my own.'

'Did she mention whether this *friend* was male or female?' Llewellyn asked.

Smythe shook his head sadly, as though at last accepting that his case was hopeless. 'I just assumed it was a man. Really pretty girls are always with a man or expecting one. They don't usually hang about waiting for a girlfriend. Only a plain girl would do that, and she'd latch on to an attractive, more popular girlfriend, hoping she'd fix her up with a man, too. Must be one of Mother Nature's more hit and miss methods of ensuring the continuation of the population, but it seems to work.'

It wasn't something that Rafferty had ever noticed, but Llewellyn was nodding his head sagely. Perhaps he'd made a study of the phenomenon in his psychology classes at university?

'She seemed nervous, strung up and wanted me to buy her another drink. I'd already bought her several and she'd obviously had a few before I arrived. I imagine I filled the waiting time for her.' His voice had a tinge of bitterness, of hurt pride that it was his destiny to be used as a convenient stop-gap till something better turned up. Rafferty could see how that would enrage a man, any man, but particularly a man of low self-esteem like Smythe. It was probably the last straw after a day filled with problems which he had found hard to cope with.

Smythe went on. 'But it was already late, well past time. I was starting to get worried that I'd be missed or that the police might come past and decide to find out why there were still so many vehicles in the car park—can you imagine Dr Melville-Briggs's reaction if I was arrested in such circumstances?'

Rafferty could, and again, the unwanted sympathy came seeping slyly back. If he was unfortunate enough to be a man like Smythe, working for a bully like Melville-Briggs, he suspected he, too, might require liquid solace.

'She'd told me earlier that she had a Citroën in the car park. I was in time to see it roar off towards town.' He sniffed away a trickle of mucus. 'I was pretty fed up myself by then and I nearly went back to the pub. But I knew it was possible that Dr Melville-Briggs might take it into his head to telephone and check up on me—he did that sometimes.' He glanced unhappily at the photo of the respectable couple on the wall. 'My parents would be terribly upset if I got the sack from here.' He sniffed again and went on. 'I'd bought a bottle of whisky from the landlord, so I decided to do what I'd originally intended and come back to the hospital for another drink.'

'What time was this?'

'About eleven thirty, perhaps a little later. I'm not sure.' He began to look less haunted, as though, like an animal, he sensed that Rafferty's determined pursuit of him was wavering. He had sufficient wit to make the most of it. 'It was dark. I hadn't had much to eat all day and I'd drunk more than usual. I fell over and broke my glasses just up the road from the pub.' A strained smile broke free from the tense set of his face. 'Amazingly, I didn't break the bottle.' The smile faded. 'After that, I was like a blind man stumbling along.'

'Your glasses weren't broken when I saw you,' Rafferty reminded him, frustrated himself now that his suspicions seemed to have led him to a dead end. They could have been broken in a struggle. But there'd been no trace of optical glass under or around the body and, according to Sam Dally, no struggle either.

Smythe's fingers touched the frames of his spectacles. 'These are a spare pair. With eyesight like mine, it's essential to have another pair for emergencies.' Rafferty nodded. It was plausible. Dropping his hand back in his lap, Smythe continued. 'Luckily, I saw the car before I got close enough to the hospital to be recognized and I pulled my collar up and...'

'What car?' Llewellyn put in sharply.

'Do you know the make? Did you see who was in it? Would you recognize them again?' demanded Rafferty.

Smythe jumped at the torrent of questions and selected one at random. 'I don't know. I never recognize makes, besides, I was too far away to see clearly. It had been parked close into the hospital wall, a little way from the side gate. Almost as soon as I saw it, it began to reverse on to that piece of waste ground opposite the hospital and was driven off towards town. I kept my head down. The driver might have been someone from the hospital and I was scared I'd be recognized. All I wanted was to get back to my office before someone discovered I was missing.'

'You recognized the Citroën, though, didn't you?' Llewellyn put in quickly.

'Yes, but that was only because she'd told me what it was and she was the only person to have left the bar. Besides, the lights from the pub car park caught the name as she sped off.'

'But you'd broken your glasses,' Rafferty pointed out.

'That was after.'

He hadn't managed to shake him. But as he no longer thought Smythe was the murderer, he hadn't expected to. 'Do you remember the colour of this car at all?'

'It was a lightish shade and I remember there was only one person in it, no passenger.'

'What happened next?'

'I had a bit of trouble with the lock on the gate. I unlocked it, or thought I did, but it wouldn't budge. I tried again and it opened.'

'Perhaps you'd forgotten to lock it when you came out?' Llewellyn suggested, glancing at Rafferty.

Smythe shook his head. 'I don't think so. I didn't forget to lock it behind me when I came back, even though I was far from sober. I hadn't gone more than a few paces into the grounds when I fell over again. Only this time it was a body I fell over. The feet were right across my path and tripped me up. I remember touching the toes as I scrambled up. I thought at first it was just a funny-shaped branch, but the moon came out just then and as I got up, I could see her face quite clearly. It had all been smashed most horribly.' Rafferty had to strain to hear; Smythe's voice was now the merest whisper and his eyes stared straight ahead, as though he was reliving the moment, its horror clearly etched in his face. He shuddered and, taking a deep breath, tried to collect himself. 'She was still warm. She could only have died a short time before.'

'You're sure she *was* dead?'

The pathetic dignity returned as Smythe met Rafferty's eyes. 'I know you don't think me much of a doctor, Inspector, but I can still recognize a dead body when I fall over one. Believe me when I tell you she was quite, quite dead.'

And Rafferty could recognize the truth when he heard it. 'Go on,' he encouraged dispiritedly.

'Someone—her killer, I suppose—had removed all her clothes. Anyway, I couldn't see them anywhere.'

'What did you do next?'

'I left her there.' With obvious reluctance, he met Rafferty's eyes. 'I know it was a despicable thing to do, but I couldn't help her. She was already dead.' He dropped his eyes. 'I—I wasn't thinking clearly. I was drunk, distraught.'

'Oh, I would say you were thinking clearly enough, Doctor,' he remarked and watched, unsurprised as the dull red flush of shame stained Smythe's pale cheeks. But, even after listening to the ready excuses for the inexcusable, Rafferty could still feel sorry for him. It wasn't reasonable to expect more ethical conduct from someone so browbeaten as poor Smythe. Confronted by the problem of confessing his dereliction of duty, together with his proximity to a newly dead body, it was no wonder he had put self-preservation first.

It was interesting about the car. They hadn't found any tracks, but then the weather had been very dry recently, unseasonably warm and muggy. There were no shops or houses just there to explain its presence. Only the hospital and the pub a good two hundred yards closer to the main road. There'd have been no reason for any of the customers to go that way, certainly not by car, as the road petered out into a dead end. Of course, it was always possible that one of the staff had been dropped off at the illicit side entrance. But he didn't think so. The night staff came on duty several hours earlier and how many other people could have been prowling around the hospital at that time of night? It was possibly a courting couple, but Smythe had mentioned only seeing one person in the car, and however blurred his vision, he was unlikely to make a mistake about that. Once the car began to move away, two separate shapes would have become visible, not just one.

He'd get the house-to-house team on to it directly. He'd also have to put out an appeal for this other girl that the landlord and Gilbert had described, see if she came forward. And perhaps it was time he indulged himself with interviewing Melville-Briggs? Perhaps *he* could shed some light on who the other girl in the pub might be?

The fact that several points of Smythe's story checked out made the story about the car more credible. Smythe wasn't streetwise enough to blend truth and falsehood in order to give a cohesive strength to his story. He was the type who would tell either the whole truth or a complete pack of lies. And he'd tried the lies. As they already knew some of his story was true, Rafferty was the more inclined to believe the rest was also.

If only he hadn't broken his damned glasses, he might have been able to tell them who had been in the car. It might well have been the murderer.

Smythe's head was still bent like a penitent as though he was awaiting Rafferty's absolution. His pink scalp showed through the thinning blonde hair. It looked soft, pleading, vulnerable.

Rafferty sighed. He believed Smythe's story, but he might as well tidy up the loose ends before he ploughed on with the investigation. 'What were you wearing that night?' he asked.

'What . . . ?' Comprehension dawned. 'This suit.'

It was a plain, lightish blue with a rather distinctive stripe of darker blue. If, as he had said, he had fallen over the girl's feet, it would explain the lack of blood.

If he had attacked the girl with the ferocity which her injuries suggested, the suit would surely have blood on it, a lot of blood. If he was telling the truth and this was the suit he had worn, of course. Perhaps Gilbert or the landlord would remember it?

'I'll have to ask you for the suit, Doctor, and your shoes and the other clothes you were wearing that night.' He paused, then demanded, 'I suppose you know you've committed an offence? Several offences I shouldn't wonder.'

Smythe nodded miserably, then his watery eyes gazed pleadingly at Rafferty. 'I suppose it'll all have to come out? My career ... I was hoping ... You couldn't ... ?'

Rafferty stared at him incredulously. Even now, Smythe still clung to the pathetic remnants of his professional dignity. The realization temporarily cured him of compassion and he observed bluntly, 'If I were you, Doctor, I'd be more concerned that someone in the pub remembers that you *were* wearing that suit, rather than another one that you could have since destroyed. Otherwise ...' He let the awful warning hang on the air for a few seconds before he turned to Llewellyn. 'Take him home and let him get changed, then take him to the station for a signed statement and a session with the identikit man. See if he can come up with a face for the girl in the pub.'

Watching Llewellyn take Smythe away, Rafferty reflected that, as Alice had said, this case was getting curiouser and curiouser. Perhaps, as well as speaking to Dr Melville-Briggs, they'd do well to see Charge Nurse Allward again?

NINE

CHARGE NURSE ALLWARD was a cool customer all right, Rafferty decided. He sat, legs crossed and perfectly at ease, in their cramped little office, his glossy looks managing to make the room look even shabbier than normal.

'What made you decide to become a nurse, Mr Allward?' Rafferty asked suddenly, as Allward settled, hoping to ruffle his smooth feathers by an unexpected beginning to the interview. 'It's hardly the automatic career to appeal to a man like yourself, I would have thought.'

Allward smiled. 'You overestimate my talents, Inspector. But, to answer your question; nursing's as good a career as any, and even with Health Service cuts, it seemed a reasonably secure profession to enter. Why do you ask?'

'Just curious.' In fact, he was *damned* curious. Allward struck him as a type who would be more at home in a city office wielding a computer and three phones than a bedpan in a psychiatric hospital, even if it *was* a private one. Did he hope for a mention in a few of the older patients' wills? Rafferty wondered. He was the type to appeal to old ladies. 'You're on permanent night duty here, aren't you?' A hint of wariness entered Allward's eyes as he nodded. 'Is there any particular reason for that?'

Allward raised his elegant shoulders. 'I see less of Dr Melville-Briggs that way.'

Rafferty shot another dart at him in an attempt to shake his composure. 'It wasn't the opportunity for illicit rompo that appealed to you, then?' To his annoyance, Allward merely laughed, with what appeared to be genuine amusement.

'Have you been listening to gossip, Inspector?' he enquired drily, seemingly not at all shaken by Rafferty's tactics.

'I listen to anything, sir,' Rafferty replied in a tight voice. 'If it's relevant to the case.'

'I wonder if I can guess who's been telling tales?' Allward's gaze rested thoughtfully on Rafferty. 'Simon Smythe looked even more hangdog than usual when I saw him earlier. *And* he had a policeman in tow. Been in here, had he?' he questioned in a light voice. 'Done a bit of snitching?' Rafferty said nothing and Allward continued. 'The rest of the staff have got Smythe jailed already. Especially Melville-Briggs. He looked positively smug when he heard Smythe had been carted off to the police station. I expect he'll be in to congratulate you when he gets back from his conference, though I suspect his gratification is a little premature. If you thought you'd got your man, you'd hardly be questioning me again, would you? I suppose Smythe couldn't wait to tell you all about my nocturnal activities? But I'm only following the boss's example, Inspector. Old Melville 'Do as I say and not as I do' Briggs. Still,' he mused, as though determined to demonstrate his lack of concern, 'I can hardly blame Simple Simon for not covering up for me.' He gave Rafferty another smile, but this time the charm failed to conceal his spite. 'Especially as he would appear to be a few answers short of an alibi himself.'

Rafferty ignored this. 'And what about *your* alibi, Mr Allward? Aren't you a few answers short as well?' He consulted his notes. 'According to your last statement, you were fifteen minutes late back from your early tea-break.'

'I've already explained about that.'

'So you have. What a shame no one but a senile old man can vouch for you.'

Allward's eyes narrowed, but, outwardly at least, he retained his composure. 'Even if I had been with a girl, it's hardly a crime, Inspector.'

Rafferty wanted to see Allward's assurance crumble, that way he might get some interesting answers. 'No,' he remarked slowly, 'but murder is.'

'Are you accusing me, Inspector?' Allward quirked an enquiring eyebrow. 'Should I have my solicitor present? You instigated this interview because you've discovered that I like a little diversion during the long nights. So what if I do? It doesn't make me a murderer.'

'No. But it does make you that much more interesting to suspicious policemen. I want to hear your statement again.'

Allward heaved a long-suffering sigh and repeated what he had already told them on the occasion of their previous interview. He'd had his tea-break at 11.15 p.m. and had returned at 11.45 p.m., having been delayed by a patient for a quarter of an hour. 'I've told you all this before, Inspector.' Allward sounded wearied by the repetition. 'I was tending to one of the patients, as I said, not having fun and games with a local working girl.'

'So you said. Old Mr Tompkinson, wasn't it?' The patient with the convenient memory. Whose room was

also handily situated near the back entrance to the bedroom block, to which Allward would have a key. He
could easily have slipped out. How convenient that it
had been Mr Tompkinson whom he claimed to have
been tending. They'd already discovered that the old
man was very suggestible. Had Allward told the patient that he'd woken from a bad dream on Friday night
as a cover, sure that the patient would be too fuddled to
contradict him? 'I believe you said he was a particular
favourite of yours?'

'What of it?' Allward replied smartly. 'I didn't realize the time of death had been pinned down to one of
my breaks.'

'All the staff are being asked to account for their
movements, sir,' Llewellyn remarked politely.

'Where do you take these breaks?' Rafferty questioned. 'In the staff lounge?'

'Sometimes,' came the guarded reply.

'And on Friday night—were you in the staff lounge
then?'

'No.' A defensive tone had entered Allward's voice.
Rafferty was pleased that he had at last managed to
rattle the man. 'I put my feet up in one of the empty
rooms in the male bedroom block. I was tired and
wanted a short nap.'

Llewellyn raised his eyebrows at this. 'Surely that's
against the hospital rules?'

Allward gave a cynical laugh. 'You'd be surprised
what goes on in hospitals at night, Sergeant: drinks,
parties, gambling clubs, a fair amount of naughties.
Don't tell me it's not the same at cop-shops? It's difficult to believe that the "boys in blue" don't get a kick
out of watching confiscated porno movies. I thought it
was how you earned the nickname.'

'We're not here to discuss what the police have to do to prove an offence has been committed, sir,' Llewellyn replied stiffly. 'I believe we were discussing what *you* were doing?'

'I've already told you I was in one of the spare bedrooms.'

'Alone?'

'Unfortunately, yes.'

'Yet, surely, with Melville-Briggs safely out of the way, you had an ideal opportunity?' Rafferty suggested. 'What stopped you from providing yourself with a little entertainment?'

Allward's eyes met Rafferty's boldly. 'I just didn't feel like it, that's all. We can't all be super-studs like the old man, you know. Of course, the rest of us don't have our virility stimulated by the thought of profit in the way that he does. I should imagine it's a great aphrodisiac.'

'The dead girl was a prostitute. A psychiatric hospital at night is not the obvious choice for a pleasant stroll. Not the likeliest place to pick up a john. Presumably she was expecting to see *someone* on Friday night. Have you any idea who?'

'No.' Allward was beginning to sound a little sullen, as though he was no longer finding the interview quite so amusing.

'Perhaps she was part of a midnight sewing bee?' Rafferty suggested sardonically. Allward said nothing and reluctantly Rafferty let him go, but remarked to Llewellyn when he had gone: 'I think we've found the "medical man" Linda's father mentioned telephoned.' He snorted. 'Probably told Linda he was a doctor. Some of the other staff must be aware of what Allward gets up to at night, Staff Nurse Estoce, for instance. I think, with a little encouragement, she might forget that touching loyalty for long enough to drop him in it.'

Llewellyn looked doubtful. 'He's good-looking, confident, hardly the type to turn to a prostitute. And he's not the sort to lose his head—Smythe yes, but not him.'

'He might have been between girlfriends,' Rafferty suggested. 'Perhaps he rang Linda to fill a temporary gap. She said herself that the medical type who rang her was one of her men friends—a regular? And even if *he* hadn't used her services before, it seems likely he'd have heard of her.'

'But what if there wasn't a phone call at all?' Llewellyn threw in. 'Sidney Wilks isn't completely above suspicion himself, remember? He could have invented that phone call to avert suspicion from himself. Of the two, I favour him.'

Rafferty shook his head. 'Even if Wilks *did* lie, it doesn't alter the fact that she must have known *someone* at the hospital to have come here in the first place. Otherwise why come? I want Allward's clothes checked by forensic, just like Smythe's,' he added decisively. 'He's too clever to refuse and of course, if he did it, he'll have got rid of the ones he was wearing by now, but it'll rattle him and that's what I want.'

SIMON SMYTHE had been telling the truth after all and they would have to cross him off their list of suspects. Although the pub landlord had been unable to confirm what he had been wearing, forensic had discovered a few tiny splatters of Linda Wilks's blood on the bottom of his trousers, presumably picked up from the grass around the body which indicated that he *had* merely fallen over her body rather than killed her. There were signs that he'd tried to remove the stains, but minute traces had still clung to the fibres. Simon Smythe might be many things, but he wasn't a murderer. The only things he was guilty of being were a coward and a bit of a dummy, and they carried with them a punishment far longer and more severe than most courts would give out; a *real* life sentence in fact. Allward's clothes, too, were free of suspicious stains, though in his case that proved nothing, merely that he was smarter than the younger doctor and not nearly so likely to incriminate himself.

So Rafferty was back to square one. Some questions had been answered only to find another crop springing up in their place. For instance, why had the killer gone to the trouble, not only of removing all Linda Wilks's clothes, but also of taking them away with him? 'Maybe the clothes the victim was wearing were an important clue,' he suggested to Llewellyn. Perhaps, Rafferty pondered, in some desperation, they were dealing with a necrophiliac—a tidy necrophiliac, who also collected the clothes of his victims. Perhaps he had gone out to his car for something before he began his vile practices, had seen Smythe coming up the road, recognized him, knew his 'fun' was cancelled, and drove off? Rafferty sighed. Perhaps he was being fanciful again. It couldn't have been easy to strip the body, he reflected. He'd have expected bruises from rough handling, but there had been none. Had the murderer *cut* the clothes off the girl? If so, it pointed to premeditation and that indicated that whoever had phoned her had also killed her. *If* there had been a phone call at all. Damn. Rafferty frowned. Why hadn't they checked with Mrs Wilks? By now, if her husband had been lying about that call, he'd have had ample time to browbeat his wife into supporting his story. Still, it was worth trying. Perhaps, he thought, if they could ask the question when her husband was at work, they'd be able to winkle the truth out of her.

'Did the murderer fear the victim would be more easily traced through her clothes?' he asked Llewellyn. He couldn't imagine why. From what the parents had said, they'd been pretty nondescript, the sort lots of young girls wore. 'What other reason could he have had for taking them?' he asked Llewellyn, that fount of all knowledge.

'Perhaps he reads crime fiction and was worried about the possibility that he'd left hair or spittle on them.'

Rafferty drummed his fingers on the table. 'If only we could be sure what the girl was doing there; who she'd come to see. I still fancy Allward.'

'We haven't seen Dr Whittaker at the Holbrook Clinic, yet, sir,' Llewellyn reminded him. 'Unless we want to upset Dr Melville-Briggs . . .'

Rafferty grunted as Llewellyn's voice trailed away. 'We'll see him this afternoon. I want to speak to his lady friend first, though, Gwendoline Parry. Let's have her in.'

RAFFERTY SETTLED the Hospital Administrator as comfortably as the rickety chairs would allow. He was surprised by a feeling of recognition. He felt he had met her before somewhere and then it came to him. Big-boned and with the rather old-fashioned bun hairstyle and practical short nails, she reminded Rafferty of one of his former school teachers, a Miss Robinson, who had fallen in love, late in life, with the new French master. She had been an intense woman and had fallen hard, and he remembered with a trace of shame how he and the rest of the school had sniggered over the affair, how they had mimicked the adoring eyes of Miss Robinson at assembly. She must, like Miss Parry, have been in her early forties; 'Miss Robinson's last chance' the affair had been called. The man had let her down, he recalled, and she had left the school soon after. He wondered whether Miss Parry had found *her* last chance and if she was prepared to fight for it. According to Gilbert, she had a widowed, invalid mother at home, so would be unlikely to have many more such opportunities.

'I understand you've just returned from a few days' leave, Miss Parry?'

Gwendoline Parry nodded.

'Do anything nice?' Rafferty enquired casually, aware that a few interested, non-threatening questions relaxed an interviewee no end, but this time, his technique failed abysmally.

For some reason Gwendoline Parry's fair skin blushed a delicate rose, though she replied calmly enough. 'I had some work I wanted to get on with at home, Inspector.'

'Doing a spot of DIY, were you?' he asked, reminded of the necessity to soon do something about the depressing yuppified magnolia walls of his own flat. He fancied something cheery like sunshine yellow or terracotta.

'No. As it happens I was typing up some research notes.'

'Surely Dr Melville-Briggs doesn't expect you to do extra work when you're on holiday?' he queried sympathetically, though Rafferty wouldn't put it past him.

Gwendoline Parry smiled faintly. 'No. Luckily, Sir Anthony isn't in need of my amateur typing skills. He has a perfectly competent secretary in Mrs Galvin.'

Rafferty had a good idea who *was* in need of some free assistance. He couldn't imagine Simon Smythe went in for much in the way of research, he had as much on his plate as he could handle already. But Gilbert's tongue had proved obligingly indiscreet on various topics, not least who was sweet on whom and Miss Parry's love and loyalty didn't rest with Sir Anthony. However, for the moment, he didn't pursue the question. 'You've heard about the murder, of course?'

She gave a grimace of distaste. 'How could I not? The papers are full of it. Still are.'

Rafferty felt guilty, as he remembered his reassurance of Linda's mother, but there had been no way he could have kept Linda's double life out of the papers. 'You understand that we have to check up on everyone's movements for Friday night?'

She nodded. 'Of course. As for myself, I was at the George in Hamborne from seven thirty p.m. till two a.m., Inspector.'

'The doctors' do? I didn't know administrators got an invite.'

'They don't. I was a guest of Dr Nathanial Whittaker. He runs the Holbrook Clinic,' she explained. 'It's a few miles from here. Perhaps you've heard of him?'

Rafferty nodded again. Between Sam Dally and Gilbert, he knew all about Dr Nathanial Whittaker. Owner of a rival private mental hospital, he was a truly dedicated doctor, but a driven one. His father had been a brilliant surgeon until struck down with Alzheimer's Disease when Whittaker was a teenager. The boy had adored his father and the cruel, undignified death had apparently made a deep impression on him; he had abandoned his long-planned career as a surgeon and decided instead, after his general medical training, to specialize in the psychiatric field, studying mental illness, its causes and treatments.

Once trained, he had dedicated his life to finding a cure for Alzheimer's. The research had taken its toll on his health, his marriage, and his money and the Holbrook Clinic nowadays barely kept its head above water. His wife had left him six months ago and he'd been pretty cut up about it, according to Sam. The house had been sold—there had been no children—and he'd ploughed his share into the hospital, where it was being swallowed up with the same dispatch as the rest of his money.

By a curious irony, Whittaker might be a dedicated and respected psychiatrist, but, according to Sam Dally, as a researcher, he was singularly inept. For all the long hours he devoted to the work, he lacked the plodding patience and meticulous attention to detail necessary, which explained both his lack of success and his inability to attract funding. Whatever money he made from his hospital was ploughed into his research work. Inevitably, his patients and their relatives had gradually turned to more comfortable establishments, where their ailments, real or imagined, were given that number one priority they felt they deserved. As Gilbert had so graphically put it, 'Not even a lunatic would pay good money for group therapy on couch-grass when he could have gymnasiums and jacuzzis just up the road.' He was right of course. Whittaker had presumably done his best to keep the standards of his hospital to a certain level, but then, according to Sam, when his wife had left him, things had begun to slide downhill. Whittaker had

turned more and more to his research work, burying
himself in it almost. Rafferty wondered how long the
relationship between the doctor and Gwendoline Parry
had been going on. He'd forgotten to ask Gilbert. Now,
he signalled to Llewellyn to take over the questioning.

'What time did you leave the George, Miss Parry?'

'I stayed till the convention ended, Sergeant.'

'I see. But Dr Whittaker didn't?'

She shook her head faintly, as though unwilling to
confirm the matter, but, aware that there were plenty of
other witnesses who would, she elaborated. 'He left
around ten thirty.'

'You didn't mind?'

Miss Parry raised her eyebrows. 'Why should I
mind?'

'Most women would expect to be escorted home after being invited out, particularly at that time of night.'

'I *am* an adult, Sergeant. Dr Whittaker knew I was
perfectly capable of taking a taxi.'

The sharp retort failed to conceal the fact that she *had*
minded and Rafferty's opinion of his sergeant's interview technique went up a notch. Who'd have thought
that seemingly dedicated bachelor would appreciate that
most women *would* mind? Perhaps there was more to
this psychology lark than he'd thought? It had been a
very swish do, by all accounts, probably looked forward to for weeks, and he remembered vividly his dead
wife Angie's reaction when he had had to leave her at
some social function or other. He couldn't believe the
elegant, if slightly repressed, Miss Parry would be anything but extremely miffed in similar circumstances. She
would surely find it even more humiliating that her boss
should witness it? Particularly as there was no love lost
between the two doctors.

Rafferty wondered if Miss Parry and Whittaker had had a row. If so, no one had so far mentioned it. But that could be because the one between Melville-Briggs and Whittaker had been much more spectacular—fisticuffs, no less. Still, it would be worth making a few enquiries. Now, with a sensitivity that surprised Rafferty, the Welshman abandoned this interesting sidelight and returned to the main beam of the interview.

'We believe that the victim entered the grounds of the hospital by the side gate, Miss Parry. As you probably know, Gilbert, the lodge-porter, took it upon himself to give out unofficial keys to this door. I believe you have one?' She nodded. 'May I see it?'

Surprisingly, for such a neat-looking lady, her handbag was a large affair and she rummaged through it for some time with a worried look before admitting defeat. 'I'm sorry, but my keys don't appear to be here.'

Rafferty's interest was sparked by this admission. 'You're sure? Perhaps you'd better check again, Miss Parry.'

She tipped everything out on the scarred table: pens, tissues, purse, make-up bag, diary, notebook, more tissues, a stray lipstick, and finally a small set of keys. Rafferty pounced on them.

'They're the keys to my office and the filing cabinets, Inspector,' she explained. 'I've always kept them separate from the main ring.'

'So when did you last see the other set?'

She frowned. 'I'm not sure.'

'Perhaps it'll help if I ask when you last *used* them? Would it have been last Friday? I believe you worked that day?'

Her lips pursed, and with a degree of reluctance, as though realizing that there was no way she could conceal the fact, she agreed that that had been the last time she had seen them. 'I had to work late, so I arranged for Dr Whittaker to pick me up at the side gate as it's more convenient for the Hamborne road. I had to use the key to get out.'

Rafferty flicked a finger at her large handbag. 'And did you take that with you to the dance?'

'No. I had a small clutch bag. I had to work late and knew I would have no time to go home and change. I left this bag locked in Nathanial's car. Luckily, I remembered it and managed to catch him in the car park before he drove off.'

So, Rafferty mused, Nathanial Whittaker *had* had the opportunity to help himself to the keys. Did Miss Parry suspect as much? Was that why she looked anxious? he wondered. He would have known she would be on leave till early the following week and therefore unlikely to miss the keys till then. 'How did you get in without your key when you returned from leave?'

'I generally use the main entrance. I have a car, so I mightn't have known the keys were missing for some time.'

'Perhaps they fell out of your bag into the car and Dr Whittaker found them?' he suggested gently.

'He *did* call round the next day.'

Rafferty frowned uncomprehendingly. 'Didn't he say?'

She flushed again. 'I didn't open the door. I was busy working, as I told you. I didn't want to stop and risk being delayed for hours. I live with my widowed mother, Inspector, but she was out on Saturday morning. I thought it might have been one of her friends and they have a tendency to linger. The flat is so designed that it's impossible to see who's at the door.'

'It might as easily have been Dr Whittaker come to return your keys,' Rafferty remarked, trying to catch her out. She didn't fall for it. Now, she seemed subtly to withdraw from him, as though his attempted trick had somehow disappointed her.

'I only saw that it was Dr Whittaker when I went to the window overlooking the car park. But as I was unaware that I'd lost the keys, Inspector, I wasn't to know that he'd call round.'

Touché. 'So you weren't.' Rafferty gave her a rueful smile. 'What a memory I've got.' She gave no answering smile. It was apparent to Rafferty that she was very preoccupied about something. Could Whittaker have engineered an argument between them so he could sneak off and keep an appointment with Linda Wilks? He'd had the opportunity to get the key to that side gate; had he, fired by his fight with Melville-Briggs, decided to make old Tony the butt of scandal-mongers for a change? Did Gwendoline Parry suspect something similar? he wondered. Was she trying to protect him from the consequences of his own folly?

Perhaps it was about time they saw Dr Whittaker. He might have some serious explaining to do or he might not. He could have turned up at Miss Parry's the next day simply to kiss and make up, not to return the keys before she'd noticed they'd gone. Either way, he'd been unlucky.

TEN

THE HOLBROOK CLINIC was crying out for money, that much was obvious as Rafferty and Llewellyn drove through the open gates. The grounds were a lot smaller than at the Elmhurst Sanatorium, but they were badly neglected. Couch-grass pushed through the gravel of the drive and the only plants were hardy shrubs that were capable of looking after themselves. As Gilbert had said, there were no gymnasiums or jacuzzis here.

The Victorian buildings, too, had a shabby air of rather faded grandeur, and, like the minor gentry from that era, attempts were made to keep up appearances; like the freshly painted black metal gates and the smartly uniformed gate-porter—surface shows that cost little. But the further one penetrated, the harder the pretence was to keep up and no attempt had been made to repoint the red brickwork or paint the many windows. It looked like the county asylum it had once been and still sported the grandiose turreted style the Victorians had favoured for such institutions.

A passing nurse escorted them to the doctor's office. They introduced themselves, and with an air of distraction Dr Whittaker gestured at the two uncomfortable-looking chairs in front of his desk. Rafferty wondered if they were chosen specially to deter visitors from staying too long and interrupting his work. They would do the job admirably, he reflected as he sat down. The stiff, presumably horsehair, padding didn't give an inch. Studying him, Rafferty realized that, in his youth,

Nathanial Whittaker must have been quite beautiful, with his thin and elegant features and soulful dark eyes. He was still a fine-looking man, but now he had a care-worn air, the thick dark hair was greying rapidly; it was quite long and when it fell over his forehead, he pushed it back with long and impatient fingers; surgeon's fingers. Rafferty wondered if he regretted his youthful vow because his research work over twenty years and more had achieved little. Perhaps it was as Sam had said, and his lack of success in the research field was because his work was driven by the grief of a personal loss rather than by a true vocation.

'You'll have heard about the murder at the Elmhurst Sanatorium, Doctor?' Rafferty began hastily, as, having sat them down, Whittaker seemed to promptly forget them. His gaze drifted down to his papers and he looked set to become immersed.

'What?' He raised his head, frowning slightly as though he had forgotten why they were there. With a sigh, he shut the file and sat more upright, looking from Rafferty to Llewellyn and back again before he nodded. 'Yes, yes. A couple of the staff mentioned it.' He glanced at Rafferty with an air of bewilderment. 'But I don't quite understand why... ?'

'Just routine, Doctor,' Rafferty reassured him. 'You didn't know the victim yourself, I take it?'

'Me? No. I didn't know her.' Rather naively, he added, 'She was never a patient of mine,' as though he couldn't imagine any other circumstances in which he might know a woman.

'I understand you were at the George on Friday night?'

Dr Whittaker nodded again. 'Yes. I didn't want to go, there's too much work to do here to waste time attending such self-congratulatory nonsense, but I knew it was too good an opportunity to miss. I hoped someone might put in a good word for me about research funds.' His face darkened and his sensitive features were distorted by an expression of such intense hatred that Rafferty was taken aback. 'It was a waste of time, of course, any chance I had was ruined before I got there. Anthony Melville-Briggs saw to that, as usual. I suppose you heard all about the fight I had with him?' Rafferty nodded faintly and waited for further enlightenment. It wasn't long in coming. 'He made sure if there were any research funds up for grabs, *he'd* get them. He's too clever to ever accuse outright, but I knew it was him all right. Sly innuendo and locker-room jokes are more his style. Impossible to fight against, of course. That was another reason for going to that convention. I knew I was isolated. Unfortunately, socializing's important in my line, as it is in most professions, but I couldn't face most of it, knowing *he'd* be there, full of urbane charm and social ease, doing his best to make me look foolish.'

He fiddled with the cover of the file, the pens, and other paraphernalia on his desk, his fingers never still for a moment. It was a wonder he didn't wear himself out, Rafferty reflected.

'I was in one of the toilet cubicles at the George when I heard the latest gossip doing the rounds. Now he's implying I go in for late abortions here as a useful sideline and use the foetuses for research. That I keep them wired up to machines to keep them alive so I have a steady supply of cells for my work. I was blazing. I found him, intending to have it out with him, once and for all, but he just laughed. And the madder I grew, the more contemptuous he became. In the end, I threw a punch at him. Of course I missed. His friends dragged me away. I left soon after. That would be about ten thirty p.m., I suppose.'

Rafferty and Llewellyn exchanged glances. Surely the man couldn't be *that* naïve? mused Rafferty. Didn't he realize that he had just provided them with an excellent motive for murder? Had he killed Linda Wilks hoping to incriminate Melville-Briggs? At the very least, he could be sure that Sir Anthony would get some very damaging publicity, even if he wasn't suspected of the murder. Or was he being disingenuous, he wondered; knowing there was no way the argument could be concealed, had he hoped to cast doubt on such suspicions by his very openness?

The murder victim had been pregnant, although only two months along. Her father had mentioned that Linda had received a phone call around 10.30 that evening from a man. If he had been telling the truth, could it have been Whittaker phoning from the foyer of the George asking to meet her? he wondered. Her diary had been less help in tracing her clients than he'd hoped. She'd used a code, a crude, schoolgirlish thing, but it might have been as cryptic as *The Times* crossword for all the success they'd had with it. He returned to Whittaker's complaint. 'You're a psychiatrist, not a surgeon. Why should anyone believe . . . ?'

'Any butcher can do abortions, Inspector.'

'But surely late abortions are dangerous?'

Whittaker's dark eyes looked sadly into his. 'Don't you know? Apart from my other evil habits I'm supposed to offer these late abortions to desperate women—drug-addicts, the homeless, the dregs of society, the implication being that I wouldn't worry if they died. Melville-Briggs knew very well that I've tended to cater for the poorer, more wretched elements of society, especially since my wi—' He broke off for a moment and a shudder seemed to pass through him before he began again, an anguished expression on his face. 'He always managed to add a certain measure of truth to his lies.' He sighed and looked down at his fingers where they clutched at the file. Slowly, he straightened them out, but almost at once they involuntarily tightened their grip again. 'The evidence was all circumstantial, but people would wonder if there *might* be some truth to the rest.'

Rafferty was wondering about that himself and he looked at Whittaker with new interest.

Whittaker laughed harshly. 'There's no need to look at me like that, Inspector. It's not true. You can search the place if you like. Besides'—his mouth turned down—'even if I'd contemplated such research, I wouldn't have the money for it. Do you know how much such machinery would cost? *He* could afford them, of course. The work I do is far more valuable, yet *he's* the one who gets the funding. And for what? That stupid study of the drug-addictive personality, while I'm starved of funds for vital research. I could tell them the type of people who become drug-addicts; it's the weak, the stupid, the gullible. I sympathize with them, I treat them, after all, but their illnesses are self-inflicted. I don't know if you're aware of this, em, Inspector, but my father died of Alzheimer's Disease. He . . .'

Rafferty nodded. 'I heard about your father, Doctor. I sympathize. My grandmother went the same way. It's a terrible thing to have to watch a loved one go like that.'

Whittaker gave him a grim nod. 'A man like my father could have had many useful years ahead of him—

valuable years of helping others, saving lives, easing suffering. Instead, he was condemned to an undignified and degrading end. Sometimes, when I see how easily Melville-Briggs gets research funds, I despair.'

'But there's plenty of research going on in that field now. Aren't they finding some interesting results with...?' Human foetuses, he had been about to say before he thought better of it.

Whittaker nodded. 'But that's other people's research. Not mine. I want to contribute something. Something important. It would make up for a lot.'

'Does it matter who finds the cure as long as it's found?' Rafferty asked gently.

'It matters to me, Inspector.'

From the expression on Whittaker's face, it mattered very much. Melville-Briggs's accusation against him was beginning to look as though it might have a little more substance than he'd originally thought. This man might just stop at nothing to nobble a rival, particularly one whom he had good reason to hate. Rafferty cleared his throat. 'Er, to get back to the night of the murder, sir. You said you left the George early?'

'Yes. If I'd stayed and got drunk I'd have probably murdered the bastard.' He stopped abruptly, as if he had just realized what he had said.

Rafferty wondered if he'd murdered Linda Wilks instead, leaving her body on his enemy's doorstep; an apt revenge for Melville-Briggs, that user of women. 'Where did you go, Doctor, when you left the George?'

'I came back here and continued with my work.'

'Did anyone see you once you left the George?'

'I don't believe so.' Whittaker raised his head as though he had suddenly wondered why he was being questioned about his movements. 'Why do you ask?'

Rafferty stared at him, once again wondering if Whittaker could really be that naïve. Circumstances were again building a case around Nathanial Whittaker and this time not simply for questionable professional activities, but for murder. Melville-Briggs had forcefully implied that Whittaker was capable of the most desperate measures in order to get back at him. Rafferty had assumed that Sir Anthony suffered from paranoia. Now he wasn't so sure. 'A young woman has been murdered, Doctor,' Rafferty reminded him softly. 'We need to question everyone, however remotely connected.'

'And you suspect me?' Nathanial Whittaker gave an incredulous laugh. 'God,' he demanded roughly of the ceiling, 'what else can that bastard do to me?'

Rafferty shuffled guiltily on the hard chair, his own suspicions making him uncomfortable. Whittaker's wife had left him, his work, to which he had devoted a lifetime, was not going well, and he had to suffer the derision and public success of a man he regarded with contempt. Whittaker was a man frustrated in both his personal and professional life. Had that frustration and resentment led him to murder?

Linda Wilks had been one of society's dregs, as described by Melville-Briggs. *And* she had been pregnant. Put the two together and you had the ideal victim for Whittaker if he chose to make use of her. Had *Whittaker* been the medical man who had phoned her? Had she met him and sought his help to get rid of the baby? Perhaps, through contacts at the Elmhurst Sanatorium, she had heard about the rumours that Dr Melville-Briggs had spread about his work and mentioned them. Even if he hadn't met her with the firm *intention* of killing her, it was possible this had brought back the fury raised earlier that evening. Had he struck out at her in a blind rage? Had he, with a dead body on his hands, done some quick thinking and mutilated her? He had access to a key to the gate. But if the murder had happened like that, it smacked more of premeditation than sudden rage, for he'd have had to obtain the keys *before* he met Linda, knowing full well why he would need them. If he'd merely made the appointment with Linda for sexual gratification, he would hardly choose to meet her on the enemy's doorstep. Rafferty could imagine the play old Tony would make of *that* if Whittaker were caught with a prostitute.

Rafferty wondered about his relationship with Gwen Parry as he gazed at the now bent dark head. It appeared very one-sided. She typed up his research notes and made herself available on the occasions when he required an escort, but to Rafferty it seemed Whittaker made nothing more of her than a convenience and she was apparently happy to let him. A strange relationship.

He'd left the George early and alone and had seen no one. And he had a big grudge against Melville-Briggs. Means, motive, and opportunity, as the crime writers put it. Now Rafferty gave the nod to Llewellyn to take up the questioning.

'Dr Whittaker?' The dark head raised and bleak eyes gazed back at him. 'I'm sorry that this has been a painful experience for you, sir,' murmured Llewellyn softly, with every evidence of sincerity. 'But it is necessary, I hope you understand that?' Whittaker nodded. 'I believe you escorted Miss Gwendoline Parry to the dinner at the George?'

Again Whittaker just nodded. It was almost as though he had lost interest in the conversation. But Llewellyn's next words regained his attention.

'I understand you called round to Miss Parry's home on the Saturday morning after the murder?'

Nathanial Whittaker stared at him. 'How did you know that?'

'You were seen,' Llewellyn replied, without elaborating. 'Did you often call at Miss Parry's home?'

'No. Not—not often.'

'What sort of relationship do you and Miss Parry have?'

'We're—friends, I suppose you'd call it.'

'Not lovers?' Rafferty put in.

The suggestion seemed to horrify him. 'Of course not.' Whittaker blinked rapidly. 'I fail to see . . .'

'You're both adults, both free,' Rafferty went on. 'There's nothing to stop you.'

'My relationship with Miss Parry wasn't like that, I assure you. We were friends, nothing more.' He frowned. 'Surely Miss Parry hasn't given you the impression that she was any more to me? I thought she understood. My work . . .' His voice trailed off and he looked embarrassed.

Poor Miss Parry, thought Rafferty. It was obvious that Nathanial Whittaker's intentions towards her were only too honourable, if a little selfish. Had she been hoping his intentions would grow a little more *dis*honourable? A little more passionate? He had abandoned her at the dinner, which indicated that his feelings about her were just as he had described. He had neglected his wife, who had apparently been quite a looker, a wife, whom everyone that Rafferty had spoken to, had claimed Whittaker loved, as much as he was capable of loving anyone. Had Gwen Parry really believed she would fare better at his hands? Like Miss Robinson, Rafferty's old school teacher, she was doomed to bitter disappointment. Research used up all his passion. He would have none left for the Gwen Parrys of this world.

Llewellyn continued his questioning. 'Perhaps you'd like to tell us why you called round that particular morning?'

The question seemed to trouble him. He gazed around the office as though seeking an answer in the dark and dusty corners. 'I—Miss Parry was typing up some research notes of mine. I—I wanted to see how she was getting on.'

'But she could hardly have made a start on them by then, surely? I understood that she intended to spend the whole of the weekend on them? Had taken a day's leave to finish the job.'

'Had she?' Dr Whittaker looked startled, then annoyed as though this latest evidence of Gwendoline Parry's devotion was altogether too much.

'So why did you go round there?' repeated Llewellyn doggedly, when Whittaker made no attempt to answer his question.

Whittaker became agitated at his persistence. 'Why are you asking me all these questions? Does it matter why I went round to Miss Parry's house? What has that got to do with this murder?'

'That's what I'm trying to establish, Doctor,' replied Llewellyn. 'You see, Miss Parry's hospital keys have gone missing. Naturally, we need to find out what happened to them. Did you see them, by any chance?'

'Me?' For once Whittaker's fingers stilled. It was as though he had finally realized the precariousness of his position and was worried about betraying any anxiety.

Ironically, the unnatural stillness achieved the opposite of what he intended.

'Miss Parry wondered if they could have fallen out of her bag into the boot of your car. We thought that might have been the reason you had called round to her flat.'

Whittaker slumped back in his chair, as though he no longer had the strength to fight off their suspicions, as if he no longer even cared. 'There's no need to be so delicate, Sergeant. What you really want to know is if I stole them in order to gain entrance to the Elmhurst Sanatorium. Isn't this what all these questions are about?'

Llewellyn didn't deny it. 'And did you?'

'No. I did not.'

They'd got all they were going to get out of him today and Rafferty stood up, calling the interview to a halt. 'You understand, Doctor, that we'll have to speak to you again?' Whittaker nodded mutely.

As they left, Rafferty looked back. Whittaker was still sitting at his desk, but now his papers were ignored and he stared into the middle distance with haunted eyes. Rafferty shook his head sadly. In many ways, he could sympathize with Nathanial Whittaker; both their marriages had failed because their work and their wives were incompatible. But Whittaker wasn't tormented by guilt, his wife was still living, unlike Angie, who, although dead now for two years, was in some ways still with him, still reaching out from beyond the grave to wound him.

Into his mind flashed a vivid picture of his wife as she lay dying in the hospital. It should have been a time when mutual regrets softened the resentments, but even in death, Angie hadn't been gentle. She had used her remaining breath to ensure the time of her dying lingered painfully in Rafferty's memory. He should be happy now, she had told him, now she would no longer be able to come between him and his precious job. What wife could make a greater sacrifice? she had asked, determined to make her mark on him in death far more effectively than she had managed in life.

Because he *had* wished death on her during one of their rows—had actually said that he had wished her dead, so when she *had* received a death sentence from the cancer, she had accused him of causing it, as a kind of wish-fulfilment.

' "Heav'n hath no rage, like love to hatred turn'd," ' Llewellyn murmured philosophically from behind the wheel as they drove back to the station.

'What?'

' "Heav'n hath no rage, like love to hatred turn'd," ' Llewellyn repeated, but before he could continue, Rafferty voiced the rest of the quotation for him.

' "Nor hell a fury, like a woman scorn'd." '

'William Congreve,' Llewellyn added *sotto voce*.

'Is that what you think?' Rafferty asked.

'I was just wondering if Miss Parry finally realized on Friday night that she meant nothing to Dr Whittaker. I wondered if she could have lied about losing her keys. Whether, rather than trying to shield him, she's been deliberately trying to lead our suspicions to him as a punishment for not desiring her.'

'You're a deep one, aren't you?'

Llewellyn shrugged wordlessly.

'Perhaps she killed the girl herself,' Rafferty threw in a suggestion of his own for good measure. He didn't want Llewellyn getting above himself in the ideas department. 'And got back at both Melville-Briggs *and*

Whittaker, both of whom probably used her in different ways. After all, she was hardly a prominent guest at the George and unlikely to be missed.'

'But she had no transport,' Llewellyn objected. 'She'd hardly take a taxi from the George to the hospital, tell the driver to wait while she killed the girl, and then calmly drive back as if nothing had happened.'

'Mm. That's true. But, I think we ought to investigate Miss Parry's alibi a little deeper. She picked up her car from the hospital some time over the weekend. Why not that night? She could have overheard Whittaker arranging the meeting with Linda and been overcome with jealous rage. She could have paid the taxi off at the hospital, murdered Linda and driven away in her own car.' He sighed. 'Perhaps we ought to check out the cab firms? See if anyone at the hospital noticed her car missing from the car park on Saturday morning.'

Llewellyn nodded and asked, 'So you think it's a case of "*Dux femina facti*"?'

'What?' Rafferty scowled at Llewellyn's smart-arse comment.

Llewellyn sighed. 'Or "*Cherchez la femme*", if you prefer.'

Rafferty preferred plain English and told him so.

ELEVEN

BY THE NEXT DAY, they'd managed to turn up nothing on the cab firms and the hospital staff were extremely vague about precisely when Miss Parry had picked up her car; but that was about par for the course, Rafferty reflected wearily. None of the staff, nor those patients whom they'd so far spoken to, had admitted to knowing Linda, either. Nor, at the hospital or anywhere else, had anyone identified the girl in the pub from Smythe's photofit—at least, they hadn't identified her to Rafferty, whatever they might have suspected privately, and he wasn't hopeful that anyone would. That was why, when the telephone rang, he anticipated only further failures, especially when he heard Llewellyn's voice on the other end. Incredibly, for once, the Welshman had a result for him and brought about a complete revival of Rafferty's optimism. At last, someone from the hospital *had* recognized the photofit of the girl in the pub.

'Keep them there,' Rafferty ordered ebulliently. 'I'm on my way.'

'But sir, I think I should warn . . .'

'Not now, Llewellyn. Whatever it is will keep. I'll get there as fast as I can.' Grinning, he replaced the receiver and made for the door. No doubt, Llewellyn was worried about his precious car and imagining the squeal of brakes and the smell of burning rubber as Rafferty tore through the miles separating them. Well, he'd have to bear it as best he could. This might be the breakthrough they'd been looking for and he wasn't going to waste any more precious time pandering to Llewellyn's idiotic sensitivities. God knew they needed a breakthrough, because ironically, although they were overloaded with suspects, they had no firm evidence against any of them. The latest news might make all the difference.

EAGERLY RAFFERTY made his way through the empty passages and pushed open the door of their temporary office. He stopped short when he saw the woman with Llewellyn and shot his sergeant a reproachful glance. Was *this* the witness in whom he'd placed such hope? he wondered incredulously.

She must be eighty if she was a day, he guessed. Dim, rheumy blue eyes peered vaguely out at him from a mass of wrinkles and her head nodded continually on her thin neck. It seemed likely she'd have difficulty remembering her own name, much less anyone else's.

Rafferty's eyes swivelled to the right, and he frowned. Nurse Wright sat silently by the door, while her charge was interviewed, as though she didn't trust them not to browbeat the old lady. She needn't think she was going to listen in, Rafferty vowed. Her behaviour over the note had already irritated him and he wasn't inclined to conduct the interview with her listening in. 'Please wait outside, Nurse,' he said sharply. 'Llewellyn, escort Nurse Wright to that little waiting room we've arranged and then come back. I'll call you when we're finished, Nurse.'

Nurse Wright opened her mouth to protest, but after one look at Rafferty's implacable expression, she shut it again. Stopping only long enough to direct a dirty look in his direction, she flounced out.

When Llewellyn returned, he nodded at Rafferty to confirm the nurse was safely ensconced on the other side of the bolted door. Turning to the old lady, Rafferty smiled, swallowing his disappointment, as Llewellyn introduced them.

She inclined her head in a gesture meant to be gracious, but there was more of pathos than regality in the movement and it touched a nerve of memory in Rafferty that ensured his voice was gentle. 'It's very good of you to come and see us, Mrs Devine.'

'That's quite all right, young man. Only I do hope it won't take long. Only, you see, my daughter's coming to see me today. She always comes to tea on a Friday,' she told him. 'Four o'clock prompt. Never misses. And I *do* want to make sure everything's perfect.' With a glance at the door, she confided in a loud whisper, 'It isn't always, you know.'

'Please don't worry, Mrs Devine. This will only take a few minutes.' He pulled a chair up and sat beside her. 'Now, perhaps you could start by telling me when was the last time you saw her?'

The question seemed to trouble her a great deal. The smile faded to be replaced by a worried look, as though she had been found out in some deception. Her head shook more agitatedly than before and her eyes filled with the easy tears of the very old.

'Take your time, ma'am.' Moved by compassion, Rafferty spoke in comforting tones, as Llewellyn, clearly embarrassed, shuffled his feet. The old lady's behaviour seemed to make the Welshman uncomfortable, but Rafferty was used to the very old. Hadn't his grandparents ended their lives in the cramped Rafferty home? Many a time as a teenager, he had spoon-fed his grandmother her food, wiping the dribbled food and saliva with a cloth; many a time, too, he'd comforted her when she'd wet her bed and cried befuddled tears from an indistinct feeling of shame. Then his tenderness had sprung from a wealth of fond memories of childhood when his Gran had gamely bowled to his fantasy Colin Cowdrey batting. She hadn't been half a bad bowler either, he remembered.

It was those fond memories that now served to remind him that Mrs Devine, too, was maybe somebody's loved granny and patiently, he attempted to rekindle her recollection. 'Perhaps it was here in Elmhurst?' he suggested gently.

Llewellyn made an attempt to overcome his own discomfort. 'You said you met her in London,' he prompted, in the loud tones some people use to the aged, as if they are all hard of hearing.

Rafferty could see comprehension and something like relief fight their way through Mrs Devine's clouded brain and he stifled a grin as she directed a look of scorn at Llewellyn.

'I didn't think you meant *her*,' she informed him tartly.

For a few seconds, intelligence gleamed out of the rheumy eyes; the nodding head stilled and Rafferty caught a glimpse of the woman she must once have been, before old age had caged her sharp mind in a fog. He bet she'd been a bit of a tartar; the sort unwilling to suffer fools at all, never mind gladly. As Llewellyn had just discovered.

'I thought you were talking about my daughter.' She gave Rafferty a coy glance. 'Are you married, young man?'

'No, ma'am.' Not any more, thank God, he thought.

'Then you must come and take tea with us. With my daughter and me. You'll like her. She's such a thoughtful girl.'

'That's kind of you, Mrs Devine. Perhaps another time, when I'm not so busy?' He took the photofit from Llewellyn. 'I understand you recognized the girl in this picture?'

Mrs Devine's nose wrinkled faintly. 'Oh her. That's Miranda . . . Miranda . . . I can't recall her other name. I used to see her regularly at Dr Melville-Briggs's London consulting rooms, before, before—' She broke off.

Before her family had had her put away, Rafferty concluded. Her face was anxious, as though she realized deep within her that there *had* been a time when she had been very different. The realization clearly upset her and although, not surprisingly, she was reluctant to bring past and remembered reality into her present unhappy situation, somehow she gathered a tattered dignity about her and went on, quite lucidly.

'I had a weekly appointment and she saw Dr Melville-Briggs after me, which I thought a little strange as *I* always asked for the latest appointment, and by the time my consultations finished, the staff had left. I often suffered from giddiness and used to retire to the ladies' room till I felt more composed and generally, I'd find this Miranda lurking in there, quite furtively, as though she didn't want anyone to see her. Very odd it was. She wasn't a very pleasant young woman. On the few occasions I tried to engage her in conversation, she was unpleasant, really quite rude, in fact. So unnecessary.' She looked distressed for a moment as though the memory was particularly unpleasant and etched for ever in her mind. 'I recall her eyes glittering at me quite furiously as though I had no right to be there.' She handed the picture back with a look of distaste and, rising unsteadily to her feet, made for the door.

'Just a moment, Mrs Devine. Llewellyn, ask Nurse Wright to come back, please.'

Nurse Wright returned just in time to hear Mrs Devine repeat her invitation to Rafferty. For some reason it made her smirk.

'I'll expect you for tea with my daughter next Friday then, young man. At four o'clock. Anyone will direct you.'

'I'll look forward to it, Mrs Devine.'

The nurse hovered in the doorway as though torn between Rafferty and her charge. Rafferty won. 'You don't want to believe everything Mrs Devine says, you know,' she advised sharply. 'She wanders in her mind.'

Rafferty's mind did a little wandering too, to the interesting question of why she should seek to convince him that the old lady was unreliable as a witness. 'Her mind seemed sharp enough to me,' he remarked tautly.

The nurse gave a derisive smile. 'You think so? She invited you to take tea with her daughter, Inspector, but I wouldn't bother turning up next week if I were you. She hasn't seen her daughter once in the nine months that I've worked here. The visits are as much fantasy as whatever she dragged you over here to listen to. She's probably seen you about the hospital and wanted to look you over to decide if you were suitable husband material for her daughter. Match-making is one of her obsessions, unfortunately.' Nurse Wright grimaced. 'I suppose she'll be ringing up caterers next to arrange the wedding. She did that last year when one of the doctors took her fancy. We had the devil of a job convincing the firm that the wedding was all in her mind. So you see, you can take whatever she told you with a large pinch of salt.'

'I'll bear it in mind,' he told her drily, reluctant to let the nurse have the satisfaction of the last word. 'Though she seemed lucid enough to me. The bit about the daughter was wishful thinking—dreaming—we all do it. But the other part seemed real enough. She didn't particularly *want* to remember'—he grinned teasingly at the nurse's avid look—'whatever it was she told us. You see the difference?'

She gave him a withering look as though to say, 'Not another amateur psychologist?' Then she shrugged and remarked tartly: 'Believe what you like, Inspector. Only I still wouldn't bother turning up for tea next week. She'll have forgotten all about you and it by four o'clock *today*, never mind next Friday.'

'Perhaps. But if Mrs Devine remembers anything else, I want you to tell me.'

The nurse looked as if she would like to tell him what he could do with his wants and her attitude angered him. 'One girl has been murdered,' he reminded her sternly. 'Information can be dangerous. It's better passed on to the police. I'd like you to remember that.'

'But you've arrested Simon Smythe for the murder. I hardly think...'

'Dr Smythe has not been charged with murder,' he told her with quiet satisfaction. 'Nor do I anticipate that he will be.'

Nurse Wright's mouth dropped open in a perfect 'O' of surprise. 'But Gilbert told me he saw him being driven off to the police-station. He hasn't come back to the hospital since and Gilbert said...'

'Never mind what Gilbert said,' Rafferty snapped. 'You might tell Gilbert that *I* said that if he's not careful someone might just sue him for slander.'

The nurse nodded quickly and shut the door behind her, no doubt eager to pass on the latest news about Smythe.

Rafferty went over their latest information. Smartly dressed and nicely spoken, was how the landlord had described the girl in the pub; something of a looker, too, he understood. Smythe had suggested she had been waiting for someone. Mrs Devine had identified Smythe's identikit picture as this Miranda; could she be the same girl who had given Nurse Wright the note for Melville-Briggs? She certainly sounded the type who might appeal to the doctor and it seemed she'd made a point of seeing him *very* privately. If she *was* this Miranda, presumably she had been hanging around the scruffy neighbourhood bar waiting for *him*, not realizing that he was out on the town. It seemed an unlikely venue for the self-important Sir Anthony. Even if he'd been available, Rafferty couldn't imagine him being willing to rub shoulders with the celebrating darts players.

He despatched Llewellyn to the local nick to get more copies made of the photofit with orders, when he got them, to go to Dr Melville-Briggs's London consulting rooms to interview the staff there. Surely, if anyone had occasionally stayed late, they might have seen this Miranda? If Mrs Devine's mind had really been as clear about the identification as it had seemed and they *were* one and the same girl.

If Rafferty could locate this Miranda, she might turn out to be a valuable witness. It was surprising that she hadn't already come forward voluntarily, it wasn't as if

the case hadn't received enough publicity, as the tabloids had seized on the story like sensation-starved can-
nibals. It was possible, of course, that she was trying to
protect someone and that someone could only be Melville-Briggs. The man seemed to bring out such an
instinct in too many women for Rafferty's liking. Perhaps, when Llewellyn returned from London, he would
rattle the doctor's cage a little?

RAFFERTY LOOKED AT his watch for the third time in as
many minutes. Damn Llewellyn. It was eleven o'clock,
he should be back by now. He'd rung yesterday afternoon to say he would have to spend the night in town.
Some of the staff at Sir Anthony's London consulting
rooms had left quite recently and he was having trouble tracking them down. But surely there couldn't be
that many people employed in one doctor's rooms?

Not for the first time in his career, Rafferty cursed his
impetuosity. It was rather a pity that he'd given way to
the satisfaction of telling Nurse Wright that Smythe
hadn't been arrested for murder. She wouldn't have
known any different if he'd kept quiet, as Smythe was
off duty for a few days and wouldn't have been expected at the hospital in any case. The element of surprise might have been useful when he saw Sir Anthony.
Still, he mused, it was still possible that he didn't know,
as he was attending a conference in the midlands and
wasn't expected back till lunch-time today.

Rafferty had agreed that Llewellyn should kill two
birds with one stone, as it were, by going to see the
Melville-Briggses' son at his business—not that it
seemed likely that Timothy, as described by Gilbert,
would be likely to have any doings with a prostitute,
leastways, not a *female* one, but they might as well

check it out. But if Llewellyn was wasting time chatting about vintage cars at that garage . . . ! This was the only positive lead they had—slight though it might be—and Rafferty didn't want to tackle Melville-Briggs till Llewellyn got back. The frustration only increased his impatience. For, otherwise, their investigations had scored a big fat zero. They had yet to find the murder weapon or Linda Wilks's clothes, and in spite of the press coverage, no one but Smythe had seen the car parked outside the hospital. Added to that, the house-to-house had yielded zilch in the way of more information and no one calling herself Miranda had so far come forward.

Too late, he realized that he should have gone to London himself. It would have been better than hanging around waiting for Llewellyn to dig the dirt—if he was even *capable* of something so grubby, though surely even Llewellyn realized that they needed answers and needed them quickly. Pressure was building from every angle; press, public, hospital staff— especially its leading light. Once Melville-Briggs discovered that Simon Smythe wasn't going to be charged with the crime, he would be sure to make his displeasure felt. He had made it clear enough that he wanted a quick and convenient solution and Rafferty wondered if his only reason was concern about what the bad publicity would do to the hospital and its profits. Had the girl in the pub really been this Miranda come down to see him? It seemed possible as, apart from Mrs Devine, no one else admitted to knowing the girl before that evening. Not that Melville-Briggs had either, of course—yet. Miranda was a loose end and he didn't like loose ends. He consulted his watch for the third time in as many minutes. The hands seemed to be crawling.

LLEWELLYN HAD FINALLY returned, but he was minus any good news, which didn't altogether surprise Rafferty. Timothy Melville-Briggs was out of the running—not that he'd really been in. And, needless to say, no one at Sir Anthony's London consulting rooms had recognized the girl in the photofit picture. Still, Rafferty consoled himself, that didn't necessarily prove anything. Perhaps she and the aging Lothario had been up to after-hours naughties—hadn't Mrs Devine said the girl had always had a very late appointment, after the staff had gone home? After all, it was unlikely that the doctor would confine his amorous activities to the countryside. Although Rafferty was disappointed not to have something more on Melville-Briggs, he was still determined to tackle him. Perhaps he would yet be able to bluff him into some revelation?

Sir Anthony hadn't yet returned, though he was expected imminently, but at least Mrs Galvin had made them tea while they waited. Picking up his cup, Rafferty asked, 'Have you worked for Dr Melville-Briggs long?'

'Three years.'

He gave a low whistle. 'Really? That long? You surprise me.'

She looked steadily at him. 'I fail to see why.'

'Human nature intrigues me,' he explained. 'What people do, why they do it. I find they often have the oddest reasons for their actions.'

'I'm afraid you'll discover nothing to intrigue you about mine,' she replied. 'I work here because I need the money.'

'Surely you could get much better paying work in London?'

She shrugged. 'Perhaps. But I have other considerations to bear in mind, like suitable housing. My husband is an invalid, Inspector. He was paralysed over two years ago. I doubt if we could afford to equip another house with the necessary aids.'

'I'm sorry to hear that. How did it happen?'

'A car accident,' she replied briefly.

It was obvious that she didn't want to talk about it. Like Melville-Briggs's unfortunate junior doctor, here was another member of his staff unlikely to find another suitable job, Rafferty reflected. She was trapped as surely as Simon Smythe and would have little choice but to continue to hold on to her position here. No doubt Melville-Briggs made full use of his knowledge of her circumstances. She'd already made her statement; not that it amounted to much beyond saying she was at home all evening with her husband on the night of the murder. It hadn't been corroborated, yet, in her case, he had thought it would be just a formality, but when he mentioned it, her reaction surprised him.

'Surely that's not necessary?' she queried sharply. 'You don't imagine that I . . . that a woman would attack a young girl in such a brutal fashion, Inspector?'

In his experience, anything was possible and Sam *had* said a woman could have murdered the girl. She came over as a woman of strong passions behind that calm exterior—certainly capable of killing. Mary Galvin might be slim, but the skinniest murderers generally managed to find the required strength if the motive was strong enough. And if she *had* been one of Melville-Briggs's mistresses, sexual jealousy would be as good a motive as any and better than most. The women in this case struck Rafferty as particularly strong-minded and wasn't it true that the gentler sex were often less squea-

mish than mere males when it came to disposing of a
barrier to happiness? 'We have to check out everyone
who had a key to that side gate,' he told her. 'It doesn't
mean that we suspect you of anything. Your husband...'

'I've already told you that he's a cripple, Inspector,'
she retorted even more sharply than before. 'The only
time he leaves his wheel-chair is to go to bed. Surely you
don't suspect that *he* murdered the girl?'

Her agitation worried him. The intercom on the desk
buzzed. Saved by the bell, he murmured. But Mary
Galvin's reaction to his questions was turning out to be
something of a mystery and he wouldn't be happy till he
got to the bottom of it.

Her hand pressed the appropriate button and Anthony Melville-Briggs's smooth tones caressed their
ears. 'I'm back. Any messages?'

After passing on the messages, Mary Galvin added,
'The police are here, Sir Anthony. Inspector Rafferty
and Sergeant Llewellyn. They'd like to see you.'

'Of course. I've been expecting them.' The tones of
satisfaction didn't escape Rafferty and a little tingle of
pleasure tickled his spine. It seemed he might have been
lucky and old Tony *hadn't* heard the latest on Smythe.
'Show them in at once. I don't want to be disturbed, so
keep back all calls. And Mrs Galvin, I'm sure they'd
like some coffee.'

TWELVE

Sir Anthony beamed at them as they entered his office. 'I understand you've got some good news for me? I must say, I never thought...' Diplomatically, he bit off whatever he had been going to say, but Rafferty guessed it would have been less than complimentary about his detecting abilities. 'Ahem, do sit down. It's a great relief that you've discovered the culprit,' he went on. 'And so promptly. It's obvious that Smythe was the man, of course. He's just the type to need to turn to prostitutes for sexual gratification.' Melville-Briggs appeared to have forgotten his slanderous accusations against Nathanial Whittaker, Rafferty noted with amusement, as the doctor continued smoothly. 'And although I appreciate your courtesy in keeping me personally informed, surely you should be at the station, interrogating him?'

Rafferty was grateful that his impetuosity hadn't met its deserved reward and he intended to get maximum enjoyment out of the situation. It wasn't often he got the chance to be one up on someone like Melville-Briggs. He allowed his face to register surprise and his voice to assume a lightly ironic, teasing tone, out of sheer devilment. 'I'm afraid you're a bit out of date, sir. I assumed you'd have heard.'

'Heard?' Sir Anthony's face stopped beaming. 'Heard what? What are you talking about, Rafferty?'

'Smythe wasn't arrested at all, he was merely helping us with our enquiries. I imagine he'll be at home if you want him.'

'What?' Sir Anthony leaned forward over the desk as though he was about to psychoanalyse him. 'Have you gone mad?'

'I don't believe so, sir. Smythe was just unfortunate enough to be in the wrong place at the wrong time, that's all. He hasn't murdered anyone.'

Melville-Briggs made to open his mouth again, but the telephone buzzed and he snatched up the receiver. 'I thought I told you not to put through any calls? Do I have to. . . ?'

Mrs Galvin must have said something soothing in his ear, for instead of continuing to carp, he merely said peremptorily, 'Oh, very well. Put her through.' To Rafferty's amusement, when he next spoke there was no trace of annoyance. It was apparent that when it came to well-heeled clients, he could be quite charming, a veritable fount of patience and solicitude.

'My dear Lady Harriet, how very nice to hear from you again . . . How was your holiday? Nothing at all to be alarmed about, I assure you. We all know how the press exaggerate . . . No, no, just some foolish girl who managed to get into the grounds. Probably turn out to be a lovers' tiff, nothing more. In fact—' He broke off and it was apparent that he'd been interrupted once again. It seemed the Lady Harriet was rather more astute than Melville-Briggs had thought. She seemed to find his explanation hard to swallow, for he was forced to go on in this placatory vein for several minutes.

Although Rafferty still listened to the one-sided conversation, he let his gaze wander around the room. Not for *Melville-Briggs* the interview conducted in a drab

and comfortless basement, he wryly mused. The good
doctor had decreed early in the case that if they wanted
to see him, they would have to come to *him*. Rafferty
concluded that he had been so insistent because he had
believed the splendour of his own office would the better impress on him that he was a man of wealth and influence—something Rafferty would rather forget. It
was strange that a practising trick-cyclist didn't realize
that, to Rafferty, the opulent office acted more as a red
rag to a bull than a reminder that respectful deference
was the required response.

The spacious first-floor room had presumably once
been the drawing room. It still had the original encir-
cling cornice and panelled wainscot, the polished wood
floor was covered with a rich oriental carpet in golds
and blues, and either side of the marble fireplace two
matching mahogany bookcases, the height of the ceiling, contained expensively-bound medical text-books.
Enormous gilt mirrors decorated the walls, and whichever way he turned Rafferty could see himself and
Llewellyn reflected, over and over again. His own bemused expression so disconcerted him that he swivelled his head away, but not before noting that his red
thatch was badly in need of a cut. He was also somewhat put out to discover that, beside his well-groomed
sergeant, he looked a bit of a scruff. The discovery disconcerted him even more and, determinedly, he concentrated his gaze on the window-facing wall behind the
doctor's desk. Unfortunately, it did nothing to improve his growing irritation.

A veritable photographer's gallery of framed prints
was on display there and he let his eyes take in the col-
oured photographs of the doctor with various members of the royal family and others, where he posed with

white-coated and presumably distinguished medical men. Perhaps, reflected Rafferty cynically, he should be grateful Sir Anthony didn't have a large colour picture of himself posed with the Chief Constable for good measure. Now that *would* have had good intimidation value.

An even more impressive array of medical qualifications were grouped together in the centre of the display and Rafferty squinted as he tried, without success, to read them. Surely they couldn't *all* be proper qualifications? Perhaps Melville-Briggs had bought some of the certificates as he'd tried to buy him, he speculated. A man like Sir Anthony thought the entire world was for sale. Sadly, most of it *was*. As he thought of Simon Smythe's pitiful collection of honours and memories, he felt a gush of fellow feeling. Unlike Sir Anthony, the poor sap couldn't even buy himself a much-needed bottle of whisky without the world tumbling about his ears.

He brought his full attention back to Sir Anthony's dulcet tones. By the time he had finished, even Rafferty was beginning to believe that the facts of the murder were just an exaggeration on the part of the gutter press. However, this happy illusion lasted no longer than it took Melville-Briggs to wish the lady a pleasant adieu and put the receiver down. Reality then again took over from the delights of make-believe.

At least, the telephone call had given Sir Anthony time to get his disappointment in perspective and now he sat back into his chair, drumming his fingers testily on his desk. The desk didn't suit the elegant proportions and restrained plaster-work of the room, Rafferty noted, unreasonably pleased that, beneath the surface sophistication, Sir Anthony's tastes reflected his

Brummie origins. Like him, the desk was large and showy. Seven feet long, its top was covered with maroon leather and around the edge the mahogany was inlaid with a flamboyant quantity of what looked like gold-leaf. It was almost as though Melville-Briggs had determined to thrust his own forceful personality on the room.

Behind the desk, Sir Anthony sat in a high-backed, thronelike chair, from which he could look down on lesser mortals. Perhaps his more anxious patients approved of such an arrangement, they probably found such dominance comforting. Rafferty did not, it merely made him more keen to prick the ego on the throne.

'Of course,' he remarked, 'in view of the news about Smythe, you'll understand that it's necessary to interview everyone again? Perhaps you'd like to enlarge on your previous statement about your movements on the night of the murder?' Rafferty suggested.

'Enlarge on *my* movements?' Melville-Briggs glowered. 'What game are you playing, Rafferty? You've let a perfectly good suspect go, now you're plunging round desperately trying to find a replacement. Well, I'm not it. And if you try to make me one, I'll create the biggest stink on either side of the Atlantic since Watergate.'

'Surely that wouldn't do the reputation of the hospital any good, sir?' Rafferty remarked calmly. 'Besides, it's hardly necessary. Can't we be civilized about this?'

'It's not very civilized to come in here and accuse—'

'No one's accusing you of anything, sir,' Llewellyn put in politely, with a pained glance at Rafferty. 'It's just that...'

Melville-Briggs ignored him and concentrated on the organ grinder. 'I didn't even know the girl.'

'That may be so, sir,' Rafferty remarked, glad he'd managed to disturb Sir Anthony's equilibrium, 'but without investigating, we can hardly be sure of that. After all, it's common knowledge that you have many women friends. The victim, as far as we know, could have been one of them. You must see,' he added with an air of sweet reason, 'the necessity of investigating the possibility?'

'As I was at the George all night, it would appear the possibility is more of an *im*possibility,' he reproved. 'I have a foolproof alibi, Rafferty. You won't succeed in breaking it.'

'I expect you're right,' Rafferty responded pleasantly. 'But even foolproof alibis have to be closely scrutinized, sir.'

Melville-Briggs laid his hands flat on the desk and leant forward. 'If you doubt *my* word'—by the tone of voice, it was apparent that he thought the idea absurd—'you can ask your own police surgeon, Dally—he was there.'

'I see. He was with you the entire night, was he, sir?' Rafferty didn't bother to edit out the sarcasm, even though he knew it was unwise and that if Melville-Briggs's alibi should turn out to be as sound as he claimed, he would pay for it.

'No, of course he wasn't with me all night.' Melville-Briggs's face was slowly becoming a marvellous match for the maroon leather of the desk. 'I don't like your tone, Rafferty. I don't like it at all.'

Rafferty didn't much care for his either. The man was too confident, a confidence that sprang either from innocence or the knowledge that he had bought and paid for an alibi that couldn't be faulted. But surely even Melville-Briggs couldn't bribe half the medical men who had been at the George that night? 'I'm sorry about that, sir,' he replied quietly. 'But if, as you say, you weren't with your wife, Dr Dally, or anyone else all night, it would seem that your alibi isn't quite as strong as you implied. In a crowded room even a man of your *eminence*,' he gave the word an ironic stress, 'wouldn't be missed for half an hour or so.'

The thin lips settled in a sneer. 'Nathanial Whittaker would be far less likely to be missed than myself.' Sir Anthony's tone was icy as he returned to his earlier and too hastily abandoned suspicions. 'As you've decided to swallow whatever lies Smythe's told you, you'd be better advised to ask *him* to account for his movements that night. Especially as he left early.'

'We already have, sir.'

'And?'

'As with all the rest of the possible suspects, we're continuing our enquiries. He'll be interviewed again, just as you are being.' Silently he added, but for the moment, we're trying to find out *your* possible motives for murdering the girl. 'I hope you'll bear with me, while I run through a possibility or two?'

Sir Anthony waved his hand irritably in the air, as though to say, 'Do what you like', and subsided heavily in his chair. Rafferty picked his next words carefully, selecting the ones most likely to push the doctor into unwise disclosures. 'Let's say you were having an affair with the murder victim. Perhaps you were afraid Lady Evelyn might find out about it and you feared she would divorce you? Perhaps you felt you risked losing all this?' His arm took in the splendours of the room.

Melville-Briggs gave a derisive snort. 'Do you really believe that I was having an affair with this wretched little tart? That after having my wicked way with her, I tossed her aside, and she threatened to tell my wife? Is that the best that your bourgeois little mind can conjure up, Rafferty?' Rafferty sat stone-faced at Melville-Briggs's amused contempt. Beside him, he heard Llewellyn give a heavy sigh as though regretting his chief's lack of finesse. Sir Anthony held out his hands in a gesture of innocence. 'My hands are clean, Rafferty.' He gazed down at them complacently. They were strong hands, expertly manicured, rich and smooth like the rest of him. 'Everyone knows that my wife and I live virtually separate lives and have done for some years. It's no secret. It suits us both rather well. My wife has the Hall and her church committees. I—I have another hobby, as you have discovered—women. But not cheap tarts, Rafferty. My tastes run to something a little more up-market.'

Frustrated that his words hadn't had the desired effect, Rafferty was, for the moment, content merely to listen. 'My wife knows and accepts that I have certain—needs, needs which she no longer wishes to satisfy. But we still manage to live fairly amicably. Besides, apart from anything else, I know my wife would never divorce me. Perhaps you weren't aware of it, Rafferty, but the Melvilles are an old Catholic family. There's never been a divorce and my wife is not the sort of woman to end a centuries-old tradition.' He leaned back in his thronelike chair, effortless superiority well to the fore once more. 'So you see, even if I had known the dead girl, I knew "all this", as you call it, was perfectly safe.' Sir Anthony picked up a slim manila file from his in-tray, as though to indicate that the audience was over. 'Now, if I might be allowed to get on with my work?'

Rafferty ignored the hint. After a wait of thirty seconds, Sir Anthony raised his head and fixed him with a haughty glare.

'Was there something else, Rafferty?'

The arrogant way he ignored his rank and called him by his surname riled Rafferty, it had done all along. He might have been the butler, dismissed once he'd brought the after-dinner port. Normally, he was a relaxed, easygoing man, with a quirky sense of humour, but now the quick temper of his forebears was aroused and demanded some retaliation. Trying to keep his voice as bland as Melville-Briggs's better efforts, he remarked pointedly, 'I'm sorry you should be so antagonistic, sir. I would have thought a man in your position would recognize his duty to help the police.'

Melville-Briggs fixed Rafferty with cold eyes and for a few brief moments, the real man behind the cultivated urbanity showed through clearly. 'A man in my position recognizes only one thing, Rafferty—the importance of staying there; and I find it offensive to have my good name besmirched, my professional colleagues questioned about my movements. It invites speculation and gossip of the crudest kind.'

'Most people would find murder more offensive, sir,' he said roughly. 'Or don't you think a common tart has a right to justice from the law?' Melville-Briggs waved the suggestion aside and Rafferty continued. 'We can't be sure that another young woman won't meet the same fate.' Suddenly, sickened by the whole business, he decided to play his wild card. Taking the photofit picture of the girl in the pub, he threw it on the desk. 'Miranda, for instance.' Had he imagined Melville-Briggs's loss of colour? he wondered. It seemed likely as the doctor recovered quickly and called his bluff.

'Miranda?' he questioned softly. 'Miranda who?'

Rafferty didn't intend to let on that he didn't know. It was possible that Melville-Briggs might merely be testing the extent of his knowledge and it wouldn't do for him to realize that both his information and his informant were far from reliable. Taking his own acting skills out, Rafferty dusted them off. 'Let me get this straight, sir—just for the record, you understand. Are you saying that you know nobody who bears any resemblance to this girl? Nobody by the name of Miranda?' He allowed a note of faint surprise to enter his voice as he tried to imply that he had information to the contrary. 'It's not a very common name.'

'I cannot recollect anyone of that name who resembles this girl,' the doctor replied suavely. 'Perhaps you would like me to make a few enquiries?' he suggested with a biting irony.

'That won't be necessary, thank you, sir. Our own enquiries are proceeding very nicely. Very nicely indeed,' he repeated with an air of satisfaction.

This time there was no mistaking the quickly concealed dismay. Rafferty assumed an even more omniscient air and decided he could risk exaggerating the extent of their knowledge. 'We believe this Miranda had connections with your London clinic. We know she was in this area on the night of the murder and expected to meet someone, which is rather odd, because, so far, we haven't found anyone from round here who admits to knowing her. Perhaps she had intended meeting the dead girl or perhaps not, but it's strange that she hasn't chosen to come forward.' He let his eyes meet the doctor's. 'I imagine Nurse Wright told you about the young woman who gave her a note for you?'

'I believe she did mention something of the sort,' the doctor replied with every appearance of untroubled calm. 'But as she threw the note away, I've no idea who the girl might have been. I have a large circle of friends and acquaintances, Rafferty, a lot of them females, as your investigations have revealed. The girl could have been any one of them.'

'Don't you think it strange that she hasn't come forward?'

He shrugged. 'That's easily explained. I move in very successful, well-travelled circles, Rafferty.' Melville-Briggs sounded smug. 'This woman could have been out of the country at the time news of the murder broke. It's possible that she isn't even aware that you're looking for her, yet you seem determined to make it look suspicious and—'

'It's just that I wondered why she didn't telephone first if she wanted to see you, instead of turning up out of the blue.'

'You know what impulsive creatures women can be, Rafferty. They don't always stop to think.'

Melville-Briggs's plausible answers irritated Rafferty and he couldn't resist a little reminder. 'Still, if your friend *is* abroad, I expect she'll turn up shortly and then we'll find out the truth, won't we, sir?' He leaned forward. 'Now. Just for the record. Are you quite sure you knew neither the murdered girl, Linda Wilks, nor this Miranda?'

'Quite sure.' Melville-Briggs glared at him. 'Now, I have work to do—if there's nothing else?'

Sir Anthony's voice was now tightly controlled and Rafferty felt disappointment seep into his soul. Now what? He hadn't succeeded in rattling him. He'd played his wild card and had nothing left to throw. But even if he had nothing in his hand but duds, he could still finish the game with dignity. 'Not at the moment, sir,' he conceded. 'But when we have, we'll be back.' He felt balked of victory, but perked up a little as he remembered that even the most cast-iron alibis had been known to be broken. He would give a great deal to see Sir Anthony humbled. After he had sketched an ironic bow at the pointedly bent head, Rafferty and Llewellyn took their leave.

'Well?' Rafferty burst out when they were out of earshot. 'You were watching him, what do you think?'

'His alibi seems sound enough, sir.' Llewellyn pursed his lips thoughtfully and directed a reproving glance at Rafferty. 'But we already knew that, that's why I don't understand why you pushed him so hard. He doesn't even seem to have any motive. Or at least, none that we've been able to discover. Besides, he doesn't strike me as a man who'd soil his own hands with murder. He'd more likely bribe someone else to do his dirty work for him.' Llewellyn's eyes darkened and his expression became enigmatic. 'I know you don't like him, sir, but rest assured, whatever his sins, he'll pay for them eventually. Every guilty person is his own hangman, according to Seneca.'

'Well, that's a comforting thought,' remarked Rafferty sardonically. Although he was impressed by his sergeant's summing-up of Melville-Briggs, he wasn't in the mood to compliment him. Especially as he was aware that his own behaviour during the interview had been a bit over the top and, if old Seneca was right, retribution was sure to follow. 'It's a pity your mate Seneca won't be about with his reassuring comments when matey-boy in there starts complaining to the brass about me,' he observed sourly.

Sensibly, Llewellyn made no attempt at commiseration. What would be the point? Rafferty mused dispiritedly, when they both knew that Superintendent Bradley, a gruff, no-nonsense Yorkshireman, hadn't got where he was by treating his *junior* officers with kid gloves when they threatened his comfortable niche. Rafferty concluded that not only could he soon expect a flea in his ear, but that all the flea's friends and relations would come along for the ride. And, although he had the nous to keep the rest of his opinions to himself, it was obvious that Llewellyn would think it served him right.

THIRTEEN

THE OLD MAN wanted results, did he, Rafferty grumbled to himself as he entered his office and slammed the door. It would serve Superintendent bloody Bradley right if he got them, gift-wrapped.

As he had anticipated, retribution had been very swift. And he didn't need two guesses as to who had stirred the shit. Even though he'd been warned off treading too heavily on those particular corns, he, for one, would enjoy tying Melville-Briggs up in presentation red ribbon, even if he got reduced to the rank of sergeant for his trouble. Disgruntled that Llewellyn seemed to number a knack for disappearing when the flak was flying among his other talents, Rafferty slumped dejectedly in his chair. The trouble was he had *too* many possible suspects. Sidney Wilks, for instance, was turning out to be a very interesting possibility, as he'd tried to explain to the superintendent, in an attempt to halt Bradley's Vesuviuslike eruption. It didn't help that Wilks had been the Welsh Wizard's preferred choice, rather than his own.

According to Tina, the absent Streatham flatmate, Sidney Wilks wasn't the solid citizen his privet hedge proclaimed, but had used his respectability as a shield for something far from seemly. Linda had confided to her that her father had regularly abused her sexually as a child. Was it true, though, he wondered, and if so, had Daphne Wilks known? Rafferty's nose twitched, once—an infallible guide—and he nodded slowly. Wilks was capable of such an act. And Daphne Wilks? Wasn't it true that those who denied knowledge of such a dreadful act denied it most strongly to themselves? He viewed the coming interview with distaste, but consoled himself with the unkind thought that Llewellyn would relish it even less than he would.

THE NETS WERE twitched discreetly aside and as quickly twitched back before Mrs Wilks opened the door, flattening herself against the wall out of sight; as soon as Rafferty and Llewellyn were safely gathered into the hall she slid the door shut again. The whole operation had taken only moments.

'Is your husband home, Mrs Wilks?' Rafferty asked as she let them through to the flowery claustrophobia of the living room. He knew very well that he wasn't. It had seemed sensible to question his wife without risking any promptings from Wilks. However, hoping to get under her guard, he kept up the pretence.

'Sidney?' Her eyes were wary as they darted from Rafferty to Llewellyn and back again. 'Why do you want to see Sidney?' she demanded. 'What's he supposed to have done?'

'I didn't say he'd *done* anything. I just want to speak to him. Is he here?' She shook her head. 'When do you expect him?'

She shrugged. 'He didn't say when he'd be back. He's gone up to the Hall, you know, the home of that doctor who owns the hospital where my girl was killed.'

Rafferty frowned. 'Gone up to the Hall? Why's that?'

'He does the occasional bit of work up there. Can turn his hand to most things, my Sid.'

'I see.' He gave her a careful scrutiny. 'Close were they, your husband and Linda?' he asked quietly.

Daphne Wilks stiffened. 'I don't know what you mean.'

Rafferty met Llewellyn's bleak gaze at the defensive answer. 'Look Mrs Wilks, there's no nice way to put this, but was your husband *unnaturally* close to your daughter?'

Mrs Wilks took a step back. 'Who told you that?' she demanded. 'It's a wicked lie,' she asserted. 'A wicked lie.'

Rafferty took her arm. 'Come and sit down. Getting yourself all upset won't help matters. Suppose you tell us all about it?'

After dabbing at her eyes with a delicate lace-edged handkerchief, Mrs Wilks proceeded to screw it into a ball. She stared down at her lap and began to speak, forcing out the words as though each one might choke her. 'He was always cuddling her, as fathers do, there was nothing in it, but Linda got it into her head he'd done something wrong and told me he—did things to her.' She raised her head and stared at them defiantly. 'I gave her a smack for telling such wicked lies and I heard no more about it after that.'

'You didn't believe her, then?' asked Llewellyn gravely.

'Of course not!' In spite of her denial, her eyes avoided the Welshman's. 'Little madam was always making up tales. Liked to imagine herself important, you know how kids do?' She gave a sniff. 'As if my Sidney would do such a thing. He's a respectable man and she's shamed him, shamed us both.'

Rafferty sighed. 'Did Linda accuse her father of doing these things at any particular time?'

Daphne Wilks looked defiantly at him. 'Crafty she was. Told me he went up to her room when I was at work. I used to help out at the hospital part-time in the evenings.'

Interesting, thought Rafferty. Here was yet another hospital connection. 'So your husband and Linda would often be alone here?' he questioned.

Unable to disagree, she burst out, 'But he didn't do anything, I've told you. She made it up to get back at him.'

'Why should she want to get back at him?' asked Llewellyn.

Daphne Wilks sighed and began to pull at the lace of her hankie. 'He was always a bit strict as a father, my Sidney. Spare the rod and spoil the child, he used to say. Linda was a naughty child and used to get spanked regularly.'

'Did you never punish her yourself?' Llewellyn questioned. 'Surely, it's more usual for a mother to punish a daughter?'

'Oh no, Sidney always said that was his duty. Said I'd be too soft. He used to take her into the dining room and shut the door. He told me he didn't want to upset me. Mind, the spankings worked. She'd always be good for a long spell afterwards.'

'Did you never think she might be telling the truth about what her father did to her?' Rafferty demanded, unable to conceal his repugnance at her giving the nod, as it were, to her own daughter's abuse.

Her face flushed an ugly red as she briefly met his eye, mumbling, 'No, of course not,' before looking away again.

'I see.' It was hopeless, she would never admit the truth, not even to herself. Rafferty stood up, now wanting only to get out and sensing that Llewellyn felt the same way. But, before they went, he had one or two more questions for her. 'About that phone call on the night your daughter died.'

Daphne Wilks looked wary again. 'What about it?'

'Who answered the phone?'

'My husband.'

'Did he say he recognized the voice? Did he say if they'd rung before?'

The unexpected questions seemed to bewilder her. 'Why should he? We were both far too upset to think about such a thing.' She frowned suddenly. 'Do you think the caller might be the one who killed her?' The possibility seemed to cheer her immensely, Rafferty noticed. Perhaps she had also suspected her husband of killing Linda? 'Do you know, it never occurred to me, but I suppose you're right. Why didn't I consider it before? Such wickedness to ring up and invite her to her own murder.' Mrs Wilks looked at them indignantly, as if they'd been the ones to issue the invitation. 'Because that's what he did, you know. I remember, it rang three times before Sidney answered it. Just like the three cock crows in the bible.' With a stunned look, she stared at them. 'It was a bad omen.'

At least, it seemed to confirm, that there *had* been a phone call. Rafferty didn't think her *that* accomplished an actress, no matter how much her husband might have primed her. Surprisingly, she seemed to want to talk now she'd satisfied herself that her husband was in the clear and it was a good ten minutes later before they managed to make it to the door of the living room.

'Perhaps you'll tell your husband we called?' Rafferty suggested. 'And that we'll be back.' She gave them another defiant look, as though to challenge them to make her change her story. 'We'll see ourselves out.'

Once outside, Rafferty rubbed a hand over his face as though to wipe off the feeling of disgust. 'She knew what her husband was doing all right. Linda wasn't lying. Poor little bitch. Who could she turn to if her own mother wouldn't believe her? I wonder if she brought it up during their row? Accused her father of pushing her into prostitution? It's possible. Perhaps she told him she wasn't going to keep quiet about what he had done to her any longer?'

Llewellyn nodded. 'He'd have been terrified of discovery. He could have followed her, waited for her to open the hospital's side gate and pushed through after her. He was working on his car. It's quite likely he still had one of the tools in his hand so he would have had a weapon.'

Rafferty shook his head. 'You're the car buff. Do you know of any mechanic's tools similar to a rake or a fork?' Llewellyn admitted he didn't. 'Even if he had such a tool, I still don't see him doing it,' said Rafferty. 'If the attack had been done in a mindless and frenzied passion, her body would have received blows as well as her face, and it didn't. And another thing,' he continued, well into his stride now. 'If her father were the murderer, surely, he would have removed her fingerprints? After all, he had just discovered she was a prostitute; for all he knew, she had been picked up for soliciting at some time. Do you think a man who could cold-bloodedly remove her face would then be so careless as to risk the possibility of her fingerprints being on record? He'd want to remove all chance of any association between them being traced. He couldn't be sure that Linda hadn't revealed what he'd done to her to one

of her girlfriends. He'd want her to disappear; an un-
identifiable body would ensure it. "She's moved to
London," he'd say to his neighbours when they asked
after her.

'No,' he added slowly, 'I think we have to look elsewhere for our killer. Someone who didn't know about
Linda's double life; someone who had no reason to
think she had a record; someone who thought we'd
discover *their* identity once we knew the girl's. But we
haven't, dammit.' He brought his fist down with a
frustrated thump on the roof of the car and Llewellyn
winced. 'Why?' he demanded. 'Where are we going
wrong?'

Llewellyn didn't answer, but he still looked doubtful
when they got in the car. The trouble with his sergeant,
thought Rafferty, was that his knowledge of psychology was all text-book, whereas his own was practical.
And, whatever Llewellyn might think, he found it hard
to believe that a man who relieved his sexual frustra-
tions on his young daughter rather than an adult and
possibly demanding mistress would be bold enough to
kill. Of course, he could be wrong.

CAUTIOUSLY, conscious of his chief's strictures, Rafferty continued his digging into Melville-Briggs's alibi,
but to his chagrin, it seemed ever more impeccable. Although it wasn't substantiated for the entire night, so far
they had been unable to discover any long period when
he wasn't vouched for by someone. He had appeared to
stay with the same cronies for most of the evening,
punctuated only by very short breaks in order to rid
himself of an excess of good wine. As though to drive
the fact of the impenetrable alibi more forcefully home,
Sam Dally, their own police surgeon, was a prominent

witness—one amongst many unfortunately, all eminently respectable professionals who were prepared to swear on their Hippocratic Oaths that the good doctor hadn't left the George all night.

Rafferty's prediction that the press coverage of the crime would create more fear in the town than the actual murder was becoming horribly true. As they drove through Elmhurst, he could see the huddled groups of women on street corners and Rafferty, sensitive about his continuing failure, was only too aware of the accusing, hostile stares. Unhappily, he wondered if the worst aspect of the crime wasn't what it did to the living. What had been a small and—for this part of England at least—a remarkably close-knit community had been split apart in a matter of days. Where before there had been trust there was now overt suspicion. Any man who had been absent from home on the night of the crime was the subject of doubt and speculation; husbands, brothers, sons—everyone looked sideways at his neighbour.

All this made Rafferty more harassed by the hour, and the feeling that he was getting nowhere fast didn't help. He supposed Simon Smythe must be feeling the strain even more acutely than himself, especially as Melville-Briggs had sacked him, thereby increasing his neighbours' suspicions. No smoke without fire, was the generally accepted reaction to his sacking. The stupid police mightn't be able to prove he did it, but the general feeling was that his boss must have good reasons for getting rid of him. Poor Simple Simon. Poor Rafferty, too, he reflected, for the pressure on him to solve the crime, combined with the lack of any conclusive lead, put him in danger of losing his previously sunny disposition. Much more of this, he thought, and there would be little to choose between him and Llewellyn.

When they reached their headquarters, Rafferty slouched along to his first-floor office and flung himself in his chair. He was barely aware of Llewellyn as he followed him in and sat unobtrusively in front of the desk. Disconsolately, Rafferty gazed through the window. It was too much to hope that someone, *anyone*, had noticed old M-B sneak out of the George with a large clawhammer clutched in his lily-white hand. He'd even begun to *dream* about arresting the smug b— Straightening up, he pulled the pile of doctors' statements towards him. There must be *something* he'd missed. If he went through them just one more time... Rafferty sensed Llewellyn's disapproval. However, the Welshman made no comment and Rafferty did his best to ignore him, aware that his sergeant's nose was getting more pinched and his lips more thin and bloodless with each turning page. Finally, he could stand the silent reproach no longer. Slamming the file shut, he demanded, 'All right! If you've got something to say, say it. Don't just sit there looking like a squeezed lemon. You think that I'm out to get the bastard because he's well-heeled, successful, and I don't happen to like him, don't you?'

Llewellyn looked down his nose at this ungrammatical outburst. 'Aren't you perhaps a trifle obsessive about the gentleman, sir?' he queried. 'There *are* other suspects.'

'Yes—no—I don't know!' Glowering, Rafferty flung himself back against his chair, aware that Llewellyn was right. But only up to a point. It wasn't *just* for those reasons that he felt an overwhelming desire to follow his mother's advice and slap the cuffs on him. He was a wrong 'un. Instinctively Rafferty knew it. All right, so far, it seemed, he wasn't into murder. But he had *something* going, Rafferty's nose told him so, even as he recognized that he wouldn't get the controlled, enigmatic Welshman to take notice of such a thing as intuition.

To Rafferty's way of thinking, a man who cheated on his wife cheated in other ways. And Dr Melville-Briggs didn't just cheat on his wife. He cheated on his mistresses as well. Rafferty was prepared to concede that a man in Melville-Briggs's position might require the occasional diversion, but, from what they had discovered so far, the doctor's diversions occupied enough of his time to look more like a second career. They'd traced eight ex-mistresses so far, thanks to the indefatigable Gilbert's appetite for other people's dirty linen, and Rafferty, sure there'd be more, had been disappointed to discover that Mrs Galvin, the cool, self-contained, and efficient secretary, was one of them. Somehow, he'd thought she'd have been more discerning. But, as he'd be the first to admit after his own disastrous marriage, he was no judge of women. According to Gilbert, she'd been making permanent noises and it had only been her husband's accident that had ended it. Rafferty wondered if Gilbert had a soft spot for Mary Galvin. He'd been reluctant to dish the dirt on her, and the information had been prised from him only with difficulty. Andrew Galvin had been paralysed from the waist down and she had been driving. Was it only duty and a guilty conscience that had persuaded her to return to her husband, he wondered, or the realization that her lover was too self-centred to ever allow anyone to put his so convenient marriage at risk? Was her love for the doctor of the obsessive variety that would make no bones about murdering a rival?

Mary Galvin had given an Elmhurst address. She and her husband lived alone. She had the opportunity to kill the girl and she didn't strike him as the sort of woman who fell in love either quickly or easily. Did that quiet exterior conceal a jealous rage? As mistress succeeded mistress, had that rage finally erupted in an orgy of violence? Had Linda Wilks been the victim of that fury, unlucky in death as she had been in life?

Rafferty couldn't begin to imagine what appeal the smooth, unctuous Sir Anthony could possibly have for any woman. Yet he seemed to have them eating out of his hand—the accommodating wife; the outwardly unassuming and apparently loyal secretary; the massed ranks of discarded mistresses, as well as the hopeful future ones. For the life of him, Rafferty couldn't see what *they* got out of it. But then he was a simple man; given to sudden bursts of passion and hot temper that passed as swiftly as they came—how could he ever hope to understand the complicated morals of more sophisticated souls?

Was the doctor some sort of esoteric gigolo? he asked himself. Did he, rather than flex his muscles, flex his bedside manner instead? And had he flexed it once too often? And if so, how the hell did he prove it? He looked thoughtfully at Llewellyn. 'You're an educated chap, Taff. Tell me—what would happen to a doctor who forgot to keep his bedside manner *this* side of the sheets?'

'He'd get struck off, of course,' Llewellyn replied guardedly, apparently not pleased to discover that Rafferty's mind was still on the same tack.

Rafferty nodded happily. That was what he'd thought. If Melville-Briggs lost his right to practise medicine, he lost everything of value to him.

Llewellyn sighed softly and looked wearily at his chief. 'You're not still suggesting he's the culprit?'

Stung by the implied criticism of his professionalism and miffed by Llewellyn's desire to use nothing but logic to solve the case, Rafferty raised eyes innocent of such an intent to Llewellyn's. '*Would* I?' he queried acidly. 'That sweet, kindly, white-haired old man? Shame on you, Taff. The very idea.'

Rafferty was amused by his own whimsy and Llewellyn's determinedly pursed lips. Who'd have thought the coolly logical Llewellyn would have the knack of restoring his good temper? Perhaps he'd keep him after all. He had his good points, even if they only extended to providing bait for his own barbed wit. Rafferty was an instinctive copper and every one of his instincts told him that he was heading in the right direction—even if the path at present seemed to have as many twists and turns as the way through a maze. A maze had a heart and he was convinced that Dr Melville-Briggs lurked at the centre of this particular leafy conundrum. It was just a matter of turning up each path till it proved to be a dead end, eliminating it from the route plan and trying the next. He couldn't expect Llewellyn to be willing to follow him on the often circuitous journey necessary to reach the goal. After all, Rafferty told himself complacently, he lacked the necessary nose and all the degrees in the world wouldn't provide him with one. It was hardly his fault that murderers didn't go by the police book any more than Rafferty did.

Yet, he was forced to admit to himself, there had been occasions when Llewellyn had come up with a discerning judgement that had left him floundering. For all his annoying traits, from his intellectual superiority to his deflating morality, Rafferty recognized that there was a tantalizing depth to his sergeant that was intriguing. Perhaps *his* judgement had been a bit rash? He'd let his Welsh terrier have another bite at the bone. 'It's worth following up, Taff,' he remarked reasonably. 'Such a scandal could have cost him a lucrative career. Don't you think he'd consider it worth a murder, when, as far as he's concerned, the murder of someone like Linda would be a *very* little murder?'

Of course, Llewellyn immediately made him regret his generous impulse. 'But Linda Wilks wasn't one of his patients,' he pointed out reasonably. 'She was no threat to him. Besides, he's got that alibi, sir,' Llewellyn reminded him unkindly. 'I fail to see that it matters with whom he was having an affair. Besides, we've found no evidence that he even *knew* the victim. I find it extremely unlikely that he did know her. She's hardly his usual type.' He delicately refrained from remarking on the unlikelihood of Melville-Briggs ever having to pay for sex, but his point was clear enough even for Rafferty.

'Besides,' Llewellyn continued, after a short pause, 'he's not the type to commit murder himself. He's what I call a *mean* sinner, the kind who may be involved, but who hides behind somebody else. There's an old Czech proverb which goes, "It isn't the thief who is hanged, but the one who was caught stealing."'

Trust his sergeant to trot out an appropriate quote, fumed Rafferty, comforting himself with the thought that Llewellyn couldn't be so smart after all, if his wisdom consisted solely of borrowing dead men's words.

In spite, or because, of Llewellyn's proselytizing, Rafferty perversely persisted in his argument. 'All those professional men at the George had drunk their full and more. Why should their evidence under such circumstances be any more reliable than that of other drunks? 'All right,' he went on hurriedly, as Llewellyn looked set to interrupt, no doubt with more borrowed philosophy, 'I'll grant you that as she wasn't his patient, any liaison with her wouldn't be enough to get him struck off for misconduct. But surely there are other forms of misconduct which the wise doctor avoids? Consorting with a prostitute, for instance? Linda might have thought he was a suitable subject for blackmail. He was wealthy and successful, unlikely to miss a few grand; the sort of man vulnerable to such smears. And she mightn't have known that Lady Evelyn knew and turned a blind eye to his affairs.'

If only it wasn't for that seemingly rock-solid alibi! Even *his* finely honed instincts had so far found no way round that, especially when the other doctors at the do seemed determined to minimize their varying states of drunken incompetence in their statements. Still, even if none of the doctors present that evening had expressed the slightest doubt that they were telling the truth, it was only the truth as they saw it, not what they actually *knew* to be the truth. There was a difference.

'It's by chasing every snippet of information and gossip, however unlikely, that murderers get caught,' he insisted to his sceptical sergeant. 'Many a time I've known a little judicious juice-gathering dissolve the most impressive alibi. It's a matter of first gathering the fruit—the gossip and titbits—then sorting the pips from the pap; and what remains is pure juice—the truth, rich, ripe, and damning.'

'What happens when the fruit has already been squeezed dry, sir?' Llewellyn asked.

'We go out and gather some more. That's what.'

Llewellyn sniffed and, looking as if he'd thoroughly got the pip, he replied flatly, 'A second harvest, you mean?'

'That's exactly what I mean.'

The Welshman didn't look enthusiastic—but then he never did. But he'd have to lump it, resolved Rafferty. This was *his* case and he would solve it *his* way, even if he had to drag a dubious and critical Llewellyn along behind him through the entire labyrinth.

FOURTEEN

RAFFERTY'S OPTIMISM didn't last long. Far from being any nearer the centre of the maze, he hadn't even managed to find the entrance. Neither had there been a second harvest, and certainly no sign of an orange grove of juicy clues ripe for the plucking. The feeling that he'd missed something, something so obvious that he was incapable of seeing it, persisted and it didn't help that Llewellyn intimated that his blindness was caused by his growing obsession with proving Melville-Briggs's guilt. Could he be right? Was he letting his antagonism to Melville-Briggs warp his judgement? It wouldn't be the first time, of course. Luckily Llewellyn didn't know that.

His sergeant had only joined the Essex force from the Welsh borders some two months earlier, just before his own promotion. His quiet disposition didn't encourage the other officers to swap gossip so no one seemed to have told him why Rafferty had been passed over for promotion before. Although that time, too, he had been convinced he was right, it was impossible to forget that in the end, his single-minded pursuit of another high-powered suspect in a brutal child-assault case had nearly caused his suspension. Could he be heading down the same road again? he wondered uneasily. Then, as now, he had taken an overwhelming dislike to one of the suspects in the case—a man of too similar a type to Melville-Briggs for Rafferty's comfort—and he had gone charging after him with his head down, like a

rogue bull elephant. Yet, in the end, the man had been
proved innocent. Rather, Rafferty amended, he'd had
nothing to do with that *particular* crime, whatever else
he might have been guilty of.

That case had made him several enemies amongst his
fellow officers—the ones who relied for promotion on
a network of well-placed contacts: important people
whispering discreetly in the right ear. And his suspect
had been important, *very* important. They hadn't ap-
preciated Rafferty's lack of subtlety, especially when the
suspect had started shouting very loudly and very bitterly about the entire investigation and all the officers
involved in it.

That hadn't gone down at all well and some of his
fellow officers were long on memory and short on for-
giveness. One in particular, Rick Brown, wouldn't hes-
itate to do Rafferty down if he got the chance. Luckily,
he'd been seconded up north on a case that looked like
lasting some time yet and Rafferty hoped that he stayed
there—at least until this case was over.

Although he knew he must accept that Melville-
Briggs *couldn't* have killed the girl, it didn't make him
like the man any more. The way he openly sneered, not
only at him but also at the wretched victim, enraged
Rafferty. Her short life and ugly death resurrected a
deeply buried and previously unsuspected chivalrous
aspect of Rafferty's character and he resolved to find
her killer, no matter how many obstacles barred his way
to the truth. He conceded he made a poor knight—he
couldn't even ride a horse—but he was the only cham-
pion Linda Wilks was likely to get and he meant to do
his best by her.

It was quite late, and he was feeling tired and a little
sad—combinations that often caused him to wax

philosophical. They did so now as he thought about Linda and her parents. 'Funny thing, marriage,' he mused, more or less to himself. 'The strangest couples get together, promise to love, honour, etc., and before the honeymoon's over they realize they've made a horrible mistake. Why are so many people incapable of seeing the obvious *before* they make it legal?'

'Impetus,' replied Llewellyn.

'Come again.'

'Impetus,' Llewellyn repeated solemnly. 'The thing gathers a momentum of its own. Like a runaway car, beyond control. People start going out together, they continue going out together, either because no stronger force stops them or because at a certain time in their lives they're convenient for each other in some way. Before they know it, they're married with a child on the way. Even nowadays, in spite of the permissive society, most people are conventional and do what's expected of them. Most women want the white wedding and the orange-blossom. Of course, marriage is now big business; once the date's set and huge amounts of money are spent on wedding finery and rings and caterers, couples find themselves on a roller-coaster ride to the altar. It takes more courage than most people possess to stamp hard on the brakes at that stage. Little wonder there's so much divorce.'

'You seem to know a lot about it.' Though, of course, he'd not forgotten that Llewellyn had studied philosophy and psychology at university. 'I know you're not married. Did you stamp on the brakes to make sure you stayed that way?'

'Me? No, sir. I've never got close enough to matrimony to require brakes.'

'Very wise,' said Rafferty drily. 'So what was it? Did all that observation of other people's marriages put you off?'

Llewellyn shrugged and began to look decidedly uncomfortable, as though wishing he'd never started this conversation. 'Women take the order out of life,' he told Rafferty with a defensiveness that sparked his curiosity. 'Lipstick on the cups, shoes all over the hall, fripperies everywhere. And they're always expecting you to keep them amused, or else they're trying to change your ways.' Rafferty could see that for Llewellyn all that might be a problem. 'Then they tend to want children. Messy things, children.'

Strangely, Llewellyn's words lacked conviction. It was almost as though he hid his real desires behind a strongly worded support for their opposite. Rafferty wondered whether—like the plain virgin—his rejection of matrimony was more to conceal the fact that he'd never met anyone who *wanted* to marry him. Dafyd Llewellyn certainly wouldn't be to everyone's taste, he reflected.

'You want to try the older woman, Taff,' Rafferty advised. 'Someone who'd appreciate neatness after years of tidying up after husband and kids. A nice divorcée for instance.' Llewellyn's nostrils quivered with distaste and Rafferty held up his hand. 'I know—messy things divorces, right?' Llewellyn nodded. 'Widow then,' Rafferty went on in his self-appointed role of agony aunt.

Llewellyn didn't look any more enthusiastic about a nice little widow than he had about a divorcée and Rafferty wondered why he was bothering. Must be his mother's influence, he decided. Still, Llewellyn seemed lonely. It would do him the world of good to get married, a little disorder in his life might just be the making of him. Standing up, he remarked with grim humour, 'Now's your chance to observe another odd couple—Mr and Mrs Galvin. It might be a good idea to take your psychology degree out and dust it off. I wonder whether they're another couple who were overtaken by impetus,' he mused, as they headed for the car park.

They left the car just past the side gate of the hospital and walked from there. Teams of police frogmen were visible across the fields, as they searched the river for the murder weapon and Linda Wilks's clothes. Their movements were dispirited and it was clear they were having no success.

The Galvins' lonely flint-built cottage looked unkempt, and but for the thin stream of smoke from the chimney, which was quickly whipped away by the still sharp winds off the North Sea, Rafferty would have thought it was empty. It wore an air of neglect as though the heart had gone out of it. Apart from the top floors of the hospital visible over the high walls of the grounds, there wasn't another house within sight. The fields gave way to the marshland, desolate and silent apart from the continual crying of the birds—curlews and warblers and moorhens, taking off and landing, taking off and landing again, to pluck fat moist worms from the squelching mud.

The gate creaked noisily behind them as they walked up the overgrown path to the Galvins' cottage and although he couldn't make out the words, Rafferty caught the tail-end of a hastily cut-off argument. Lifting the knocker, he let it fall, pinning a friendly smile to his face as Mary Galvin opened the door. 'You remember I said I'd call?'

She nodded. It was plain she'd been weeping. Her eyes were red and sore-looking as though the tears had been particularly bitter. After taking their coats, she led them into a small sitting-room-cum-kitchen. The room had a half-finished look, one side of the kitchen had modern fitted cupboards and looked quite sleek and stylish, while the other half had an old stained stone sink and a cheap red drop-front kitchen cabinet, the sort his mother had thrown out years ago. An attempt had been made to strip the many different layers of paint off this, but patches had clung, stubbornly resistant to the paint stripper, and had been left as though the effort required to finish the job was too much.

Rafferty turned as he heard the wheel-chair behind him and introduced himself and Llewellyn. Andrew Galvin seemed a surly individual. He barely managed a nod, before he brought the chair to a halt and gazed at them with a brooding, unblinking stare.

During the course of the case, Rafferty had come to expect hostility, but this was something else again and he found himself meeting Galvin stare for stare, feeling that it was somehow important not to betray any pity. Although Galvin's legs, under the thick working trousers, might be withered, his arms and shoulders were powerful and strained against the denim shirt. A sprinkling of sawdust covered the material and Rafferty could see a trail of it leading from a door at the far end of the living-room to the connecting garage, which was an obvious later addition.

'Well now.' Rafferty unlocked his gaze from that of Galvin and began, with a mock cheerfulness that did nothing to lessen the tense atmosphere. The Galvins had the air of people waiting for the axe to fall. The house was very quiet; set amidst the fields as it was, the limited traffic on the road, several hundred yards away, passed unheard. He found the silence and isolation of the Galvins' house depressing. Coming from a large family, he was a sociable man and liked to hear the sounds of the neighbours through the walls of his flat.

How did Andrew Galvin stand being alone here day after day while his wife was at work? he wondered. But perhaps solitude was preferable to long uncomfortable silences, broken only by the next argument, to company that created strain without companionship. How many times had he felt that way about his own wife?

As he had expected, Mary Galvin's alibi was backed up by her husband, as his was by her. They had both been at home the entire evening of the murder. Whether they were telling the truth or not, Rafferty thought it would be impossible to shift them. They seemed to have decided to present a united front, yet he sensed it was an uneasy alliance and wondered if he might succeed in breaking it.

Apart from supporting his wife's version of events on the night of the murder, Andrew Galvin said little. He sat in his wheel-chair, a sullen and withdrawn presence. He was still quite a handsome man, despite the lines of pain deeply engraved from nose to mouth. The full lips were compressed impatiently as though he was only waiting till the statements were noted down in Llewellyn's little book before he burst out with some furious comment. Rafferty sensed the frustration and bitterness just beneath the surface and he guessed Galvin had been a sensual man before the accident. How would *he* feel, Rafferty wondered, if he lost his mobility, his job, the love of his wife, and in their stead suffered continual pain and the knowledge that his wife was as bitterly unhappy as himself? He had to admit he

didn't know—he, at least, had a large family to cushion him should he need it. In this man's presence he felt
suddenly ashamed that the death of his wife, Angie,
hadn't caused him to grieve either long or deeply. It was
only guilt that had caused him suffering. His family had
realized his wife was little loss to him as a human being, for they'd left him to come to terms in his own way
with the feelings of mingled self-reproach and relief her
death had brought. If he'd truly loved her and mourned
for her his family would never have been out of his flat,
especially his ma.

Yet Andrew Galvin had grieved; was still grieving.
His wife's infidelity had obviously devastated him as
much as a bereavement. Llewellyn's earlier remarks had
made Rafferty oddly contemplative and now he wondered if there had been anyone to comfort Andrew
Galvin. He let his eyes flicker casually around the room
and saw that there was no evidence of brothers or sisters, nephews or nieces; no photographs of any description. But even if there were such a family in the
background, it was usually the woman who took the
trouble to frame and display their pictures. And Mary
Galvin struck him as unsentimental, not the sort to put
such things on show, the sort of woman who would
keep her deepest feelings locked away from prying eyes.
It was strange that a man like Sir Anthony had been
able to release them. Perhaps his psychiatric training
had supplied him with a few tricks denied to lesser
mortals?

After getting their statements out of the way, they
both seemed to loosen a little of their stiff control and
Rafferty decided now was the time to get under their
guard. 'I've some—rather delicate—questions for you,

Mrs Galvin. Perhaps you'd rather speak to me without your husband being present?'

To his surprise, she shook her head, her back seemed to straighten a fraction more and she gave him a sad smile; the smile of a woman who knew she had already lost everything of importance. 'I think I know what you want to ask about, Inspector,' she remarked quietly. 'There's no need to be so circumspect on my account. I no longer have any secrets from my husband. Andrew already knows about Sir Anthony and me.' She raised her head and met Rafferty's eyes boldly. 'I'm sure you already know all this, Inspector, but you might as well have the true version rather than the more lurid gossip from the hospital grape-vine.

'I'd been having an affair with Sir Anthony for six months before the accident that paralysed Andrew. Oh, now I see him for what he is,' she exclaimed bitterly, 'but then he took the trouble to be as charming and considerate to me as he is to his rich patients. It was only later that I realized what a fool I'd been, thinking my-self in love with a man who didn't exist. He played a part, you see, and played it to perfection. It took An-drew's accident to show him in his true light. Even then I didn't want to believe it. I thought his reluctance to leave his wife stemmed from concern for me, worry about my reputation in such a small place.' Her eyes didn't flinch from his, but now, the hatred was plain in her face. 'All the time, of course, his only concern was for the social position he enjoyed through his wife. Without her, he was only another doctor—not a terri-bly good one at that. She got him his first clients.' She laughed harshly. 'I used to think it was loyalty to him that kept them. But of course I was wrong.'

She didn't elaborate, but left Rafferty to come to his own conclusions. He could believe that it was loyalty to Lady Evelyn that brought his patients back time and again.

He wondered again if Mary Galvin could have killed the girl, her personality corroded by seeing her now hated ex-lover day after day, and having to watch as he paraded his latest mistresses under her nose? Had she decided to hit him where she could do most damage—in his reputation? It would explain why the victim's body had escaped the blows. She didn't hate her ex-lover's latest mistresses, why should she? She knew they would be replaced in time, as she had been. But she was astute enough to realize that a 'Faceless Lady' would catch the imagination of the press and guarantee far more damaging publicity, and that would surely be what she wanted?

Had she known the girl would be coming to the hospital that night? Had Sir Anthony delighted in telling her about his mistresses? Rafferty didn't find it hard to imagine that he would get pleasure from such casual cruelty. Had he intended to slip away from the George that night to meet Linda? And had she known about the assignation and decided to meet the girl herself and kill her? Looking at her sitting calm and composed as she related the details of her affair, he realized she was fully capable of it. The thought brought the realization that if he wanted answers, he would have to get tough with her. She might yet regret that confident assertion that she had no secrets from her husband.

'You must have felt very angry when Sir Anthony told you the affair was over,' he remarked. 'I can imagine what a traumatic time it must have been for you; your husband crippled, your realization that Sir Anthony didn't love you. A lot of women would brood over the unfairness of it all, maybe even want revenge. Is that what you wanted, Mrs Galvin? How many lonely nights while your husband was in hospital did you scheme to get back at him?'

'I didn't,' she protested. 'I . . .'

'How many mistresses did he parade under your nose before you snapped?' he demanded remorselessly. 'Was it one? Three? Six?'

'No, I tell you. It wasn't . . .'

'Come on, Mrs Galvin. You can't expect me to believe that a woman passionate enough to have a love affair wouldn't also have enough passion to kill. I understand your husband was paralysed from the waist down in the accident. You must have felt very frustrated after Sir Anthony dumped you. Did you channel that frustration into planning murder? One that . . .'

'Stop it!'

Startled, Rafferty stared as Andrew Galvin raised himself from the chair and launched himself at him. He tried to protect his head from the man's fists as they rained blows down on him.

'Leave her alone. Leave her alone, I tell you. Of course, she didn't kill that bastard. I know damn well she didn't because . . .'

Llewellyn had finally managed to drag him off and Galvin stood in the middle of the room, breathing heavily and swaying, before he turned and flung himself back in his chair.

There was a stunned silence that lasted all of thirty seconds after Galvin's outburst. Llewellyn was the first one to gather his wits. 'When did you discover you could walk, Mr Galvin?' he asked quietly. 'Was it before the murder? Or after?'

Andrew Galvin's painfully rasping breath was now the only sound. As though satisfied that his outburst had caused sufficient shock, he wheeled his chair away from them and spat out a single word. 'Before.'

Rafferty shifted uncomfortably in his chair. The man's manner seemed to challenge them to arrest him. Rafferty wondered why. Was he trying to protect his wife? Or was there a deeper reason? Andrew Galvin had been discounted from the murder investigation. The man couldn't walk, or so they had thought. Apart from the difficulty of manoeuvring his wheel-chair through the undergrowth and trees planted at the perimeter of the hospital, there had been no sign of any tracks, no sign of vegetation flattened by the passing of such a vehicle. But if he could walk . . .

Although he might find the feat difficult, it wouldn't be impossible. Was that why Mary Galvin had kept up the pretence of his paralysis? Had she secretly suspected? He remembered that she'd become very defensive when he'd told her he would have to check her alibi with her husband. Did Andrew Galvin secretly want to punish her for her infidelity? And was being arrested for the murder of one of her ex-lover's mistresses the method he had hit on? Bemused that so many possibilities should fall into his lap at once, Rafferty glanced at Mary Galvin. Her face was chalk-white and anguished. Her eyes, when they met his, were pleading.

'Well, what are you waiting for?' Galvin demanded, when the silence had dragged on a little longer. 'Aren't you going to arrest me?'

'Why?' Rafferty asked. 'Did you kill the girl?'

The reply was slow in coming. 'No.'

'Then why should I arrest you?'

Andrew Galvin looked helplessly from Rafferty to his wife and back again. Then he shrugged and slumped back in his chair, a defeated expression on his face.

Rafferty took a deep breath and began to question Mary Galvin again. 'How long have you known your husband could walk?'

'Since just—after the murder. I came home unexpectedly and found him in the shed. His chair was in here.'

'Did you suspect he might have killed the girl?'

Pain-filled eyes met his. 'I didn't know what to think. I only knew how much torment I'd caused him. How bitter he had become and...' Her voice trailed off before beginning again more firmly. 'I couldn't let him be suspected of murder as well. I owed him that much. It was bad enough that I'd caused the accident which paralysed him, but when he discovered about Sir Anthony and me...' Her throat muscles worked up and down spasmodically and she gave a particularly joyless little laugh. 'I really thought he loved me, you know. I was—dazzled, I suppose. He showed me a life style I'd never experienced before. Andrew and I were going through a rocky patch and it was as if the scales had fallen from my eyes and that life didn't need to be so dull, so dreary. For the first time in my life, I began to have fun. I was stupid not to realize that all fun has to be paid for and not by the Sir Anthonys of this world. You could say that after Andrew's accident, the devil called in his debt. I knew then that he didn't love me at all, or if he did, it was only as a very poor second to his upper-crust life style.'

She was being brutally honest, stripping herself of pride in a way that was embarrassing to watch. Up to now, her husband had sat silently listening to her outpourings, but now he looked at his wife's tear-wet cheeks with a shocked expression on his face.

'Did you really think the police would suspect I killed the girl in some fit of blind rage?' he asked.

She nodded once, her features taut with emotion.

'God!' He put his head in his hands and tugged at his hair as though he would wrench it out by the roots. 'How can you not have realized that if I'd wanted to kill anybody it would have been him?' He wheeled himself over to her and took her hands in his. 'Oh, I told myself I hated you, perhaps I did for a little while, but that was nothing beside all the grief I felt for what we had lost. I couldn't hate you.'

She looked at him as if not quite certain she had heard aright. 'What are you saying, Andrew?' she whispered.

He gazed at her pleadingly. 'That I still love you.' His voice hoarse with the intensity of his emotions, he added, 'That I don't want you to leave me, now or ever.'

'Oh Andrew. My love.' With a sob, Mary Galvin flung herself into her husband's arms and they clung together with a kind of fierce desperation.

Quietly, Rafferty signalled to Llewellyn and they let themselves out of the cottage. Cynically, he wondered if it was possible that they had staged that touching little scene for his benefit? They'd certainly had plenty of time to plan it and he thought Mary Galvin's mind was sufficiently cool for the job. But even if their emotional display had been genuine and not merely intended to divert suspicion from Andrew Galvin, it still didn't bring him any closer to making an arrest. Sourly, he reflected that the case would have caused him a damn sight less trouble if *Melville-Briggs* had been the one to be found murdered.

FIFTEEN

RAFFERTY HAD KEPT away from the hospital all the next day so he wouldn't be tempted to interview Melville-Briggs again. Not that he had anything new to tackle him with, anyway. He didn't even have any solid proof that the so far untraced Miranda and the girl in the pub were one and the same. Even if the girl in the pub proved to be this Miranda, it added nothing to the investigation; rather it confused matters. Given Dr Melville-Briggs's womanizing, there might be any number of unexplained females, however tenuously connected with the case, still to come out of the woodwork. But even if a couple of battalions of women appeared, none of them would be Linda Wilks. Dr Melville-Briggs hadn't murdered her and he'd better accept it if he was ever to solve the case.

It wasn't as though he was short of other candidates for the crime; if anything, he had an over-abundance of them, and would have been happier if their numbers were less and the pointers to someone's—anyone's—guilt more conclusive. But as wishful thinking wasn't going to solve the murder, he decided to ring through to the station to see if, by some miracle, the killer had confessed. His radio was on the blink and when he finally found a phone that worked, it was to find a message from his mother awaited him rather than a murderer's confession. She had been trying to contact him for several hours, apparently. 'You're sure she didn't say what she wanted?' he asked the desk sergeant.

'She said it was a private matter. You want to get round there, sir. She sounded a bit breathless to me— agitated like. Didn't she have those heart palpitations last year? Anyway, she said you was to go as soon as you got the message.'

The heart palpitations had turned out to be nothing more than indigestion. Rafferty wondered briefly why she hadn't phoned one of his sisters, and then shrugged. He'd find out soon enough. He hoped it wasn't a ruse and that he wouldn't discover Maureen concealed in a cupboard when he got there. She could be as crafty as any double-dealing diplomat, his ma. Still, she wasn't getting any younger and she'd never summoned him off a job before. Perhaps this time she really was ill. He'd left Llewellyn holding the fort in the office so he instructed, 'Tell my sergeant I'll ring him if it looks as though I'm going to be a while.'

Rafferty left the call-box and put his foot down all the way to his mother's house, but when he got there he found her sitting in her favourite chair by the window, watching the world go by and looking a damn sight more hale and hearty than he felt himself. His eyes flickered suspiciously when he saw that she was in her best navy-blue crimplene dress and his ear cocked for the sound of footsteps emerging from the cupboard under the stairs. 'What's going on, Ma?' he demanded. He felt hot and cross and not in the mood for any romantic games.

She stood up, arms akimbo, and he didn't need his policeman's nose to sniff trouble. 'What's going on, he asks,' she demanded caustically of the living-room ceiling. 'Little enough from what I hear,' she went on.

'Where've you been? I've been ringing that station all morning.'

'My radio's on the blink so they couldn't get hold of me. Anyway, I'm here now. What's the problem?'

'The same one,' she told him flatly. 'Jack.'

Jack! He'd forgotten all about him. He must have been charged, he realized guiltily, and would probably be in the remand cells at the Harcombe nick awaiting trial about the stolen whisky.

'You said you'd see to it, but you haven't. According to Deirdre you haven't been near nor by. I was that ashamed when she told me. So much for my son, the Inspector,' she mocked. 'And to think I promised Deirdre she could rely on you. Do you want the poor thing left standing at the altar?'

'It won't come to that, Ma,' he muttered feebly.

'No?' Her voice was sharp with annoyance. 'It seems it will if *you've* got anything to do with it. I was going to go to the station myself and wait for you if you didn't turn up.'

'I'll see to it, Ma,' he vowed desperately. 'I'll see to it this afternoon, I promise.'

'Yes, well,' she sniffed. 'See that you do. I promised that poor girl,' she repeated. 'Would you make me go back on my word?'

His mother had always had the knack of making him feel like a guilty schoolboy, he reflected. Perhaps all mothers were the same, but his was expert at cutting him down to size. At the moment, he felt about twelve years old and he scowled, but that, of course, only encouraged her to rub salt into the wounds.

'Why couldn't you have been a builder like the rest of the family?' she demanded plaintively. 'Then at least I might have been able to get hold of you when I wanted

you. But oh no, you were set on becoming a policeman, wouldn't listen to your mother.'

She made it sound as though he had joined the police solely from a perverse desire to annoy her, yet having a son in the police force had been almost entirely her
idea. The free boots for his expensively large feet had
held a strong appeal for a widow with five younger
children to feed and clothe.

'Now look at you,' his mother was in full spate. 'Not
only have you no time to ring your mother, but you're
in charge of trying to catch a dangerous murderer at
that loony-bin. I don't like it, Joseph. I don't like it at
all.'

He was getting progressively less keen on it himself as
the case went on, but he wasn't prepared to admit it to
her. 'There's more than me standing between chaos and
the forces of law and order, Ma,' he remarked soothingly.

'That's as may be, Joseph, but I'd feel much easier in
my mind—if you *must* be a policeman—if you had a
wife to look after you. A nice sensible girl. Like your
Uncle Pat's girl, Maureen, for instance.'

Here we go again, he thought, and sighed. However,
to his relief, having put across her feelings in her usual
forceful fashion, she relented and for once, didn't pursue the point.

'I don't suppose you've eaten?' Another guilty flush
crossed his features. 'I thought not. The kettle's on.' She
looked closer at him. 'How's your murder going, anyway? Any nearer to catching the wicked creature?'

'No,' he admitted flatly.

'Well, it's early days yet. Look at some of the cases
you read about, drag on for weeks they do.'

Rafferty gave his mother a weak smile. 'Thanks, Ma. You're a real Job's comforter. That's sure to keep the Superintendent sweet when next he wants a report on my progress.'

'Well, if he thinks he can do any better, let him try.'

That was the trouble, Rafferty reflected grimly. He just might. 'I ought to be going, Ma.'

'A few more minutes aren't going to make any difference,' she insisted. 'Let that Superintendent cool his heels for a bit. You might as well take the wedding present while you're here.' She pointed to a beautifully wrapped parcel sitting on an occasional table by the kitchen door.

'What is it?'

'A crock-pot.'

'How much do I owe you?'

'Ten pounds.'

'That's cheap, isn't it?' he asked suspiciously. 'It's not knocked-off, is it? If it is . . .'

'Of course it's not,' exclaimed his mother vehemently. 'It's bankrupt stock. With so many businesses going to the wall these days, there's a lot of bargains about.'

Bargains—the very word made him uneasy. His mother's love of 'bargains' didn't stop at the January sales unfortunately and, although, like most of the rest of the family, she was honest enough after her own lights, she saw nothing wrong in buying the occasional questionable item. Everybody did it, she defended herself when he tried to remonstrate with her. But of course, with so many relatives working on building sites, she had more opportunities than most. Little had changed it seemed. Why should she pay over the odds just because her son was in the force? she often demanded. And her on a widow's pension. She knew how to turn the knife, his ma. No wonder he'd been glad to leave home early and move into the section house. He could hardly have arrested his own mother for receiving, yet neither could he pretend to uphold the forces of law and order when his dinner was heated on a 'hot' infra-red grill. He sighed. A policeman's lot in the Rafferty family was not a happy one.

An hour later he was finally able to escape, after finishing his tea and picking up his present and promising, once more, that he would see to Jack straight away. At least by doing as he was bid in this it would give his mother one less excuse to persuade him into her parlour and he might be able to get on with solving the murder in relative peace.

RAFFERTY POPPED his head round the door of his office. 'I've got to go out again. Some checking up to do,' he explained quickly, shutting the door behind him before Llewellyn could offer to come with him. This was one task he wanted to see to by himself.

He turned into the car park at the Harcombe police station, ready, if not wholly willing, to do his familial duty. But as he knew he'd never hear the end of it if he didn't at least make the attempt, he gritted his teeth and put a good face on it.

'Morning, Tom,' he greeted the desk sergeant with false bonhomie in an attempt to cover his awkwardness. 'I rang earlier about a fellow called Jack Delaney. The constable who answered the phone told me he'd been charged and was back in the cells on remand. I'd like a word with him.'

'Oh yes?' The sergeant eased his bulk off the counter and looked at Rafferty with interest. 'I didn't know you were involved in this case, Inspector. You know Brown's back from the case up north and has taken over the investigation?'

Rafferty hadn't and now he swore silently. The desk sergeant whistled and obtained the services of the nearest constable to escort Rafferty down to the cells. 'Brown's in his office,' the sergeant told him slyly. 'You'll want to see him, of course. Out of courtesy, like.'

'Of course,' Rafferty muttered, trying to stop himself from glaring at his persecutor. In his late forties, the desk sergeant was only hanging on for his pension. He knew all about the little feud between Rafferty and Rick Brown, and, having long since given up on getting beyond the rank of sergeant, it amused him to pass the years till retirement fomenting trouble amongst his superiors, the 'clever young buggers', as he called them. He wasn't partisan, he despised them all without particularity.

Affecting an air of unconcern, Rafferty said, 'I'll see chummy first,' and followed the constable down to the cells. Before he'd learned that Brown was in charge of the case, he'd still had a faint hope of emerging from the station with his pure policeman image virgo intacta. But once he discovered their distant family ties, Brown would plunder his most secret cranny with all the finesse of a mad rapist. Rafferty knew well enough that Rick Brown was still looking for an opportunity to get his own back and here he was with no choice but to present it to him, gift-wrapped.

The constable unlocked the door of the cell and let Rafferty in, banging the door shut behind him. Luckily, Jack waited till then to express his joy at their reunion, leaping to his feet as relief chased the worry from his face. 'Long time no see. Sure an' you're a sight for sore eyes. Are they lettin' me go then?'

'No. Not yet.'

The expression on Jack's face was that of one whose trust had been irretrievably shattered. 'But Deirdre said...I thought you'd come to get me out,' he reproached. 'What's going on?'

If it hadn't been for Jack's fiancée, Deirdre, a sensible girl who didn't deserve such a husband, he wouldn't have bothered his head about his gormless relative. But he consoled himself with the thought that Jack was taking his bride back to Dublin with him after the wedding. It could be worse. 'Why don't you tell me all about it,' he encouraged.

With a face as deceptively blameless as a choirboy's, Jack chorused in his peculiar high-pitched voice, 'They're fitting me up, Jar, I didn't do it, as God's me witness.'

'Let's save God for the real witness-box, shall we?' Rafferty suggested tightly, annoyed by Jack's use of his old childhood nickname. 'I'm sure he's got enough on his plate at the moment worrying about your nuptials. Right. Where and when is the crime of the century supposed to have taken place and what were you doing at the time?'

'It was last Friday night, way over near Colchester. But I wasn't anywhere near there.'

Rafferty's drooping head jerked up at this. 'You mean the night of the murder?'

'Was that the same night?' Jack grinned, his troubles evidently forgotten. 'Well, well, you were kept busy then, one way and another. Poor old Jar. Still,' he added airily, 'if you will join the pigs you've only yourself to blame.'

Rafferty looked pityingly at him. The eejit didn't even have the nous to keep his usual insults to himself. Now he said flatly, 'If you want this particular pig to squeal in your defence, you'd better remember your manners.'

The tactlessness of his remark must even have penetrated Jack's thick skull, for he murmured, 'Sorry, Joseph,' in a suitably chastened manner. 'Slip of the tongue.'

'Try not to have any more,' Rafferty advised, 'or there's a good chance *I* might have a slip of the foot and slide right back out that door, leaving you this side of it. Wedding or no wedding. Now,' he sat down on the thin mattress, 'why don't we make ourselves comfortable and you can tell me the rest.'

'I didn't do it, Joe, honest, I didn't. Admittedly, the money would have come in useful for the honeymoon, but I was casin' a joint out at Elmhurst that night.'

'And that's your defence, is it?' Rafferty sighed. 'It won't do. It won't do at all. Let's start again. You were *out for a walk* on a particularly fine spring night...'

Surprisingly, Jack had caught his drift. 'Right. I was out for this walk, like, me and Deirdre and—'

'Hold on, hold on. Let's get this straight. Do you usually take your fiancée out with you when you look over a likely prospect?' It seemed a strange thing to do, but then, with Jack, anything was possible, the dafter the better.

'It was only a *general* once-over.' Jack defended himself from the slur of unchivalrous behaviour. 'We'd been to the pub by the loony-bin. Deirdre knows the landlord and I fancied me chances of gettin' afters.'

Rafferty's instincts went into overdrive at this. 'What time was this?' he demanded. 'What time did you leave, I mean?'

Unnerved, Jack was, for a moment or two, incapable of getting his small vocabulary together, but at last he managed it. 'I dunno. Bout half eleven or thereabouts, I s'pose.' He pulled a face. 'Deirdre knocked the idea of afters on the head. Shame, as it was a good night, too. Anyhow, sure an' we was walkin' back up the road to where I'd left me car and...'

'You hadn't left it in the pub car park then?'

'Course not! Do you think I'm daft?' Rafferty forbore to comment. 'I'd had a few drinks, hadn't I? It was after hours and the landlord's late with his backhanders this month. Deirdre was worried the cops might pounce out of spite. You know how the bast—' Jack's voice trailed away and a sheepish grin decorated his face. 'Sorry,' he mumbled. 'Anyway, the car was up the road, across the way from the madhouse on that patch of waste ground.'

Rafferty broke in. 'Why didn't you tell the police you'd been in the pub with a bar-full of witnesses at the time someone was ripping off the lorry?'

'I told you,' he explained patiently. 'It was after hours. I'd have got them all in shtook, wouldn't I?' Apparently Jack's capacity for making instant friends hadn't changed either. He thought the whole world was his bosom buddy. 'I'd a still been there meself, only Deirdre kept on at me till I agreed to leave.'

Rafferty reminded himself that he was related to this cretinous individual, even if only distantly, and counted to ten before he allowed himself to reply. 'I see. So in your opinion, it's better to go down for another five stretch than to nark on your mates for after-hours drinking?' It wasn't as if they'd been that much over time, but perhaps his cousin had a point. Back-handers were a way of life and some of the uniformed branch could be most unpleasant about any delay in receiving their dues.

Jack nodded, quite impervious to the sarcasm. 'That's right. I'll tell you somethin' else, an' all. Deirdre said I'd 'ad enough to drink—you know how women do—anyway, when I saw the bleedin' monk I thought she might 'ave a point. Perhaps I ought to lay orf it for a bit. What do you think?'

'Monk? What monk was this then? Friar Tuck?' Rafferty was beginning to wonder if the low-wattage lightbulb of his cousin's intelligence hadn't finally flickered out altogether.

'I dunno,' Jack answered in all seriousness. 'He 'ad his 'ood over 'is 'ead. I only saw 'im for a second. Gave me quite a turn, I can tell you.'

Rafferty decided to humour him. 'This monk,' he asked patiently, 'where did he go?'

'Into the nut-house.'

Rafferty didn't believe it. It couldn't be happening. Surely God wasn't so kind as to reward his good deed with such charity? Could it be, was it possibly—a lead? He felt a taut shiver of awe run up his spine as he looked at Jack's vacant features. What was it the Bible said? Something about the least of his creatures? Out of the mouths of babes and the simple minded? Llewellyn would know, of course, but Rafferty had no intention of bringing him into this little tête-à-tête. Careful, he warned himself, as he felt the urge to grab hold of Jack and shake him. Don't spook the witness. Take it nice and slow. 'You didn't, by any chance happen to see a car parked outside the hospital gate as well did you, Jack?'

'A car?'

'You know, one of those painted jobs with a wheel on each corner,' he enlarged sarcastically, saintly patience quickly forgotten.

Jack's mouth dropped open. 'How did you know that? Bloody 'ell. You're smart and no mistake.'

Rafferty smiled smugly. 'I try. Any idea what make it was?'

'Can't remember.' Jack gave a sheepish shrug. 'I'd just come out of the pub, remember? One of those sleek jobs though. I'm thinkin' of getting one meself,' he added.

Stealing one, more like, thought Rafferty. 'Get a glimpse of the licence plate, did you?'

Jack shook his head again. But it wouldn't have made any difference if he had. Rafferty had nearly forgotten that eleven years of schooling had failed to teach Jack even the rudiments of the alphabet. Perhaps Deirdre would know.

'You've been lucky, Jack,' he told him, as he got up and knocked on the door. 'I'll tell the inspector your story myself, it'll save Deirdre the trouble.' If he'd known his cousin had been with his girlfriend that night, he could have saved himself the unpleasantness of sorting it out. Women, he generally found, didn't worry overmuch about the shamefulness of snitching. Practical creatures, women. Still, he'd done himself a bit of good as well as Jack, so he shouldn't complain. 'You'll be out of here in an hour or two, I shouldn't wonder.' Ebullient, he nearly told Jack he could buy him a pint when he got out, but stopped himself in time. That wouldn't be such a good idea, he realized. The fewer people who saw them together, the better he'd like it.

The constable let him out and Rafferty walked thoughtfully back up the corridor, stopping abruptly as his mind strove manfully to connect the tenuous strands of the case to the latest information. There was something, some glimmer of a connection. Was it, no wait a minute, could it be...? Something heavy lurched against his shoulder.

'Sorry Inspector.'

The constable grinned apologetically for his clumsiness and walked swiftly away as Rafferty scowled ferociously at him. Whatever his mind had been reaching for was gone. A few seconds before he had felt puffed up, good deed for the day performed and smug with the self-righteousness of the properly rewarded, now he felt horribly deflated. Slowly, reluctantly, he walked towards Rick Brown's office. But at least he wouldn't have to admit to a delighted Brown that Jack was his relative. Just checking out a possible witness in a murder case, wasn't he? And he had a whole bar-full of drinkers to back him up.

SIXTEEN

RAFFERTY HAD JUST got back from Harcombe when Llewellyn gave him the latest news. Melville-Briggs was dead. It took him a few minutes to take in. Apparently, he'd wrapped his car around a tree at Wivenhoe, taking with him any faint remaining chances of charging him with murder. Llewellyn had been right when he'd quoted that old bod's words. How had it gone? Something about every guilty person being his own hangman? Well, Rafferty concluded sombrely, it certainly looked as if Sir Anthony had been his own executioner, whether or not his sins had included murder.

He supposed it fell to him to break the news to Lady Evelyn. To Llewellyn's undisguised relief, Rafferty told him to remain at the office. Picking up WPC Green on his way, he drove to the Hall. The butler let them in, and after briefly stating they were there on official business, they followed his broad black-clad figure into the winter parlour.

'Inspector.' Lady Evelyn seemed pleased to see him and he stared guiltily at her. 'What can I do for you? Have you come to see over the house? I'm sure I've got time if...'

Rafferty shuffled his feet. 'No, ma'am. Er—that is...' he began awkwardly. To fill in the gap while he remembered his carefully rehearsed words, he introduced his companion. 'I'm afraid I have some bad news for you, ma'am.'

Lady Evelyn frowned. 'Bad news? What do you mean?'

'It's—your husband, Lady Evelyn. I'm sorry to have to tell you this. He's had an accident—it seems his car went out of control.'

'How . . . how bad?' Rafferty shuffled his feet again. 'Please. Just—tell me.' Her voice was faint as she asked, 'Is he . . . is he dead, Inspector?'

'I'm afraid so, ma'am.'

Lady Evelyn sank down slowly on to one of the chairs. Bleakly, her eyes rested on the array of family photographs on her desk and her lips tightened as she struggled for control.

'It—it would have been very quick though,' he told her in a desperate attempt at comfort. 'He wouldn't have suffered.'

'I see.' She shuddered slightly and then sat up straight in her chair. 'Thank you for coming to tell me. I understand how difficult it is to break such news.'

She seemed dazed, but apart from a faint white line around her tightened lips, she had taken the news with remarkable composure, much to Rafferty's relief. He had a quiet word with the butler who alerted the staff. The housekeeper took charge and she and one of the older female servants were soon plying their mistress with hot sweet tea. After quietly offering his condolences and having them as quietly accepted, Rafferty left the WPC behind with instructions that he'd send a car for her in a couple of hours and let himself out into the gathering dusk.

MELVILLE-BRIGGS'S DEATH seemed to act as a starter's pistol and, all at once, things began to move more swiftly. When Rafferty got back to the station, it was to find that Staff Nurse Estoce had finally decided to tell them the truth about Charge Nurse Allward's habits on night duty. He *had* been the one who had rung Linda that night, as they had suspected. When Linda had told him about the row with her parents, he'd promised her a bed for the night in exchange for a freebie. Staff Nurse Estoce had heard him on the phone arranging it. Yet, she was adamant that the girl hadn't turned up and had assumed that she had changed her mind. She had thought no more about it till the next morning when her body had been found. Rafferty didn't have time to dwell on this news because hard on the heels of the Staff Nurse's revelation came another breakthrough.

They had found Miranda, or rather, she had found them. She turned up at the station and demanded to see Rafferty. She'd been hiding in a cheap hotel in Wandsworth, apparently, and only now felt safe enough to leave it.

Sitting on the visitor's chair in front of Rafferty's desk, the light from the window shone full on her. Her eyes were dilated, a fine sheen of perspiration marred the pale skin, and as she fiddled with the collar of her blouse, Rafferty noticed that her fingers were trembling.

'It ... it began a year ago.' Haltingly, she continued her story.

'What did?' Rafferty asked.

'The—affair between Tony Melville-Briggs and myself.'

So—she *had* been yet another mistress. He had half-suspected as much. Rafferty mightn't have admired the *man*, but he certainly had to applaud his energy. 'I don't quite understand,' he rapped out sternly. 'What has this got to do with Linda Wilks's death? You said it was connected.'

Her eyes widened in surprise. 'Of course it's connected. It must be. Why else would he...?' She paused and began again. 'I was there the night the girl was murdered. It was meant to be me, don't you see?'

'Perhaps you could be a little more specific, Miss Raglan,' Llewellyn suggested quietly.

She nodded. 'I'd learned a lot of things about his practice when I was with him—I wasn't the only woman to whom he was giving powerful drugs.' Her voice had a vicious bite to it as she went on. 'He turned us into junkies for his own profit. Before I met him, I was only into drugs in a small way, parties and so on, but that soon changed. He made sure of it. Mostly, as my habit increased, I was just grateful for a reliable source, but later, when I realized just what he'd done to me, I wanted revenge. And I knew the perfect way to get it.

'What would be more just than to make him pay for the habit that he had created?' she asked them. 'I needed more drugs and I expected—demanded, that he supply them for nothing—or else. He just laughed at me, was convinced that I'd be so desperate to get the drugs he supplied that I'd be as cowed as the rest, only too glad to do what he said. But I'd already begun to try to kick the habit. I'd voluntarily reduced my intake, but he didn't know that. I still needed them, of course.' She looked bleakly at them out of over-bright eyes. 'Perhaps I always will. Anyway, I was soon able to convince him that I meant what I said.'

She shuffled restlessly on her chair, opened her handbag and started to light a cigarette before changing her mind and crushing it out in the ashtray. 'He soon realized he'd badly misjudged me when I put my demands more plainly. I knew he couldn't refuse.' An expression of malicious spite hovered for a second on her vapid features. 'I threatened to go to the papers. I could ruin him, you see. That's when the meeting at the hospital was arranged.'

Rafferty remembered Nathanial Whittaker's description of the character of drug-addicts; the weak, the stupid, the gullible; and in spite of Miranda Raglan's outwardly tough stance, Rafferty detected the rather foolish, insecure young woman concealed beneath the bravado.

Llewellyn broke into his thoughts. 'But he *can't* have killed her. He had an alibi. We've checked it out very thoroughly.'

'But it couldn't have been anyone else,' Miranda insisted, with a trace of hysteria. 'He was the only person who knew I was meant to be there. I'd arranged it with him myself.'

Whatever she thought, it was evident to Rafferty that someone had known. He fixed her with a grim stare. 'You were blackmailing him, you say. How did you...?'

Miranda turned up her dainty nose. 'Do you have to use that sordid word, Inspector?'

'A sordid word for a sordid deed, Miss Raglan,' Llewellyn told her reprovingly. 'Did you never think of going to the police instead of taking matters into your own hands?'

'The police?' she repeated scornfully. 'And what would they have done? Arrested me, not him, most probably. I knew he had powerful friends, you see. He threatened me with them once.'

Rafferty felt the sympathy of a fellow-sufferer stirring and quickly stifled it. 'How did you meet him originally?'

'I'd heard on the grape-vine that he'd supply drugs that other doctors wouldn't, so I contacted him. He was happy to oblige. I used to see him at his London consulting rooms twice a week, after hours, when the staff had gone home. Gradually he began to supply me with stronger and stronger tablets. I didn't realize, because he was careful to make sure that to a layman's eye the tablets looked similar. It was only when my cravings began to get out of control that I began to suspect. By then I was a helpless addict. It was costing me a fortune. So you can imagine how grateful I was when he suggested I sleep with him to reduce the price.' She gave a bitter smile. 'I gather I was one of a select little band.'

Mrs Devine had described Miranda as having 'glittering' eyes—a typical description of a drug-addict's eyes. Why hadn't he made the connection before? he wondered. But, of course, the fact that the doctor openly specialized in drug-related problems had put him off the scent. Didn't the old crime writers say that if you wanted to hide a letter put it in the letter-rack with the rest of the mail? Suddenly, he was glad he hadn't dismissed Mrs Devine as a senile old woman whose information was useless. 'So you made an appointment to meet Dr Melville-Briggs in his flat the night Linda Wilks was murdered?'

Miranda Raglan nodded.

'That was a risky thing to do,' Llewellyn commented. 'Didn't it occur to you that you might be in great danger?'

'Not then, only after. I was getting desperate.' She pulled a face. 'It's difficult to think straight when you're on drugs, Sergeant. You should try it some time.'

Ignoring this piece of advice, he asked, 'How did you arrange the meeting?'

'After phoning him to let him know just what I expected, I told him to contact me with the details. He wrote me a note. Just the time and place.' She smiled, but her eyes were empty of warmth. 'He knew he didn't have any choice. But once it was arranged, I became nervous, so I arrived early and waylaid one of the nurses as she arrived for duty and asked her to deliver a note

to him. It said I'd changed my mind and I'd meet him
in the pub up the road sometime before eleven thirty
p.m. but he never came. Obviously, that stupid nurse
forgot all about the note and never gave it to him. And
then I heard about the murder and went to ground while
I thought through what to do.'

'What time did you get to the pub?'

She shrugged. 'About ten. I'd come down a few
weeks before, just to look around, when the idea of
making him pay first occurred to me, and I'd gone in
the pub for lunch. I discovered then that they didn't
bother to call time. On the night of the murder, I waited
there for an hour and a half, being pestered by some
appalling little man, but Tony didn't turn up. I learned
why the next morning.' Her face took on an expression
of distaste. 'That's when I booked into that scruffy hotel. God knows what the girl was doing wandering
around the hospital at that time of night, but whatever
she was doing there, I'm convinced Tony killed her,
mistaking her for me in the darkness. From the picture
in the papers, we are superficially alike.'

'When did you make the appointment with Melville-
Briggs?'

'The week before the girl died.'

Rafferty frowned. Couldn't she even be bothered to
remember Linda Wilks's name? he wondered irritably.
After all, the poor bitch had died for her. But he wasn't
here to make judgements, he reminded himself grimly.
In some ways, Miranda Raglan, too, had been a victim. 'But he must have known when he arranged to see
you that he'd be at a medical dinner at the George all
night. Such important events are arranged weeks in advance. It seems likely he would check his diary before
arranging to meet you. It looks very much as though he

made the appointment knowing he wouldn't be able to keep it.'

'Are you saying that he arranged for *someone else* to murder me? Some hired assassin?'

It was possible, he supposed, hadn't Llewellyn alluded to the possibility? But somehow, with him, it struck a false note. Would Melville-Briggs be likely to place himself in jeopardy from another blackmailer? Even if a hired killer didn't blackmail him, how could he be sure that such a criminal wouldn't cop a plea in the future if arrested for another killing? No, he was still convinced that this was an inside job. But who thought enough of Sir Anthony to kill his troublesome mistress for him? His wife, who had long accepted his faithlessness and lived her own life? Simon Smythe who feared him? The Galvins, both of whom had reason to feel a bitter hatred towards him? There was no one connected with the case whom Melville-Briggs could persuade to do his dirty work. Even the obliging Gilbert, who wasn't beyond indulging in a little attempted blackmail himself if he thought he could get away with it, would shy away from murder. Besides, he had stayed in the pub till he had been chucked out at one in the morning, not that Melville-Briggs would be likely to trust his sly porter with the task, anyway.

LLEWELLYN POPPED his head round the door. 'I've got Allward in the interview room. Are you ready to speak to him?'

Rafferty slammed the phone receiver back on its rest and shook his head. 'He'll have to wait. Him and Sidney Wilks both. That was Simon Smythe. Lady Evelyn must have got him temporarily reinstated. It was all a bit garbled, but it seems someone's attacked Gilbert, the lodge-porter.'

'Who?'

Rafferty shrugged. 'God knows. Smythe hung up before I got an answer to that one.' With a worried frown, he asked, 'You don't think Gilbert saw something on the night of the murder, do you, and tried another spot of blackmail?'

'What *could* he have seen?' Llewellyn asked reasonably. 'He was in the pub when the murder happened. I hardly think the murderer would hang around after killing the girl.' Neither did Rafferty. 'I imagine the answer's simple enough. Personally, I've been expecting something like this for several days.'

'Oh?' Rafferty picked him up sharply. This was the first *he'd* heard of Llewellyn's suspicions. 'Being wise *after* the event are we?' he gibed.

Llewellyn shook his head. 'Not at all. I imagine one of the patients attacked him. Murder unsettles the mind,' he explained. 'And it unsettles the troubled mind even more.'

'I bet it unsettled Gilbert's,' Rafferty remarked grimly. 'He's all right, though. At least, Smythe didn't seem too bothered about him. Of course, that's not altogether surprising and knowing Gilbert, he's probably got all the pretty nurses giving him tea and sympathy right now.' Picking up his emerald-green jacket, he led the way out to the station car park reflecting that Llewellyn was probably right. Again. One of the patients had probably taken a dislike to Gilbert's face. Understandable really.

The hospital was in uproar when they arrived. They'd barely got through the gates before the car was surrounded by a throng of shouting, gesticulating staff, Simon Smythe at its centre. Smythe was trying to establish order, without any noticeable success. He emerged from the scrum surrounding him and a look of relief appeared on his face when he saw Rafferty. 'Thank God you've come, Inspector. It's one of the patients, Brian. He...'

'Where is he?'

'In the lodge. He's locked himself in and refuses to come out.'

'I take it you've got a hefty injection of sedative handy?' Smythe nodded. That was something. 'Come along then, Doctor.' Rafferty headed purposefully for the lodge, feeling like the Pied Piper of Hamelin as Llewellyn, Smythe and most of the still-depleted hospital staff fell in behind.

At least Constable Hanks, left on duty at the gate, had shown some presence of mind. Armed with a dustbin lid, he'd stationed himself outside the lodge, while from inside came the sound of crashes and bangs. It seemed the patient was intent on demolishing everything within reach.

'Has he tried to come out?' he asked Hanks.

'Not so far, sir. More interested in wrecking the place.'

'Damn near wrecked me 'ead,' complained Gilbert.

Up till now, Gilbert had kept quiet and Rafferty hadn't noticed him in the crowd. But as the shock began to wear off he became increasingly voluble. 'Gave me the fright of me life when I saw that religious nut, Brian, with that great lump of wood in 'is 'ands. Murder 'e 'ad in 'is eyes. Murder!'

'I was just about to try to establish what steps Gilbert took, Inspector,' Smythe interjected, in an obvious attempt to justify his less than professional panic.

'I'll tell you what steps I took,' exclaimed Gilbert vociferously. 'Bloody great big ones, of course. What do you expect me to have done?' he demanded. 'Reasoned wiv 'im? Ain't *my* job to reason wiv 'em, mate. I just let the b— in and out. Reasoning's *your* job. 'Ere,' Gilbert shot a worried look at Rafferty. You reckon 'e's the one as done fer the girl?' He went quite pale and ran his hand over his face as though to make sure he still had all the bits that belonged there.

For a moment, Gilbert's suspicions revived Rafferty's own earlier one that the mad, misogynistic Brian *had* somehow escaped the vigilance of Staff Nurse Estoce and committed the murder after all. Then common sense reasserted itself. He'd already checked and discarded that possibility. Besides, since when had such an easy and obvious solution fallen into *his* lap?

'No.' Gilbert answered his own question. 'It must 'ave been old smarmy-pants. Why else would 'e top 'imself?'

'Is that what everyone's saying?' Rafferty asked curiously.

'Stands to reason, dunnit? He certainly looked as sick as a parrot when I saw 'im, just before 'e made a concertina out of 'imself in the Carlton. Looked, I dunno— glazed, I s'pose. Almost as though 'e was drugged or something.'

Sir Anthony had prescribed himself some tranquillizers, the officer called to the scene had found them in his pocket when he'd looked for some identification; but the label said they were mild, only 2ml, certainly not enough to bring a glazed look to his eyes, not unless he'd taken a handful of them. Yet, according to the PM he must have done. Perhaps, afraid that his many sins were soon to be revealed to a censorious world, he'd dosed himself up to deaden the pain of the impact when his car wrapped itself around the tree. 'Didn't you try to stop him?' he asked Gilbert.

'Me? And remind 'im that 'e 'adn't sacked me yet? Not bloody likely!'

'So he just got in his car and drove away?'

Gilbert nodded. 'Pretty fast too, considering the patients were milling about the place.'

'Powerful car, a Carlton,' commented Llewellyn, the car buff.

'Still, it was rather out of character,' commented Rafferty. 'I understand he was usually very careful of his patients.'

'Not one to risk endangering 'is investments,' agreed Gilbert. 'Not Sir Anthony.'

By now, the sound of destruction from inside the lodge had slowly petered out. 'Sounds like he's exhausted himself,' said Rafferty. 'Right, Gilbert. I'm sure you've got another key for that door. Let me have it please.'

Gilbert released a key-ring from his belt. Selecting one, he handed it over to Rafferty, with the comment, 'Mind you let me 'ave it back, now. I'm responsible fer it.'

Given his less than zealous guardianship of the other keys under his protection, Rafferty was sorely tempted to make a sharp retort. Instead, he wordlessly took the proffered key and crept up to the broken window and peered in. Brian was taking a well-earned rest and was calmly sipping a piping-hot brew from Gilbert's personal mug, which had somehow escaped the ravages suffered by the rest of the equipment. To Rafferty's relief, the patient's destructive storm seemed to have blown itself out. Unlocking the door, he stepped inside the lodge. Brian continued to sip his tea and Rafferty remarked quietly, 'I like the mug.'

Brian raised his eyes suspiciously. 'It's *mine*.'

'Oh? I wouldn't have thought the wording on it would appeal to you.'

'Why? Work *is* a four-letter word. The Lord's work. Why was that blasphemer Gilbert using it?' As Rafferty shrugged noncommittally, Brian finished his tea and, with the help of a couple of nurses, Smythe managed to sedate him. He went off between them as quietly as a lamb, still clutching Gilbert's mug, much to the porter's vexation, and Rafferty and Llewellyn were left alone to survey the ruins of Gilbert's little castle.

Brian had made a thorough job of wrecking the place with the amazing strength of the deranged. The table was overturned, lists and rosters were torn to shreds, even the key-cabinet had been wrenched off the wall and the keys scattered all over the floor, some of them large and rather cumbersome. They reminded Rafferty of something, and as he struggled to remember, suddenly into his head popped a conversation he'd had some time ago and all at once he knew who the killer was; a double murderer, for he was now convinced that Sir Anthony's death hadn't been suicide. He knew who and how—he even knew why. The means, motive, and opportunity were all there. All that remained was to carry out the arrest.

SEVENTEEN

THE NURSERY was quiet; it was 6.00 p.m. and the toddlers had long since gone home. Rafferty had had a word with the elderly caretaker who lived in the flat above and he had gone off, quietly grumbling to himself. They waited in the ground-floor play-room. Large and airy, it was decorated with a jolly Disney cartoon mural. Its colourful characters seemed mocking and, for once, Rafferty managed to look even more long-faced than his sergeant.

In the silence, they heard footsteps approaching down the linoleum-covered hall, but instead of the door to the nursery opening, the suddenly increased roar of the traffic told them that the front door had been opened. Seconds later the roar slackened off again as the door shut with a soft click. Rafferty and Llewellyn exchanged a questioning look that turned to alarm as the unmistakable whish-wishaw of air-brakes hurriedly applied was followed by a deathly silence. They rushed to the street door.

The body lay mangled under the front wheel of a huge juggernaut. The driver was in his fifties. White-faced and shaking uncontrollably, he clutched the small silver crucifix around his neck as he told them in a dazed voice, 'Done it deliberately. Looked straight at me and made the sign of the cross before stepping off the pavement.' He brought his sleeve across his suddenly wet eyes. 'I couldn't do nothing.' Shock was clearly taking a hold for he kept repeating, over and over, like a stuck gramophone record, 'I couldn't do nothing.'

Rafferty checked the pulse, but had guessed before he tried that he would find none. Telling Llewellyn to ring for an ambulance, he left the distraught driver to the tender mercies of the caretaker. Walking over to the car, he took out the car rug from the back seat. Normally used to protect the covers from the destructive tendencies of his myriad nephews and nieces, he now had a more urgent use for it.

'*Noblesse oblige,*' he murmured softly as he laid the red tartan over Lady Evelyn. Its bright colours made the pooled blood seem less gory. In an odd contrast to Linda Wilks's death, although Lady Evelyn's body was a mess, her face hadn't been touched and it looked as composed in death as it had in life. He thought she'd have been glad about that. Unlike her husband, Lady Evelyn accepted that all privilege had its penalties. She had tried to protect her family—the honour of its glorious past and her hopes for its future. But she had failed and had realized that her continued existence would be a liability to her line. Predictably, she had done the honourable thing.

Llewellyn returned. 'The ambulance is on its way.' Rafferty nodded and settled the rug more cosily around the body, tucking it in so no draught could touch her.

'Messy method to choose,' Llewellyn remarked mournfully.

Rafferty didn't look up from his study of the tartan-shrouded figure on the ground. 'For her it was the cleanest way, the best way. She must have guessed why we had come and didn't want a verdict of double murder and suicide—might blot the family escutcheon, whatever that is.'

'It's a shield for a coat of arms,' Llewellyn told him, dispensing information a little more solemnly than usual.

Rafferty nodded. 'It'll be labelled accidental death, of course, she knew that.'

'Here on earth, perhaps,' stated Rafferty sombrely. 'But she was a Catholic. Whatever label is applied won't alter the fact that her God would know the truth of it.' With a shake of his head, he turned away. 'Did you ever hear of Bloody Mary, Inspector?'

Bemused, Rafferty stared at his sergeant. 'The drink?'

'No. The queen.'

Rafferty's face cleared. 'Henry VIII's elder daughter, you mean?' He had heard of the lady. Llewellyn wasn't the only one with an interest in the past, he reflected grimly, as he guessed what his sergeant was about to say.

Llewellyn nodded. 'If you remember your history, duty ruled her life, much as it must have ruled Lady Evelyn's. She was a Catholic, too, and she felt it was *her* duty to rid the county of heretics. Hundreds died in the Smithfield fires. Their deaths were no less repugnant because they died from one woman's dutiful desire to glorify God. He would have condoned their deaths no more than he would condone the ones Lady Evelyn was guilty of. Murder is murder, however high-principled the murderer may be.'

Llewellyn was right, as usual. Lady Evelyn had murdered two people, but Rafferty still felt more pity than anger. Even if he couldn't condone her actions any more than God would, he felt he could understand why she had done it. Poor, sad, disillusioned lady, the burden of her duty was, to her, equally heavy and equally strong— the upholding of the family honour. After all, God had looked after the Melvilles for five hundred years and countless deaths, insurrections, and wars. But, even with God's help, no one held on to their property during the dangerous years after Henry VII's death and the religious turmoil that was to come without getting plenty of blood on their hands. In comparison two murders must seem a trifling matter.

'Didn't you tell me that the Latin of her family motto translated as "Honour above all"?' he asked his sergeant. Llewellyn nodded slowly. 'She must have thought God would understand and approve,' said Rafferty softly. 'She sacrificed herself for the dynasty. The next link in the chain was her son, but from what Gilbert said, he was a weak link. Unless he married a strong woman who shared Lady Evelyn's ideals all that she had worked for risked being broken up. I imagine she pushed him into the engagement with the Huntingdon girl. She held the family purse-strings, of course, she probably used that to persuade him to agree.' Rafferty still gazed at Lady Evelyn's shrouded form. 'You'll see, first he'll postpone the wedding—out of filial respect naturally—but somehow I doubt if another date will ever be fixed. Next, he'll put the Hall on the market. Now he's got the money he can start indulging his own dreams instead of his mother's. I imagine he'll find that mechanic of his, Harry, far less demanding than all that rich blue Huntingdon blood.'

As Llewellyn nodded agreement, Rafferty realized how dreadfully lonely Lady Evelyn must have been. Perhaps it might have been different if her husband had loved her, for who would give all their love to a building—however magnificent—if they had a human being worthy of their cherishing? In the end her obsession had taken over her life, wrecking it, as well as the lives of several others. Such was the nature of obsessions, of course. Ultimately, they were always destructive. That was why they were so dangerous. Rafferty knew the servants all slept in a separate annexe over the old stables of the Hall and now he pictured Lady Evelyn in her echoing and empty home, carefully drawing up a tapestry of murder, stitch by stitch, until she had made her own shroud. With a sigh, he stood up. Now he could hear the sirens in the distance. A few minutes later, the ambulance had drawn up and the attendants gathered Lady Evelyn's body in the back. Rafferty found his shoulders straightening and his hands making the sign of the cross automatically, as he had been taught to do as a boy in the presence of death.

With a start, he realized that with the case over he no longer had a valid excuse for avoiding his mother and Maureen, the good catch. His shoulders slumped. Feeling as he did, that was the last thing he needed right now. Families, he shook his head sorrowfully, they really could be bloody murder.

What he needed was to cleanse his mind and refresh his spirit in the best way he knew. Tomorrow, he promised himself, he would visit a building site, the new one at Colchester. The gaffer of the masons laid his bricks with a deft rhythm that soothed the soul and Rafferty felt sorely in need of such balm.

EPILOGUE

'IT WAS SOMETHING that my mother said that made me realize the truth,' Rafferty remarked to Llewellyn several days later as he gestured to his sergeant to move into the passenger seat and got behind the wheel. Jack's wedding was over, thank God, and he only had the reception to get through. He'd arranged for Llewellyn to pick him up around the corner from the church. Luckily, he'd been able to sneak away before the photographer was able to record the relationship for posterity, discarding his button-hole on the way. 'She mentioned a mother's pride in her first-born son. How much greater, do you think, would that pride be for an *only* son?'

Had he suspected all along and not let the suspicion rise above his subconscious? He hadn't wanted to believe Lady Evelyn was the murderer, neither had Llewellyn. It was only the second time he had felt himself in sympathy with the man since he had met him. That embryonic empathy was the only good thing to come out of the case. Neither of them had thought her capable of what looked like a particularly vicious crime, but of course, she hadn't killed the girl that way from choice. It had been essential. It must have sickened her as much as it had them.

Llewellyn returned to Rafferty's last comment. 'But the son wasn't even threatened. It was Sir Anthony who was being blackmailed and faced with exposure.'

Llewellyn's investigative nose had still to learn in which direction to wrinkle, reflected Rafferty. After turning on the ignition and nosing the car bonnet out on to the road, he explained, 'You forget—the son was getting married. Sir Anthony chose the wrong time to confide his little difficulty to his wife. Miranda Raglan, even *with* the drugs she craved, was hardly a stable woman. If her demands had been met and she kept quiet about Sir Anthony's unprofessional conduct, it was unlikely that she would continue to do so, and Timothy's long-planned wedding was still four months off. Lady Evelyn must have known that anything could have happened in that time.' Llewellyn absorbed this in silence and Rafferty went on. 'When Lady Evelyn discovered that Miranda Raglan was threatening her husband with exposure, she knew that her son's forthcoming marriage was in danger and that she couldn't permit. I imagine it was what she had hoped for for years—the uniting of two old and aristocratic families. It would have made up for so much. She had engineered it thus far, ignoring her son's inadequacies as a bridegroom. If she failed to bring this marriage off, she knew she might *never* manage to get him up the aisle.

'She wasn't a fool, she had eyes to see and ears to hear the rumours about her son. Her mother's love didn't blind her to the truth about his sexual preferences. But she knew that a homosexual is as capable of getting a son as any other man—a son to continue the Melville line. That was of greater importance to her than even her son's happiness.'

He was, after all, only one link in the chain that went back centuries, he reflected. It would have been unthinkable to a woman like Lady Evelyn to let *her* son be the one who broke the chain and brought the dynasty to an end. He put his foot down, biting back the wry grin when he sensed Llewellyn wincing beside him. 'Take it easy, Taff. I'm barely doing sixty.'

'But it's a fifty mile-per-hour limit,' Llewellyn pointed out uneasily.

He was right, of course. In that infuriating way of his, he usually was, and Rafferty eased his foot back from the accelerator. Still, they had plenty of time and it wasn't as though he was in any great rush to reach his destination. He went on with his explanation. 'She had been largely able to ignore her husband's womanising; her son's future in-laws wouldn't have blinked an eye at that, but what they would have blinked *both* eyes at was a *real* scandal. And Miranda threatened to blow the lid off a scandal that would bring nothing but shame. She had to be stopped.'

According to Miranda Raglan, Sir Anthony had acted as a high-class supplier, using his London consulting rooms and the hospital as covers, very profitable covers, for a still more lucrative trade—drugs. On the surface, his wealthy lady patients returned to him time and again out of loyalty, but in reality, they had no choice. He had got them hooked on very powerful drugs; no wonder they were so faithful, thought Rafferty. They were totally dependent on him and them.

They'd never be sure now, of course, but Rafferty suspected that Lady Evelyn had switched the tranquillizers in his pill bottle, replacing some of the low-dosage tablets with something stronger. He carried various drugs in his doctor's bag, it wouldn't be difficult for her to get hold of the keys. Melville-Briggs had badly misjudged three of the women in his life and had paid the ultimate price. 'He thought he had everything under control; his wife, his secretary, his ex-mistress. When Miranda Raglan threatened to crack the golden eggs and scatter the flock of fat geese with them he became badly frightened,' Rafferty went on. 'Under all that brash self-confidence he was just another weak man who needed the shelter and support of a strong wife and he confided in Lady Evelyn. From that moment, he was a dead man. But first, she had to remove the worst threat to her son's marriage—Miranda Raglan.'

'But—' Llewellyn broke in.

Rafferty was well into his stride now and he waved him to silence. 'Gilbert wasn't the only one practised in forgery. According to him, Lady Evelyn used to act as her husband's secretary when he first set up in practice. She was used to signing his letters for him, probably wrote them too. I imagine she wrote his signature better than *he* did. She was the one who wrote Miranda that note arranging to meet her at the hospital, not Sir Anthony. As she had never set eyes on Miranda, she killed the wrong girl.'

'But Lady Evelyn was at the George all night,' Llewellyn exclaimed. 'How could she . . . ?'

'Simple. She wasn't centre stage all night, in the way that her husband was. She had only to slip out for half an hour; ten minutes to drive to the hospital, ten minutes to kill the girl and clean up, and ten minutes to get back. She made sure she kept a low profile that evening so that she wasn't missed. Somehow that seemed out of character. She was the wife of the chairman, she was the one who had done all the work. Usually, they would have presented a united front, both prominent, papering over the cracks in their relationship—she for the sake of her son and Sir Anthony for his own sake. Funnily enough, Sam Dally remarked that that evening she had seemed subdued and content to stay in the background and Sam just put it down to Sir Anthony's bad mood at their being late. I imagine she engineered the flat battery so they'd be late and wouldn't have to park in the hotel car park under the door-man's eye. She could slip out of one of the side entrances and get the car without anyone noticing she'd gone.'

'But why on earth did she choose that *particular* night? Wouldn't it have been better to wait for an occasion when she wasn't so restricted by time and circumstances?'

'On the contrary, that night was the only possible time. She had to be sure that her husband wouldn't be likely to disturb her. I doubt if he bothered to give her advance warning of his movements. She could be sure he was safely at the George. Of course the limited time meant she had no opportunity to change.

'You know, at the beginning of the case, I dug back into her family history—oh, not because I suspected her then,' Rafferty admitted when he sensed Llewellyn's scepticism, 'but because I was interested. Her family have always been staunch Catholics—quite a few members in the past joined religious orders. It seemed likely that the attics at the Hall would be stuffed with costumes of all kinds. It's my guess that she covered her own clothes with the monk's habit to protect her from the blood.'

'So the drunk wasn't merely hallucinating?'

Rafferty shook his head and drew up to the road junction, glad of an excuse to avert his face. The less Llewellyn knew about that little episode, the better. Luckily, Llewellyn didn't know that Jack was the drunken witness to Lady Evelyn's arrival for her rendezvous with murder. Not that he was likely to blab, in fact, Rafferty realized suddenly, he'd never met a more close-mouthed copper. It was another thing in his favour. For the first time, he wondered whether the dapper little Welshman might not suit him very well after all. The bridal pair were toying with the idea of staying in England, and if they did, Llewellyn's discretion might just turn out to be an asset.

The weapon used for the murder had puzzled him for a long time; until the scattered keys had jogged his memory and reminded him of the weapons of war displayed in the Great Hall at Elmhurst. The mace had been amongst them and he'd remembered that he'd read in the guide book that it had been used at the Battle of Bosworth by Lady Evelyn's illustrious ancestor, Edward Melville. Rafferty suspected the symbolism of using so archaic a weapon to kill one of her family's enemies would mean much to her.

They hadn't got the results back yet, of course, but Rafferty was sure that when they did they'd find that the bloodstains on the mace were not just those from ancient foes, but from a modern victim as well—Linda Wilks.

It had been a tragic coincidence that she had been where Lady Evelyn had expected to find Miranda Raglan; one of those bizarre twists of fate that had so often dogged Rafferty's own footsteps. He wondered if, in her death throes, she had recognized that she was about to be a star at last? The star victim in a murder hunt.

'Your speed's creeping up again, sir.'

Rafferty glanced at the speedometer and eased back once more. 'I'm surprised you didn't choose to go into the traffic division,' he remarked caustically. 'Think of all those speed junkies you could collar.'

Llewellyn made an odd noise in his throat. To his astonishment, Rafferty realized that his sergeant was actually laughing. 'What's so funny?' he demanded.

'It's just that I *did* apply for traffic, but they turned me down.' His voice sounded deceptively innocent as he went on, 'Perhaps the superintendent thought that with

the police image being so important, the division would
be better served if I stayed in CID and acted as your
personal speed trap, sir.'

'Very droll.' Things *were* looking up, he reflected, his
sergeant had actually cracked a funny. Rafferty shot
him a curious glance, but although Llewellyn's face had
fallen back into its normal lugubrious folds, he was beginning to realize that there was a lot more to the
Welshman than met the eye.

'You were explaining about the murder, sir,' Llewellyn reminded him solemnly.

Rafferty was quite willing to let himself be drawn
back to an exhibition of his own cleverness. Smugly, he
went on. 'When I wondered if she could have done it, I
worked backwards and it all fitted. Several people have
commented on her efficiency and great organizational
skills. I asked myself how likely it was that Lady Evelyn could possibly have forgotten to get her chauffeur
to change his weekend off, particularly for an occasion
that had been planned so long in advance. I wondered
if she could have done it deliberately and if so why? I
realized it was essential to her plans that the chauffeur
wasn't available. Not only because she needed to get
away from the George without anyone noticing, but she
also needed the use of a car that wasn't conspicuous—
one, moreover, that she could drive, and the Bentley
was a manual. She could only drive automatics. It all
fitted.'

He pulled into the car park and turned off the ignition. Looking down at his no longer quite so smart
brown suit, he sighed, aware that, as usual, in spite of
his tasteful day-glo orange tie, his sergeant managed to
outshine him in the well-groomed stakes. 'As for removing the girl's clothes, it was a precaution, nothing
more. She knew Miranda would be unlikely to wear

mass-produced chain-store clothes, she would dress expensively, in clothes that would be much more easily traced. In the dark and with the need for speed, she wouldn't have stopped to examine whether the girl was wearing designer labels or not. Forensic found small traces of blood in the boot of her car. She probably stuffed the mace and the clothes in a plastic rubbish bag and left them there overnight, but because she was rushing, she didn't have time to be as careful as she should have been. I imagine she burned the clothes in one of those great hearths at the Hall. She had to remove all signs of her victim's identity so she couldn't be traced back to Sir Anthony. That's why she removed Linda's face and smashed her teeth. Once the victim's identity was known, the possibility of her being linked with Melville-Briggs was much greater, especially as she knew that the post-mortem might reveal the existence of powerful drugs—drugs only available from a doctor.

'It never occurred to her to remove the fingerprints. Of course, her *intended* victim didn't have a criminal record, Miranda's sort never do. She'd have been careful to check up on that and with her husband's contacts in the police force it wouldn't have been difficult. I wonder how she felt when she discovered that she'd killed the wrong girl?'

'It's strange how Sir Anthony appeared so confident through all of this,' Llewellyn remarked. 'It's almost as though he knew nothing about the murder.'

'I don't believe he did,' said Rafferty. 'Think about it. Do you seriously imagine Lady Evelyn would confide her intentions to a man who had proved himself so unreliable, so untrustworthy? She probably told him she'd bought Miranda off and that he'd seen the end of her. You were right when you said he was the type to get somebody else to do his dirty work for him,' he added

expansively and thought he glimpsed a gleam of gratification in Llewellyn's eye. 'She must have been desperate to find her when she realized she'd killed the
wrong girl, but, for once, Miranda Raglan used her
brain. She'd booked into that seedy hotel where she was
unlikely to bump into anyone who knew her and Lady
Evelyn couldn't find her. I reckon that's when she
brought forward the murder of her husband.' He wondered if she'd even handed him the extra-strength tran-
quillizer herself with a glass of water in a gesture of
wifely solicitude shortly before he left the house and Sir
Anthony had tossed it back without a second thought?
It was the sort of bold, direct action Lady Evelyn would
take and Sir Anthony was used to the adoration of
women, he wouldn't expect his previously accommodating wife to want him dead. Was it possible she'd felt
some concern for other possible victims of her action?
he mused. After all, she couldn't be sure that Sir Anthony would be the only victim. He had to accept that
it was unlikely. Those in the grip of an obsession allowed nothing to deflect them from their course, not
even the lives of others.

'It's my belief that she had hoped that by removing
her husband the blackmailer would back off and everything would be as it was before,' Rafferty began
again, preferring to leave his grim thoughts where he
had found them. 'She wasn't to know that by now Miranda Raglan was past reasoning. Her supply of pills
was running low and she was starting to get the hor-
rors—he'd been giving her some extremely powerful
drugs. She'd signed on with another doctor, but he
wouldn't prescribe anything like the strength of the
tablets she needed.'

Now he resolutely put the unhappy Lady Evelyn from
his mind. Pulling up in the car park, he leaned over and

picked up the package from the back seat before getting out of the car and slamming the door. Shoving the parcel under his arm he gestured at the imposing white-stone façade of the George. 'We've got a bit of a family do on.' He hadn't mentioned it to Llewellyn before, but somehow, secrecy didn't seem quite so important now.

'You've got a lot of relations, haven't you, sir?' Llewellyn commented.

Rafferty nodded. One too many, he reflected ruefully.

'I often wondered what it would be like being one of a large family,' Llewellyn remarked. 'I was an only child.'

He sounded quite wistful and Rafferty glanced at him in surprise. 'Speaking as one of six, that's a subject on which I *am* an expert,' he said feelingly. 'It's heaven and hell, love and hate, but mostly it's messy, noisy and totally lacking in any privacy. You wouldn't have liked it,' he told him decisively. 'You wouldn't have liked it at all.'

Llewellyn sighed. 'I suppose you're right.'

Strangely, the wistful look was still there. Was it possible that Llewellyn was human after all? wondered Rafferty. A lonely human being who secretly rather longed for some disorder in his neat and regimented existence, in spite of his denials?

Rafferty had fully intended getting rid of his sergeant once they had reached the George, reckoning on taking a taxi back. But now some instinct made him pause.

Perhaps because Llewellyn was so different from himself, he'd misjudged him? He'd already discovered a little of Llewellyn's family background and pretty bleak it sounded. How could he, with his rumbustious but loving family, imagine what Llewellyn's only child life of nannies and boarding schools and university had been like? What did he know of anybody's life, when all was said and done? Look how wrong he'd been about Lady Evelyn.

Llewellyn had mentioned that he was the son of a minister of the church. Rafferty had already discovered one of the grim duties expected of Llewellyn as a boy, now he wondered what else he had been expected to go through. Had he been forced, like a lot of church kids, in order to set an example, to spend half his school holidays at the services? Had he never gone fishing for newts in the nearest pond, bringing them home triumphantly in a jam-jar? Had he never kept green caterpillars in a match-box, waiting for them to change magically into butterflies? Had his youth been the joyless one Rafferty imagined it to be? Spent joining in doleful hymns shut inside a damp church while the world and the birds outside were singing sweeter songs? If so, it was no wonder if his youth and capacity for joy had atrophied. Perhaps it was time somebody tried to remedy that?

He wasn't really surprised, when he heard his voice saying, 'I don't know about you, Taff, but I, for one, am ready for a drink. I did say you were invited, didn't I?'

Llewellyn frowned. 'No, sir.'

But much to his surprise, Llewellyn accepted the belated invitation with something approaching alacrity and as they strode together towards the brightly lit hotel, Rafferty wondered if his second good deed in a week might not receive a suitable reward. For if Llewellyn really was lonely and looking for a mate, that was one area where he *could* help. He opened the door to the reception with a flourish. 'After you, Taff.'

He'd always liked a wedding—as long as it wasn't his own—and the discovery of his sergeant's unsuspected secret fancy for family life put new heart into him. His mother tended to collect lame dogs, and to Rafferty's mind, they didn't come any lamer than Llewellyn.

Perhaps this was the opportunity he'd been waiting for—the ingenious answer to his present little problem. Perhaps his mother would agree with him that his sergeant's need for a wife was far more urgent than his own and likely to demand her single-minded attention. He certainly hoped so.

He gave Llewellyn one of his brightest smiles. Maureen would be here. Hadn't his Uncle Pat told him that she had always had a soft spot for the serious intellectual type? Like Llewellyn, for instance.

SNOWJOB

TED WOOD

First Time in Paperback

A REID BENNETT MYSTERY

SOLDIERS ON THE SAME SIDE

An SOS from old Marine buddy Doug Ford brings Canadian police chief Reid Bennett across the border to the picturesque Vermont ski town of Chambers.

Ford, a local cop, is arrested for the murder of an attractive woman. Because he had not told anyone about the case he was investigating, no one except Reid believes he was framed.

As more murder paints the resort town bloodred, Reid uncovers a trail of dirty money that leads all the way to New York. He also realizes that the killer he's dealing with will stop at nothing to preserve his secret.

"Solid genre fare." —*Booklist*

Available in November at your favorite retail stores.

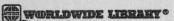

Take 3 books and a surprise gift FREE

SPECIAL LIMITED-TIME OFFER

Mail to: The Mystery Library™
3010 Walden Ave.
P.O. Box 1867
Buffalo, N.Y. 14269-1867

YES! Please send me 3 free books from the Mystery Library™ and my free surprise gift. Then send me 3 mystery books, first time in paperback, every month. Bill me only $3.69 per book plus 25¢ delivery and applicable sales tax, if any*. There is no minimum number of books I must purchase. I can always return a shipment at your expense and cancel my subscription. Even if I never buy another book from the Mystery Library™, the 3 free books and surprise gift are mine to keep forever.   415 BPY ANQ2

* Terms and prices subject to change without notice. N.Y. residents add applicable sales tax. This offer is limited to one order per household and not valid to present subscribers.

© 1990 Woirdwide Library.

MYS-94

TRAIL OF MURDER

Christine Andreae
A Lee Squires Mystery

First Time in Paperback

ROCKY MOUNTAIN MURDER

English professor Lee Squires signs on as camp cook for a wilderness outfitter hired by the wealthy and dysfunctional Strand family.

As the group begins the week-long trail ride through the Bob Marshall Wilderness, patriarch Cyrus Strand maliciously announces that he's written a new will disinheriting his spoiled and avaricious children from his immense fortune.

Suddenly, Montana's pristine beauty turns menacing as greed and rage litter the scenic expanse. And now, between whipping up elk meatballs and sourdough bread, Lee must negotiate a trail of murder that turns deadlier by the day.

"The author is remarkably sure-footed."
— *New York Times Book Review*

Available in November at your favorite retail stores.

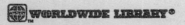 **WORLDWIDE LIBRARY®**

TRAIL